INDECENT eXposure

INDECENT eXposure

CARMEN GREEN
VICTOR McGLOTHIN
TRACY PRICE-THOMPSON

sepia™

If you purchased this book without a cover you should be aware that this book is stolen property. It was reported as "unsold and destroyed" to the publisher, and neither the author nor the publisher has received any payment for this "stripped book."

INDECENT EXPOSURE

A Sepia novel

ISBN 1-58314-709-8

© 2006 by Carmen Green, Victor McGlothin, and Tracy Price-Thompson

All rights reserved. The reproduction, transmission or utilization of this work in whole or in part in any form by any electronic, mechanical or other means, now known or hereafter invented, including xerography, photocopying and recording, or in any information storage or retrieval system, is forbidden without written permission. For permission please contact Kimani Press, Editorial Office, 233 Broadway, New York, NY 10279 U.S.A.

This book is a work of fiction. The names, characters, incidents and places are the products of the author's imagination, and are not to be construed as real. While the author was inspired in part by actual events, none of the characters in the book is based on an actual person. Any resemblance to persons living or dead is entirely coincidental and unintentional.

® and TM are trademarks. Trademarks indicated with ® are registered in the United States Patent and Trademark Office, the Canadian Trade Marks Office and/or other countries.

www.kimanipress.com

Printed in U.S.A.

One

Morning came much too fast for Julian Blake. Sure he'd had his share of nights on the town, but he should have taken his own advice and saved the a.m. hours for Saturday nights, where they belonged. He must have been out of his mind to think he could have dined at Justin's, then club-hopped into the wee hours of the morning. If Julian had been in his right mind, a pleasant dinner with his closest female friend, socialite Kelly Taylor, and Raja Jackson, the blind date Kelly'd taken it upon herself to hook him up with, would have sufficed. Having dubbed the night before the sweetest mistake he'd made all month, Julian stepped out of his lavish marble bathtub smiling and thinking, a good measure of wine, women, and song can't do nothing but make a brother do wrong. He also realized that at age thirty-eight, he wasn't a kid anymore, as it was difficult to ignore how his wavy black hair was sprinkled with dashes of gray at the temples, but he had managed to sustain the same perfectly sculpted build from his heyday while attending Georgetown Law School. All things considered, he still looked good.

As Julian toweled off, he watched his dark-skinned reflection with the muscular frame smiling back at him for some of the sly things he'd said and done merely hours before. Although he couldn't pretend his head wasn't still ringing from one hell of a party hangover, he kept right on smiling.

Moments after he'd subjected himself to numerous laps inside his monstrous walk-in closet, eyeing rows of impeccably tailored garments all arranged by color and style, Julian decided on a charcoal-gray three-button business suit. In spite of his having felt somewhat weathered on the inside and faking it, nobody wore charcoal gray like Julian. More than self-assured, he was certain of the two things that he and Kelly always swore by: they believed that clothes made the man but an expensive wardrobe made the man *fine*. If last night had served as a litmus test to support their theory, they were correct on both counts.

While he was exiting his renovated brownstone off 110th, Julian's watch chimed, informing him that it was eight o'clock and time to remove the latch from his private life, a private life that he'd guarded with extreme vigilance. However, Julian would soon discover how becoming a serious contender in the New York mayoral race blurred the lines of what he considered private once in full view of the public eye.

He pulled into traffic, thinking back on the blind date Kelly had sprung on him at a moment's notice. She was easy on the eyes, he thought at first glance. Not half bad, actually, he had to admit when he caught himself staring at her deep-colored cocoa complexion over appetizers. She was funny, intelligent, and certainly knew how to have a good time. "Raja Jackson from Brooklyn," he murmured, rewinding the tape of the previous night knowing that he would be quizzed by Kelly later that day on what he thought about "her girl."

Unfortunately, later came sooner than he could have prepared for. "Twelve messages," he sighed, as soon as his cell phone powered up. "Already twelve messages and it's only eight-oh-one. Somebody's in trouble. Big trouble." Julian set the pocket phone into the car console and pressed the speaker button. "Voice mail," he announced matter-of-factly, and the messages began to replay. One right behind the next, Kelly's voice insisted that he contact her before reaching the office. It was imperative, she reiterated, that he for one time in his life do as instructed instead of as he pleased.

While he was debating whether or not to heed her persistent advice, the twelfth message she'd left demanding that he call her back "or else" compelled him to comply.

"Kelly. It's Julian," he said, wearing the same devilish grin as before. "What's gotten you all worked up so early this morning that couldn't wait? I mean, I just talked to you a few hours ago."

"Julian, are you sitting down?" Her voice was quiet and hesitant.

"Yeah, I'm on my way into the office. What's wrong? I know something is wrong because I recognize that subdued tone in your voice and it's screaming *Julian, I'm sorry.*"

After a long stream of silence passed between them, Kelly's apologies poured out like a mighty river of reluctance. "Julian, I *am* sorry. So sorry. Please don't get upset. Try to understand that I didn't mean any harm when I called myself playing matchmaker last night. I never intended for it to blow up into some distorted front-page gossip. Actually it's on the sixth page but that's beside the point. I'm just saying, keep in mind that I wouldn't ever intentionally put you or your business out there like that."

While cruising toward Manhattan's financial district, Julian tried to comprehend Kelly's wall of words, but it came at him so fast that he didn't have the slightest idea what she was talking about. "Okay, let's try this again. Kelly, it's Julian calling about the twelve messages you left, all marked urgent. Now, tell me again what you just told me, only this time in English."

"All right but please promise me that you won't be upset when I break it down for you."

"Cool, so what's got my girl all out of sorts?"

"Nah, you didn't promise me. We've been tight for a long time, Julian. I know how you shut down and refuse to hear another word I say once you've gotten upset," Kelly told him. "So promise."

Julian thought Kelly had played her game long enough and he'd grown tired of the stall tactics. "Listen to me, Kelly Taylor, you'd better tell me what the hell is going on before I move on with my day without it." When Kelly held her ground, Julian caved in. "You're just going to sit there holding the phone until I promise, aren't you?" Silence. "Okay, you win. I promise not to get upset."

Traffic had come to a complete stop as Julian approached Ninety-sixth Street and Broadway.

"Well, since you promised, I'll tell you." Kelly knew how to work a man into a sexual frenzy. She also knew how to render him into submission with relentless pouting, if that's what the situation called for. "There must have been a photographer from *The New York Weekly* covering the entertainment beat at Justin's last night because . . . there's a very flattering picture of our happy trio on page six."

Julian whipped his car toward the curb and slammed on the brakes. "Page six of *The Weekly*!" he shouted at the top of his lungs. "Kelly, I know you didn't bring no drama into my personal space. Tell me you didn't."

"See, there you go. Whenever you start letting your ghetto show and your grammar slide, a bad attitude can't be too far behind," she huffed. "And you promised me you wouldn't get upset."

"Upset? Upset? I'm not upset. I'm livid! Livid is way past being upset. Hold on a minute, and if you value what's left of our friendship, you bet' not hang up the phone."

Several taxi drivers displayed their angst by pounding on car horns and shouting obscenities in an assortment of foreign languages as the rear end of Julian's midnight-blue BMW jutted out into the turning lane. Pedestrians scurrying into nearby buildings gawked at the well-dressed black man, who'd abandoned a 7-Series luxury sedan to bum-rush a sidewalk newsstand.

After marching up to the wooden kiosk, Julian frantically searched the periodicals. "*New York Times, Wall Street Journal, New York Post, Daily News . . . New York Weekly!*" He snatched a copy of the newspaper off the rack and ripped it open. "Page six, page six," he muttered. There it was just above the fold, a framed photo of Julian seated at a dinner table sharing laughs and cocktails with two fashionably attired women. Julian's heart skipped a beat when the realization sank in regarding just how very public his life would become leading up to the election runoffs. The story was down and dirty, short and sweet, just enough to grab readers' attention over breakfast or on the train ride into the city.

IN THE SPOTLIGHT
by Natalie Huffman

*New York City Councilman and man-about-town Julian Blake
was spotted last night at Justin's Restaurant, owned by rap mogul
P. Diddy, with the ever-lovely marketing wizard Kelly Taylor and
an unnamed beauty. Blake insists that he and Taylor are "no more
than good friends," but rumor has it that Blake is primed to make a
run for mayor of the Big Apple and that the fabulous Ms. Taylor will
be the machine that runs his campaign. Blake is known to frequent
many of the hotspots around the city with a bevy of beauties. However,
Ms. Taylor continually seems to rate high on the list of lovelies to be
found on the arm of Councilman Blake. One wonders, with all the
lady-hopping and the late nights in all the right places, when our
elected official will have time to do the job he was elected for. As the
old saying goes, politics make strange bedfellows. This reporter will
be curious to see what role, if any, the new face in Councilman
Blake's life will play in the days to come. In other news . . .*

The newsstand vendor looked on as Julian stared down at his
own image, seemingly staring back at him as well. "Hey, looky
there. That's you," the vendor acknowledged. "Whoa, the both of
your dates are knockouts. What, you famous or somethin'?" His
question was answered with an icy glare, cold enough to freeze the
Hudson.

Julian hastily overpaid for the stack of remaining papers and
tossed the wrapped bundle into the trunk of his car as if those were
the only ones left in the city, then jumped back into his car, mutter-
ing and cussing the whole time.

Kelly listened in tense silence on the other end as the man she
cared for, in more ways than one, contemplated the potential fall-
outs over having been labeled "the lady-hopping man-about-
town."

"Kelly, you there?"

She jumped. "Yeah, I'm still here. Where'd you go?"

"I had to get my hands on the story that's got me looking like
some aging hip-hop rapper who can't keep his fly zipped," he

barked into the speakerphone. "I'm making a bid for mayor. Mayor, Kelly. I've spent four long years on the city council and a lot of time building strong alliances with very important people. People who want to feel like they're backing the right candidate, not some flashy partying club pimp." Julian exhaled a heavy dose of frustration. "Look, I'm sure that this wasn't one of your little marketing schemes to get me some hot press, but articles with a nonprofessional slant can't do anything but hurt my chances with the people."

"*The people*?" Kelly repeated. "Let me hip you to *the people* who've been blowing up my e-mail all morning. I've gotten requests from nearly every television show and newspaper in the city, all wanting to interview the most eligible bachelor in New York. Now if you ask me, what the people want is a whole lot more of some Julian Blake." When Julian didn't respond immediately, Kelly's lips formed a perfect "uh-huh, gotcha" grin. "Just play with that thought for a second and let it marinade. If you handle the conservative crowd and allow me to do what I'm best at, together we can wrap this thing up in one helluva beautiful bow. You should consider Natalie Huffman's review of your date with the, and I quote, 'fabulous Ms. Taylor and an unnamed guest,' an entrée into the dinner party of a lifetime."

"Whew, this is too much and too fast," Julian replied finally. "I don't know about living my life out in the press. Those same newspaper entertainment hounds who would do anything for a story would do just that, *anything for a story*, no matter the consequences to their prey. I don't want them quizzing me about my love life, my 'female associates . . .'"

"Well, you're quite the gentleman, so that's not going to happen. You don't kiss and tell, no matter who wants to know."

Julian was smiling again, this time because there was a lot of truth in what Kelly surmised. "Yeah, you do have a point. And speaking of who wants what, how well do you know that unnamed guest you introduced me to?"

"Raja, she's real cool people. Other than what you had the chance to see for yourself, I'd say she's a self-motivated woman of the new millennium, a sista with all the right stuff that brothas want their women to aspire to be."

"Your girl was real jazzy and you know how I love that. We talked and danced into the wee hours—as they say."

"Uh-huh, hence the reason I hooked you two up. She's all that and a Cadillac," Kelly replied with quaint amusement.

"Hence the reason?" Julian teased in a jovial tone. "You must really be feeling yourself right now. Tell you what, Kelly. I'll let this sixth-page media mishap slide if you run a background check on Ms. Jackson. I don't need any more surprises."

"Yes, suh, master suh, I's gone get right on it."

Julian tossed his head back and laughed. "Yeah, you do that. Later."

Julian caught an elevator in the underground parking garage of Branson & Talbert feeling a lot better about the article and how his future constituents might have viewed his moment in the limelight. Raja was stunning, after all, and Julian had thoroughly enjoyed their witty banter over dinner. Perhaps a sneak peek into his private life wasn't so bad as long as it didn't evolve into something catastrophically damaging to his political career.

When Julian stepped off the elevator on the fourteenth floor of the highly regarded law firm, several of the paralegals, aides, and administrative assistants stopped in their tracks to take in long, extended glances. "It's Julian Blake," one of the young women whispered to a coworker at the copy machine. "Here he comes. Maybe you should ask for an autograph."

"Okay, my cousin Gina's been in love with him since she moved here from D.C." the tall willowy brunette responded. "It's too bad they've never met." She approached Julian with a copy of *The New York Weekly* folded at the entertainment section. "Mr. Blake, I know that you're a very busy attorney and I wouldn't normally bother you, but would you mind signing this for my cousin?" she asked, presenting the paper with one hand and an ink pen in the other.

It was then that he noticed for the first time there was scarcely any movement in a work area generally buzzing with energy. He glanced around the office and saw a few too many grins and batting of eyes for his tastes. Having been a crackerjack litigator at Branson & Talbert for ten years, Julian had received more than his share of accolades for winning tough cases, but nothing close to facing autograph seekers at his own office. "Are you serious?" he asked. "You expect me to sign that newspaper?"

The woman's expression displayed her newly mounting trepidations, but she stayed the steady course. "Well, yeah. You're a celebrity now, Mr. Blake, and my cousin thinks you're a hunk."

Somewhat flattered, Julian agreed to jot down his John Hancock for the cousin's sake. A signature in exchange for a potential vote might be an interesting trade-off.

"So, what's this cousin's name?" he asked, while scribbling his name.

"Cynthia," she lied. "Oh, thank you so much. She'll be so happy about this."

"Don't mention it, but going forward, let's stick to the firm's business during business hours . . ." he said. He already knew her name was Cynthia and knew the autograph was not for a cousin.

"That's Cynthia, with a *y*," she whispered, with a wink just this side of flirtatious.

Julian handed back the newspaper and quickly dismissed the whole episode as he headed to his office. Just as he was about to flash a good-morning smile at Grace, his secretary, the phone rang. He slowed his steps when she held up one finger—their secret code that the call was worthy of his attention.

"Sure, hold one minute, Ms. Taylor, he just walked in." Grace glanced up. "Ms. Taylor on two."

Justin couldn't imagine what Kelly could want now. "Thanks," he muttered. He walked into his office and shut the door behind him.

Crossing the hardwood floors, he snatched up the phone and stared out the window upon the Manhattan skyline.

"This better be damn good news this time," he said instead of hello.

"Depends on if having lunch with your best friend on the planet is good news."

He could almost see the smile playing around her mouth. He grinned. "Did somebody say food?"

They both laughed.

"Figured that was the least I could do."

"Yeah, the very least."

"Be nice. Anyway, meet me at Mong's Tips and Things."

Julian groaned.

"Noon."

Julian opened his mouth to protest, but Kelly hung up before he could give her a quick cussing out just between best friends. He hung up the phone and shook his head.

Two

The sugary scent of vanilla spice permeated the air as Raja Jackson lit the row of candles that stretched along the back ledge of her sunken tub. Born under a water sign, she began each day with a luxurious soak in a hot scented bath as both a mandatory indulgence and a sharp reminder of how far she'd come from the cold-water East New York flat of her childhood.

Slipping out of her silk robe, Raja crossed the room and stood naked before the mirror that covered an entire wall of her custom-designed extra-expansive bathroom. Yes, it had cost a small fortune to tear down all that Sheetrock and convert her spare bedroom into the area where she now stood, but as far as Raja was concerned it had been money well spent. The bathroom was where she got her head right. Where she meditated and calculated and got her scheme on, and if she wanted the details of her life to go exactly as planned, then she had to start each day out correctly. Right here in this room.

Raja was an early riser, and her apartment was on the top floor of a busy condo in Montclair, New Jersey. Outside, the sky was awakening, with just a touch of orange peeking into the new day. She enjoyed bearing witness to the sun's birth each morning, and she never closed the curtains during her morning bath. For all she knew some pervert with a pair of binoculars watched her undress on the regular, and God help him if he did, because Raja knew how to put on a show. She strutted around that bathroom like the luscious black goddess that she was, and if some lucky man out there was treating himself to a few pieces of her ebony eye candy each morning, she sure as hell wasn't mad at him.

With quiet intensity, she scrutinized her face under the flickering light reflected in the mirror, pleased with what she saw. Her brow was high and her eyebrows professionally arched. At thirty-one years old, her cinnamon-colored skin was still flawless, her lips soft and sensual, her nose neither spread out all over her face, nor too tightly pinched. Of course her hair, still covered by her sleeping cap, was the bomb. Mozelle might be the messiest, backstabbingest, cutthroat somebody in Brooklyn, but she had a Midas touch when it came to wielding a pair of scissors and choosing the right perm. Total strangers were mesmerized by Raja's hair. White men wanted to touch it, black men wanted to be touched by it, and women of all races were dying for the name of the magician who waved her wand over it every week.

Her eyes raked down the length of her naked body and she nodded in satisfaction, staring at her round breasts, then turned slightly to get a view of her hips in profile. Delicious. Just delicious. Every curve was in just the right place, and in just the right proportion.

Done with her body, Raja parted her lips in the mirror and revealed her best feature. Her smile. Bright, powerful, seductive, perfect. As well it should be. Five grand invested in bleaching treatments and Invisalign retainers was nothing to sneeze at. Her perfect smile completed her perfect package and gave Raja all the confidence she needed to stay on top of her game in a world where having a sharp mind didn't mean a damn thing if you didn't have the breathtaking looks to back it up.

Judging by the stir she'd caused in Justin's Restaurant the night before, and the sexy vibes she'd picked up from the gorgeous councilman she'd dined with, Raja had both. And she knew how to use them, too. Her entrance into Justin's had been off the hook as she arrived fifteen minutes late for a scheduled dinner with her girl-friend Kelly Taylor, and the black politician Kelly had insisted Raja just had to meet.

"Cool," Raja had said, finally giving in after twenty minutes of listening to Kelly gush about the man as if he were the best thing since the booty-shrinking body wrap. "But remember, I'm a lady. I don't show up for strange men all by myself. If you want me to meet him so bad, then you're going to have to be right there to in-troduce him."

Kelly had agreed, and set the meeting up for dinner at Justin's at 7:00 p.m. Raja arrived promptly at 7:15 looking perfect from head to toe, and gave herself a mental pat on the back as every man in the house broke his neck to get a look at her as she sauntered across the room, flashing her brilliant smile and working her designer dress six ways to next Sunday.

She'd kept up the energy throughout dinner, and by the time the evening ended she was convinced that Kelly had been right. Julian Blake was a prime catch. He was a high-profile black man who fit right in with her agenda. Single, good-looking, well connected, and ambitious. What more could a sister want in a man?

Retrieving her morning paper and a small book of personal affir-mations from the vanity near the window, Raja eased herself down into her steaming bath. The water was swirling with scented oils and creamy body softeners, and coated her skin like liquid velvet. Holding the newspaper above the water, Raja read from a page in the notebook of affirmations she'd been doodling in since her col-lege days. She chanted the affirmations out loud, and mostly from memory.

Raja Monet Jackson, you are great.
Nothing can stop you from achieving your goals.
No one but God is more glorious than you.
You have the power to do amazing things.
Whatever you pursue with all your might, you conquer.
You are black and beautiful and female, the envy of the world.

Breathing deeply and filled with a serene sense of her own power, Raja dropped the book to the floor and positioned herself against the padded neck brace she'd had specially installed at the head of the tub. She opened the newspaper and relaxed.

A social butterfly, Raja was a regular at professional and cultural society events, and her subscription to *The New York Weekly* was one way of staying abreast of the city's happenings, even if she did have to pay extra to get an early morning delivery. Besides, as the international banking manager at First American Bank, she spent the bulk of her day reading financial codes and regulations, so a few positive affirmations and an early morning dip in the gossip pool were more than justified.

Raja skimmed the paper as her pampered body appreciated the abundance of hot water that cocooned her in the tub. She paused at a column on page 6 entitled IN THE SPOTLIGHT, written by some chick called Natalie Huffman. Raja smirked. Huffman was probably some fat, frustrated frankfurter-eating white woman who couldn't snag a decent man to save her life. Her columns were usually juicy and up-to-the-minute, but nice-nasty as well. Full of veiled sarcasm but stopping just short of making you want to revert to the East New York days and call the heffah up and tell her a few things. Raja read:

> *New York City Councilman and man-about-town Julian Blake was spotted last night at Justin's Restaurant, owned by rap mogul P. Diddy, with the ever-lovely marketing wizard Kelly Taylor and an unnamed beauty . . .*

Raja sat straight up in the tub, her eyes greedily devouring the text, her heart hammering as she skimmed the paragraph.

> *Blake insists that he and Taylor are "no more than good friends," but rumor has it that Blake is primed to make a run for mayor of the Big Apple and that the fabulous Ms. Taylor will be the machine that runs his campaign. Blake is known to frequent many of the hotspots around the city with a bevy of beauties. However, Ms. Taylor*

continually seems to rate high on the list of lovelies to be found on the arm of Councilman Blake. One wonders, with all the lady-hopping and the late nights in all the right places, when our elected official will have time to do the job he was elected for. As the old saying goes, politics make strange bedfellows . . .

Why the hell was Huffman sweating Kelly so hard? Raja wondered hotly. Julian Blake had asked *her* to dinner. Fine, cultured Raja Jackson. Kelly was simply the icebreaker, an expendable tool to bridge the initial gap. And what the hell was up with that unnamed beauty label? If Natalie Huffman wanted to know who she was, all she had to do was ask. But yeah, Raja thought, settling back into the tub with a bit of satisfaction. Huffman had one thing right. *A beauty. That would be me.* She smiled and read the column's closing line . . . *This reporter will be curious to see what role, if any, the new face in Councilman Blake's life will play in the days to come.*

Raja laughed out loud at that one. Oh, she was gonna play a role, all right. That much was for sure. A leading role. The starring role. Because no matter how many cute little airhead honeys Julian Blake was accustomed to parading around town, if Mr. Man was planning to run for mayor of New York City he was going to need a woman who had it going on in all areas to complement his public package. A sister who knew the correct political protocol and who could hold her own when swimming in the high-society waters men like Julian Blake navigated.

For sure, for sure, Raja thought, dropping the paper and lying back in the tub and splashing thick suds over her high breasts. It was time to get her scheme on. The buck-toothed little girl from East New York had come a long way, had totally reinvented herself, but there was still more work to be done.

Humming a tune by India Arie, Raja trailed her fingers through the cooling water, teasing them along her supple thighs and across her firm stomach. *Brown skin . . . up against your brown skin . . .* Justin Blake for mayor would be a tough campaign for a man who had a reputation as a club-hopping playa-playa. With or without the mighty marketing wizard Kelly Taylor there to guide him. No, whether he knew it or not, Julian needed an image overhaul. A tune-up of his public perception, a shoring-up of his political image, and hooking up with a sister like Raja Monet Jackson would be the perfect way to get it.

Three

Kelly inspected each newly filled French-tipped nail with the concentration of a health inspector in a Chinese restaurant.

She regarded her index finger carefully, and the Asian technician, Mong, dragged the brush across the lip of the bottle preparing to apply a thin layer of clear polish. Kelly waved her off. Too much was almost as bad as too little.

"I always swear to God I'm never coming to pick you up at the salon, but here I am again."

Kelly blew a kiss at Julian. "Stop swearing to God."

Mong smiled at Kelly, but made pretty eyes at Julian.

Over her expertly manicured nails, Kelly observed every woman in the salon. Old, young, and every age in between, all eyes were on Julian.

He was indeed delicious eye candy. He knew it too as he casually lounged against the wall, his arms crossed over a chest many would give their husband's paycheck to lay their head against.

Ladies flowed by, a fashion show of designer this and that, and they basked in their four seconds in the sun of Julian Blake.

When the parade ended, his gaze returned to Kelly. She saw what the women saw, but when he smiled at her, she felt the heat deep in her chest.

She smirked at him, giving her nails a final blow. "Come on,

Cassanova. If we don't leave now, I'm afraid Natalie Huffman, our favorite reporter, would suffer heart failure when she had to report that she missed the orgy of the century, right under her nose in downtown Manhattan."

"That's why I love you, girl. You're always looking out for me." Julian hooked her purse over his arm, but pulled a fifty out of his pocket and paid the bill.

They headed out, and Kelly was thankful that she didn't have anything pressing to do that afternoon. She loved the fact that she called her own shots and her own hours, but the hustle of New York continued and was something Kelly never stopped enjoying.

But Julian didn't seem to be all there.

"What you thinkin' about?"

"Food. You promised food, remember?" Julian started walking, swinging her purse as he went. He headed to the curb and raised his hand for a taxi.

"Is Natalie a freaking ghost?" he asked, suddenly coming to a sharp halt. He whipped around and nearly collided into Kelly, who'd come up short behind him. "How does she know my every move?"

Kelly inhaled his scent and collected her thoughts. "Spies, baby," she said, smooth as an expensive liqueur. "It's only going to get worse when you run for mayor."

"You think she's got someone in my camp?"

"Maybe. Even the most tightly run campaigns have a weak link. But that's not the point. As a councilman you do your job. You vote on time. You push for controversial legislation and win. You're good-looking and single. You know your stuff, and you kiss babies. You're a dream. Hell, I'd vote for you."

"Your ass better. I'm not paying for manicures just so you can vote for my rival."

Smiling, Kelly stopped their easy banter. "So you own me, is that what you're saying?"

"Hell yeah. Got a problem with that?"

"I might," she replied, unable to hide her grin.

"Then give me back my nails and toes. What else have I paid for?

That ten grand I gave you last year, and you claimed it went to pay off your parents' house in Philly? I know that money went to a boob job."

Giggling, Kelly turned her face away from Julian's prying eyes. "You are so full of shit. I gave you the money back, and I did not get a boob job."

"You didn't? My bad." Julian looped his arm through hers and pulled her up the sidewalk. "You should have. Last time I saw them, they were swinging kind of low."

Laughing, Kelly gently raked her fingernails down Julian's cheek and then tugged on his earlobe.

He growled and tried to escape. "Girl, quit. You know that drives me crazy."

"Really? I had no idea."

They walked for a block in silence until Kelly couldn't take it anymore. "Can we talk seriously for a minute?"

Julian guided her to an outdoor patio and found seats in a relatively quiet corner. "If we're going to talk, I have to eat. I think better on a full stomach."

The birth of summer bathed the air in a mild breeze, beckoning winter-weary New Yorkers out to play. They strolled or jogged by, a few even smiled.

Kelly had a real appreciation for daylight, but her favorite time of day was when the sky was black, broken by a trillion little stars.

The night was her playtime, and she enjoyed that Julian was a man of the night, too. But she was concerned that their partying would hurt his mayoral campaign. Natalie had mentioned it in her column, and that meant on Monday when Julian went to work he'd hear about it from several of his fellow council members. And not in a favorable way. He was young, intelligent, popular, black, and in demand. The older, more elite members felt he needed mentoring.

Julian felt differently.

Kelly knew differently.

He was primed to be mayor, and they were running scared that they'd have to report to his young, intelligent, popular black ass.

They'd better get used to it, Kelly thought, because if she had her way, she'd see Julian in the mayor's office.

"What you havin'?" he asked, perusing the menu.

"Caesar salad, light dressing on the side, one ounce of grilled chicken on top, no Parmesan cheese."

He looked at her, the space between his eyes dented. "Why the hell don't you just order lettuce? Light dressing, no cheese," he mimicked. "That's lettuce, Kelly. Rabbit food."

"I wouldn't have this body if I ate like you."

The waitress approached and he handed her the menu. "A plate of lettuce for her and the lunch grilled tuna for me."

Kelly smiled as she dug her heel into Julian's toe. He grimaced as she gave her correct order. "Also, two bottled waters, please."

"One for me too," he said, and the waitress left.

He sat with his back to the sidewalk and leaned forward, bracing his elbows on the table. "Is Natalie correct? Are you going to be my campaign manager?"

So that's what had been bothering him. Not that they'd been to three private parties at the hottest clubs last night with Raja hanging on his arm as if they shared a common vein. Not even that Natalie had more spies on staff than the CIA.

Kelly gazed at him. He wanted to know if she'd be there to support him.

She took his hand. "Julian, my strengths are the big details of life. I'll be there to make sure you talk to the people in our circle that matter. Be seen at the right events, press the flesh with the right grassrooters that will get you the votes of thousands nobody cares about."

"You're saying no? I can't believe you, Kelly. I need you. You're underestimating your abilities to handle this for me."

He looked almost heartbroken, but Kelly had to stand strong; otherwise he'd lose. Her life hadn't been a bed of roses, and she would not be an unwanted distraction to his run for the top position of New York.

"Julian, let someone who's qualified make sure your campaign contributions are within the legal limit, file all your papers, meet every deadline, review your taxes, run background checks on the volunteers, and all the other campaign shit I don't want to deal with. I'm going to be there every step of the way, but I don't want to captain this ship. Let me work with you and the campaign manager, speechwriters, publicists, and administrative staff to ensure that your image is maximized."

"I'm not sold, Kelly. All the things you just said should be done by someone else can be accomplished by you. You know me better than my own mother. This is a prime opportunity to let your real talents show. I trust you, Kelly. We could go to the top. Together."

Her chest tightened. Julian knew how to push her buttons. But he was pushing the wrong ones.

Their food was delivered and the waitress vanished inside the restaurant with dirty plates from an older couple that was about to leave. The man took the woman's hand and kissed her fingers. Kelly tore her gaze away and looked at her salad, dipped her fork in the dressing, then speared some lettuce leaves and ate.

"Julian, I'm not the person for that job. You know my history and I know yours. Some things need to stay left behind. Period."

He ate some of his tuna and cut his asparagus into bite-size pieces. "You're talking about the date rape in college? Kelly, that was fifteen years ago. If it comes up, we'll deal with it."

"I never reported the rape. My brothers beat him within an inch of his life. He was hospitalized for four weeks. He could come forward and twist the story around, and suddenly your campaign isn't about lowering taxes, fixing roads, overhauling the prison system, or homeland security. It's about me and something that happened a lifetime ago."

"We all have skeletons."

As if summoned by negative forces, a cloud floated in front of the sun and a cool breeze swept across the patio. They held their napkins over their plates, not wanting the scummy dirt of the street to taint their food.

"Julian, I can take the heat. Hell, nothing can happen to me now, the statute of limitations for me filing a complaint has been over for years. But constituents want their candidates to have squeaky clean pasts, and the people who work for them should be invisible. The last thing you need is me overshadowing your future. I'll be by your side all the way, but I can't be your campaign manager."

His eyes said he understood. Julian ran his fingers down the side of her face and Kelly leaned into the comforting gesture.

"Do you ever regret not coming forward?" he asked.

She cocked her head to the side. "No. The law wasn't always fair to women victims and I didn't want my life in the hands of reckless attorneys. The family ass-kicking he got was enough vindication. He can't hurt me now or ever. As for you, we'll hire the best person available and after you win, we're going to show everybody how things are really done."

They both laughed and Kelly turned to her vibrating cell phone. "Hey, Raja. Where you been?"

She listened for a moment, knowing Julian was eavesdropping. He and Raja were all over each other the night before. Raja practically panted every time they drove past a jewelry store. She wanted a ring worse than she wanted air.

"Julian's right here. Want to talk to him?"

Kelly handed over the phone and signaled for the check. She paid the bill while Julian relaxed into his conversation.

Kelly leaned back in her chair, glad the moment between her and Julian had passed. She had more skeletons in her closet than a costume shop before Halloween, but Julian's past was pure as the driven snow. His intelligence and dedication garnered unprecedented support across party lines. That made him a great leader to some, dangerous to others. The press would start digging. And her rape might be found out.

For now until the end of the campaign, she'd stay classified as a close friend of the councilman's. If the media made the rape public, women and victims of crimes across the country would sympathize with her and their exposé efforts would backfire. The media would leave her alone as long as she stayed in a nonessential role.

Julian sat with his legs open, chatting with Raja like a teenager.

The cloud shifted, taking the cool air with it, but Kelly didn't feel as carefree as she had earlier.

They'd have to stop hanging out so much. The mayor's race was months off, but Julian had an image to maintain.

Julian picked up a napkin and gestured to her mouth.

"Where?" Kelly wiped her face and looked at her hands.

"Come here." He motioned to Kelly. "Raja, I'll see you tonight, baby. Later. Right here," he said to Kelly and dabbed at her mouth, their faces inches apart.

Out the corner of her eye, she saw the out-of-character movement of a man stepping behind a freestanding sign. She wasn't mistaken that he had a long-lens camera around his neck. She gestured with her shoulder. "Eleven o'clock. We've got company."

He stayed close. "A photographer?"

"Looks like one of Natalie's."

"Let's see who he is."

"Come on, Julian. I've got three parties tonight and you need to be seen in church tomorrow. Forget him."

He started backing up, smiling. He was going to chase the man. "See you later."

"You've got to go to church tomorrow, you heathen. Julian," she warned, laughing. "You're not a dog on a hunt."

The photographer was still standing there, unaware that Julian was about to pounce. He had a busy street to cross and it was likely that the photographer would get away, but occasionally Julian liked to behave like a kid. She felt sorry for the man if Julian caught up to him.

"I'll see you tomorrow," he called, backpedaling faster. "And my heathen ass will be in church on time."

Kelly nodded and he took off, the photographer freezing in shock that Julian was dodging through traffic heading toward him.

Kelly chuckled and started back toward her condo. After tonight, they'd have to get serious about his campaign. After all, if Julian was in the mayor's office, so was she.

Four

Raja waited as Julian unlocked the passenger side of the car and held the door open. His ride was sweet and powerful, the perfect vehicle for an upwardly mobile black man like him.

She slid in smoothly, taking her time and making sure Julian got a good long look at her toned, shapely legs and the hot, but demure, little black Fendi that rode sexily up her thighs. Raja crossed her legs at the knee, then gazed at Julian through her lashes, smiling inside. Yep, his eyes were wide. Her legs provoked that response from a lot of people, male and female.

"Here," Julian said softly. "Let me get that for you." Reaching across her body without touching her, he slid the seat belt into its mechanism and made sure it clicked.

Raja seized the opportunity and inhaled deeply, enjoying his clean masculine scent and the light aroma of the expensive cologne he'd used sparingly. So far she was digging everything about Julian, and even after he straightened up and closed her door, she couldn't help envisioning his body hovering over hers in other ways.

"Dinner was lovely," Raja said sweetly as Julian climbed in beside her and fastened his own seat belt. He had invited her to accompany him to a fund-raiser at Abysinnian Baptist Church, but first they'd dined at an intimate little Italian restaurant where the lights were low and the food was excellent. Raja had chosen the restau-

rant after reading about its merits in a local dining review, and decided what better way to sample the menu than to have someone
else pick up the tab?

Pulling out of the parking space, Julian paused to flash her a
quick smile. "My pleasure, Miss Raja. I'm sure we'll do it again. Real
soon."

Damn right, Raja thought and settled back into her plush seat. Of
course he wanted to take her out again. She was a quality woman.
Cultured, educated, polished . . . and it didn't hurt that she was also
beautiful. Julian knew the deal. Top shelf recognized top shelf, and
she and Julian were definitely cut from the same social cloth.

Raja tapped her foot to the tune of an easy jazz beat drifting from
the car's speakers. Growing up in the hood she'd hated anything except rap or rhythm and blues, but by the time she'd graduated from
college and broadened her political horizons, she understood how
important it was to speak the right way, wear the right clothes, and
listen to the right music.

Julian drove with confidence. He was neither overly aggressive
nor passively careful, and Raja liked that. She was feeling a bit
chatty and since conversation flowed so naturally between them she
engaged him with small talk and kept the vibe easy and upbeat.

"I just love the city," Raja was saying as they sped past bright
lights and crowds of people. "My parents wanted me to go away for
college, but I couldn't bear to leave all of this so I stayed right here
and got a great graduate degree in finance."

Julian's brow went up. "Where'd you go? Columbia, right? They
have the best finance program going and the school has a great reputation."

Raja nodded. "Yes, Columbia is an amazing school. The faculty
there seems really intent on ensuring that students have a top-
notch educational experience."

Two points for Raja! She laughed inside. She'd taken advantage of
in-state tuition rates and graduated first from Brooklyn College,
and then transferred over to Baruch where she received her MBA
in finance and investments. Columbia hadn't even been on the list
of colleges she could afford to attend. Julian should have known

better than to make assumptions, and it wasn't her responsibility to correct him.

"So how long did you live in Montclair?" Julian asked.

"Until my teens," Raja said, the lie sliding smoothly past her lips. There was no way in hell she'd claim East New York. Not even under oath. "My father worked in New York, but he and my mother didn't feel it was the right environment in which to raise children. My father commuted into the city each day while my mother ran a small business out of Montclair. I have lots of family in New York, though, so it's truly like a second home."

Julian signaled left and whipped the car around a short turn just as the traffic light changed to red. He was a man who took chances, Raja decided, which was both sexy and intriguing.

"Does your father still work in the city, or have your folks retired?"

Okay, sister, Raja counseled herself. *This is where you pour it on thick.* "No," she said, the word slipping softly from her lips. Raja turned toward the window as if in deep reflection, then stared straight ahead before speaking. "My dad was a fireman. He perished in a blaze down in Lower Manhattan. He rushed into a burning building when someone in the crowd screamed that a little girl was still inside. It turned out that the little girl had spent the night with a friend way across town, and the building was actually empty. Daddy didn't make it back out. They found his body the next day. On the floor of the little girl's bedroom."

Raja forced a tear from her eye and quickly produced a tissue from her purse to dab at it.

"Oh, Raja," Julian said quietly. "I'm sorry. I had no idea you'd suffered such a loss or I would never have mentioned your family. Thank God you had a strong mother though. She must have honored your father's brave spirit by raising you to be so lovely."

Raja shook her head, her curls bouncing with body before each strand settled perfectly back into its assigned place. "Not really. You see, Mother's soul was battered. She hated the fires that my father chased, but knew that forbidding him to do so would crush his spirit. She was a praying wife, that much is for sure, but when

Daddy left us she just couldn't bear up. She lasted about a year, but it was downhill all the way. The doctors couldn't find a thing wrong with her, and one of them told me in private that she was dying from a broken heart."

"Damn," Julian swore under his breath. "That's really sad."

"Yes," Raja said with a rise in her voice. Who the hell knew who her father really was? And her mother . . . while Raja had loved her dearly, Sadie Jackson had had some sure 'nuff undesirable habits.

Faking interest in her surroundings, Raja peered straight ahead. The church parking lot was a block up and Raja wanted to bring the mood back up before they went inside. "But their deaths were a long time ago and I've adjusted remarkably well. I've dedicated my life to being a woman that my parents would be proud of. I've taken all of their life examples and incorporated them into my own personal philosophy, and there isn't a day that goes by when I don't feel them smiling down on me with love and approval."

Abysinnian Baptist Church was large and regal. It boasted a tithe-paying congregation in the thousands, and most were fast-tracking young professionals on the rise. Raja plastered the appropriate smile onto her face as Julian led her inside. The sight of the councilman arriving had set tongues wagging, and Raja knew that with her silky hair, perfect smile, and designer dress, they were the picture of success. A perfect package.

Raja clung to Julian's arm as they moved through the crowd and into the church. They got envious looks from most of the men, many of whom wished they had the good looks and positioning that Julian had, and would have chopped off their right foot to have a woman like Raja on their arm. The church sisters were another matter. They were drooling over Julian like a bunch of hallelujah hussies, vying to get his attention while gazing jealously at Raja as they checked her out from head to toe in three seconds flat.

Raja just smiled and let her hips sway gently as she moved like a diva. She looked scrumptious and she knew it. Obviously Julian knew it too because out of all the women who could have had his attention tonight it was her hand that he was now clasping tightly as he guided her to a front table that had been reserved specially for them.

"Thanks for accompanying me," he whispered into her ear as he pulled her chair out and waited until she was seated. "If I haven't already told you a million times, you look beautiful."

Raja smiled and nodded briefly. Of course she did. But he looked good too in his custom-made suit and well-groomed haircut. The Rolex on his wrist was the real thing without being flashy or pretentious.

They had barely settled into their seats when an event organizer asked them to stand in the greeting line. Raja couldn't wait. She and Julian stood shoulder to shoulder as Julian greeted the guests and sponsors as they arrived, then smoothly introduced them to Raja before turning to focus on the next person with his engaging warmth and bright smile.

This was her chance to prove she could hold her own, and Raja wasn't about to blow it. She was charming and delightful as she shook each person's hand and called everyone by name, making just the appropriate amount of small talk and paying small but sincere compliments as the guests moved down the line.

Sisters could be vicious and catty, but Raja expected that. She turned the charm up an extra notch with those women she suspected of hating on her; the ones who lingered a moment too long while shaking Julian's hand, or whose hot smiles immediately froze when they turned to face her.

She gave it to them good, clasping their hands between both of her own and shaking firmly, pulling them slightly toward her in a power gesture designed to keep them off balance and to give herself the upper hand. She smiled sweetly at these overly made up wanna-be-a-Raja types, while her eyes told them that yes, she'd spotted that fake-ass Gucci purse, and yep, she knew that dress came straight off a rack at Marshall's, and for sure, the Negro standing next to her was officially off the market because Raja Monet Jackson was the super shit of the new millennium and every other chick with a wish and a short skirt was simply living in her shadow.

The entry line had thinned and Raja supposed she'd shaken close to three hundred hands. Julian had just taken her by one hand and placed his other in the small of her back to lead her toward their table when she spotted Kelly slipping quietly through the doors.

Five

Kelly breathed deeply and tried to tame her rapid heartbeat. This was only church. Everybody was welcome. Sinners included. *Well, that would be me*, she thought, slowing as she stepped lightly on the cement to preserve the heels of her favorite Blahniks.

She was always struck with a bit of nerves before she entered the doors of a church, because there had been a period in her life when she'd fallen out of love with God.

Those dark days had been a lifetime ago, but inside her core there was still the tiniest kernel that held the secrets to the question God had never answered. *Why me?*

"Sista, do you need assistance?"

Kelly didn't realize that she'd reached the elegant entrance of the great Abysinnian Baptist Church, nor that the tug that had ignited deep in her belly when she'd breached the property of this tabernacle was a force she couldn't control.

She had to remind herself that she was no longer that barely legal nineteen-year-old, ass-swingin' plastic-pumps-wearin' imitation of the woman she'd wanted to become.

Now she was the worm of silk, the opiate, a child birthed from the earth. Twice.

Once by God's hands. The second time by her own.

The rape had about destroyed her. Stripped her to the saddest form of human. Half a woman with half a mind.

The lady who'd found her mangled body on her doorstep had uttered over and over that half crazy wasn't nearly good enough. Go all the way, or forget the bullshit and walk on.

Kelly had walked ten days later. And every day since then. A decade and more had passed before she'd ventured through the doors of a church. Now she was what she wanted to be. There was nothing to fear. Not anymore. She was in the driver seat of her destiny, and the future she wanted was somewhere inside these doors.

"Come." The man who held the door open didn't extend his hand, and for that she was grateful.

These were her steps. Her walk. And she took them alone.

Damn, Raja thought, sizing up her friend. Kelly could be really pretty if she just took the time to do something with herself. That whole casually thrown together look she had going on was tired. If she ever hoped to land a decent man she'd have to come better than that, because the competition was a bitch out there and sisters were starting to get up much earlier in the morning to make sure they looked good from all angles.

"There's Kelly," Julian said and abruptly let go of Raja's hand. "Kelly!" he called out, waving to get her attention. "Over here!"

WTF? . . . Raja wondered. Why'd he have to flag Kelly down as if she were the last cab on a cold night in Brooklyn?

"Hey, you two," Kelly breathed with a big smile.

Julian swept her in a hug so full she absorbed his strength and let it fill up the empty places.

"Crazy girl," he chided, for her ears only. "You had to do it alone, didn't you? I would have walked in with you. But that's you. My little Harriet."

Kelly held surprising tears at bay. She was by no means as brave as the revered Harriet Tubman, but Julian knew how to bring her back from the edge.

"Let me go, now," she whispered, realizing too late that the tears were in her voice. "I'm good as gold."

She would be fine now. The hardest part was over. She hugged Raja and slapped Julian on the arm. "Sorry I'm a little late."

Julian shrugged and elbowed her playfully. "Actually, you're right on time."

Raja's eyes were slits as she watched the interaction, deliberately maintaining her own smile. "Good to see you, Kelly," she said sweetly. "You're looking good, sister-girl."

Raja moved quickly to position herself so that she sat in between Julian and Kelly. They chatted comfortably for a few minutes and sipped the homemade iced tea that some church mother had probably spent hours brewing.

"Kelly, you okay?" Raja's spicy voice asked a hundred questions. Namely, *who you think you are body-checkin' my man in front of all these people?*

Kelly played the role. She wasn't in an explaining mood. "Raja, where's the ladies' room?"

"Up those steps and through this amazing choir room. There are couches in there."

"Need my help?" Julian teased Kelly. "Or better yet, why don't you go with her, Raja?"

Kelly gave Julian's arm a secret squeeze while the banking whiz kid looked as if she'd swallowed an apple whole before leaving his side.

"Oh, sure," Raja piped up. "If you need me."

"No. Mingle," Kelly told them. "I'll catch up to you in a bit."

"We can wait," Julian insisted. "This isn't any fun without you."

"I'm good." Kelly grinned. They needed to be away from each other before one of Natalie's spies gathered enough film of them to fill the entire eleven o'clock news. She started to walk away but stopped short. "Hello, Mayor Haskins," she said, sincerely delighted at seeing him approach. She greeted Ralph Haskins, the former mayor of Virginia, like the old friend that he was—with a warm hug.

"Ms. Taylor," he said, returning the embrace. "You are just the woman I was hoping to see. I've been thinking of another run for office. If this young man isn't smart enough to hire you, I sure am."

"Is that any way to treat your godson?" Julian asked, giving one of his closest confidants a hug.

Kelly slipped away, making a perfunctory visit to the ladies' room, then easing into the crowd. She noticed right away that Raja had inserted herself as the frame of the two men, who now basked in the glow of her statuesque beauty.

Raja would be the perfect fixture for Julian and his career, she thought. She had everything society looked for in a politician's wife: brains, connections, class, and no political aspirations of her own.

Of course Hilary had kicked down that door by retiring as First Lady, then becoming a senator, but not Raja. Her aspirations were not for the floor of the capitol, but the boardroom and then the bedroom of her husband's mansion.

The way Kelly saw it, Julian needed to get serious with someone and soon. There were fifty states of single women and one high-powered, single man who wanted to be mayor of New York.

Julian wouldn't appreciate being the country's newest reality dating spectacle. Raja was the woman for him. Subtlety wasn't one of Kelly's finer attributes, but she'd have to use all the finesse she'd been born with to convince him to fall in love while seeking the job of his dreams.

Now that the good ole ex-mayor was gone, Raja thought she would have a few moments with Julian before the night got into full swing and the pesky Kelly returned. But she didn't get a chance to.

"Excuse me," Julian said abruptly, gazing across the room. "Don Gregory just walked in. I need to pitch him a proposal real quick."

Raja nodded and smiled as he stood, but a moment later her smile was completely knocked from her face. Julian had taken about ten steps when he turned around and gave a quick "come here" gesture toward their table.

"Me?" Raja said, and she was already on her feet and scooping up her tiny purse before he could respond.

Julian shook his head and motioned that she should sit back down. "No, *Kelly*," he mouthed.

Raja looked behind her and spotted Kelly. She felt her insides heat up, but she played it off like a pro. She sat back down and swung one lovely leg over the other as Kelly practically sprinted over to Julian. Their heads were almost touching as Julian whispered something in Kelly's ear, and Raja felt like slapping her friend. But then she chilled out.

Look at her, Raja thought, calming herself. Kelly was absolutely no competition. She had no rearview at all. In fact, from the back Kelly could pass for a man in drag. Besides, Raja reprimanded herself. Kelly was her friend, and a good one at that. There weren't many women she could tolerate, but Kelly was sweet and good-natured and had a lot going for her.

Raja relaxed in her chair and gazed around the room wearing the appropriate smile. She was gonna have to get with Mr. Man though, the next time he dared leave her sitting alone like somebody's afterthought. No, men didn't just walk away from a woman like Raja Jackson. They gave her their quality time and their full attention. Julian Blake might be the man of the hour, but he was gonna have to learn to toe Raja's line. She noticed some friends in the crowd, got up, and headed in their direction.

Kelly talked up Julian to supporters, touting his platform, espousing his past accomplishments. She worked the crowd until she ended up in the center of the room beside Julian.

"Where's Raja?"

"I saw her talking and laughing with a man and woman. Must be friends of hers. I must have left her alone too long."

Kelly laughed. "I'm sure she'll be back soon."

Julian looked over his shoulder and guided Kelly in the opposite direction. "I need a break."

"You've never been afraid of a sexy, gorgeous woman, so why you actin' like there's an A train after you?"

Julian pulled two glasses of sparkling cider off a tray and handed one to Kelly. "You know, Raja's fine. She's got all the best qualities going for her to be standing beside me. But people keep acting like we're about to jump the broom and sweep New York clean at the same time."

"And you want this to be about you and not your personal life. I get that. But if the public doesn't see you with someone, they're going to speculate. If you want this to be about your campaign, you *have* to be seen with her. If you've got your personal life under control, then it becomes invisible."

Several senior citizens approached and started grilling Julian about a sales tax exemption for seniors. Kelly tried slipping away again, when she felt Julian's hand on hers.

She wanted to shake him loose, but his touch was firm.

"I'd like you to meet my publicist, Kelly Taylor."

She communicated with her eyes how "thankful" she was for being pulled into the conversation. Seniors were supporting the economy just like everyone else. New York wasn't about to lose another tax base.

"It's nice to meet you. Ladies, I've got to get the councilman over to meet with the lieutenant governor. I'll make sure your concerns are brought to his attention. Julian?" she said, giving him the exit he needed.

As a couple, they slid into the mainstream of the crowd.

"Thank you," he said for her ears only.

"That's why you pay me the big bucks." Kelly sipped her drink. "I e-mailed you a list of media appearances I want to book for you. Did you review . . . Julian . . . what is it?"

Kelly responded to the sharp intake of air and the jolt of surprise that rolled through Julian and then into her arm where he held her.

"I can't believe it," he said from between his teeth. "God, what's she doing here?"

"Smile, baby, and look only at me. Who you talkin' 'bout?" Kelly scanned the crowd, not seeing anyone who'd cause such an intense reaction to the coolest man she knew.

"Someone I used to know well." He looked around, his face giving away none of the anxiety that rolled off him in waves.

Kelly finally saw what he saw. "Is that who I think it is?"

"It's Victoria."

The name and face rang a bell from their college days, but Kelly and Julian hadn't been tight then like they were now. He hadn't opened up about the infamous Victoria, but Kelly feared this woman with the smooth alabaster skin and brunette hair was the secret Julian claimed he never had.

"Let's get the introduction over with." Frankly, Kelly was curious to see who could fluster Julian so.

"We're not going to say a word until I find out why they're here."

"That her husband?" Kelly asked, referring to the man beside her.

"If so, that's Alex Nixon."

"Wha—"

Her question was cut off.

"Good evening." The voice of Pastor Douglas Wilson rang through the sophisticated sound system. "I'd like to take this opportunity to welcome everyone to Abysinnian Church, and let you know that you are welcome in God's house."

Clapping swept through the crowd.

"This evening we are blessed to have a very special young man who with our help can be the next mayor of our great city, and I have the pleasure of introducing him."

Julian's rock-hard arm tensed.

"Just keep your eyes on the prize, we'll deal with the other issue later," Kelly whispered hastily. "This is your night."

"I got it." His voice was tinged with a bit of hope, but his eyes told a different story.

This couple made him nervous and Kelly wanted to know why.

"Give me the one-sentence version, Julian. What's going on?"

"Councilman Julian Blake!" the pastor was saying.

The crowd roared and Julian waved and made his way up to the front, taking Kelly with him. Kelly wondered where Raja was, then spotted her making a desperate attempt to meet them at the edge of the crowd so she could take Kelly's place.

Kelly held back, trying to disentangle her hand from Julian's.

"You're in this with me, partner," he said and held on.

Kelly wanted to kick herself. She beckoned to Raja to take her place, but the pastor's assistant motioned her to be still.

Anticipation swelled when Julian was escorted into the grand edifice like a celebrity. Surrounded by antique mahogany wood and crimson tapestries, several cameramen adjusted their equipment, while zooming in on the man the multitude had come to see. "There he is," yelled an elderly man sitting in the front pew, as if he were paid to do so. However, pride prompted his energetic acknowledgment. An immediate round of applause followed Julian's majestic entrance. The audience became electrified when he climbed the steps, entered the pulpit, and greeted the beloved pastor with a touching embrace.

After Julian accepted the seat offered by Deacon Chaney, he settled in and enjoyed the moment. The oversized chair hand-carved from African ebony wood rested beneath Julian's long frame like a throne. Everything was befitting a high and honored guest. The pomp and circumstance he'd been showered with was in appreciation for the prominence they hoped he'd restore to the city after a drastic decline in tourism following 9/11, numerous occurrences of police brutality, and a soaring crime rate unrivaled in recent years. Expectations were high but Julian was determined to exceed them all.

Jubilation from the crowd of supporters and interested voters waned when the church minister stood to introduce the man of the hour. Pastor Wilson had been the residing pastor of Abysinnian Baptist for three decades. His sermons were legendary and it was often said that God not only walked with him but also spoke with his voice. He was the patriarch and sage of the community, a man who earned the respect of his parishioners. His smooth skin, soft-

ened with age, crown of gray, and sturdy build demanded the attention of visitors as he reached up to lower the microphone anchored
to the broad podium. "It's a good day that God has made, amen,"
the pastor said, while straightening his necktie.

"Amen," people chorused in agreement.

"I say, it's a good day and a better day than yesterday. See, on yesterday, it was rumored that a certain man was coming to lend a
hand. Our great city is in need and there's no way around that. On
yesterday, there were more questions than there were answers."
Again, the multitude nodded in unison. "But today, the rumors
have been put to rest and our questions have been answered."

"That's right, Pastor," a man's voice signified from the back of
the hallowed hall.

"Help me to welcome someone I hold in high esteem and he's
never once let me down. Without further ado, it is my distin-
guished pleasure to introduce you to the man who has come to lend
a hand, and the next mayor of New York . . . Julian Blake."

Applause resonated off the walls and erupted into chants of
"Julian Blake . . . Julian Blake." The atmosphere was searing and
Julian wasted no time in fanning the flames. He shook the pastor's
hand, bowed graciously, then stepped up to the podium.

"Who loves New York?" he roared, with his hands placed over
his heart. The cheers were deafening as he asked a second time,
above the merriment. "I said, who loves New York?" The camera
crews panned the audience to catch lightning in a bottle. "Good,
then I came to the right place. Because, I too am in love with New
York. Now, I wasn't born here but I got here as fast as I could." The
audience belted out unbridled laughter. *Lights, cameras, action.* There
was no turning back now, not even if he wanted to. "I am thankful
and inspired by your turnout today." Julian looked over the room.
"Now I need for you all to do me a favor. Would each of you stand
up and hold the hand of the person standing next to you?"

When everyone in the vast room stood on their feet, Julian gave
the people exactly what they had come for, something magical.

"Just look at this, we have all come here today to stand up for
what we believe and that's a strong, committed, determined, never

quit, never say die, can't hold us back, can't hold us down . . . New York City."

Thunderous applause began to escalate throughout as he loosened the microphone from its stand, took it, and headed down from the pulpit and up the aisle. The cameras followed Julian's performance step for step while he brought his message home.

"With your support, I will be the next mayor of this great city and I'm honored to stand among you, beside you, behind you. Let's continue standing together, working together, and winning together!"

By the time he'd finished his public address, the "Julian Blake Show" was a smash hit. The one thing that New Yorkers loved more than their politics was their superstars. With numerous news crews recording his vibrant day in the sun, Julian had successfully hit the big time.

He returned to his seat among deafening applause. He looked out into the crowd and his eyes locked onto his past.

Through pretty white teeth he spoke to Kelly. "Don't move too far from my side for the rest of the night. And get rid of Raja as soon as you can. Later, you and I need to talk."

Six

From the top of the steps overlooking the stately narthex, Kelly watched the hundreds of people who milled about. She couldn't help but appreciate why they were really all here. There were no door prizes or a luxury car giveaway. No promises that they'd get better government jobs and no promises that Julian could restore their state of security pre-9/11. There wasn't even a rapper in the house.

They were here because of Julian, and not because of what he'd said, but because of what he'd done. He'd made their lives better.

Ending the strike between the company honchos and the sanitation workers so that trash was once again picked up made people believe in him. Facilitating the talks that ended the mass transit strike made him their hero. He'd done the unbelievable. He'd become the darling of the people of New York.

Now he stood amongst his constituents, working as he'd always done, but troubled.

She eyed Victoria and Alex Nixon. What did they want? And what was it about them that put a look of momentary panic on Julian's face?

Kelly wanted to charge at them like a bull and force them out of Julian's life, but she couldn't, not until she knew their purpose, and their intentions. And her gut told her that whatever Julian wanted to talk about was going to change the game entirely.

Eighteen hours ago, Julian had been a man with private hopes of making very positive changes for millions of people. The press conference he'd staged earlier in the day was the lead-in story on every newscast in town. With the entire city taking notice, Julian was hell-bent on making the best of his golden opportunity, and now Victoria had resurfaced with her rich husband in tow. Not certain what their sudden appearance meant, Julian feared that it reeked from the worst kind of politics, *airing dirty laundry*.

He continued shaking hands and offering cordial thanks to his supporters, but his painted-on grin began to fade behind the underlying thoughts circulating within him. What had just happened? he wondered. What was to happen next was a hell of a lot more important, he reasoned, but in the meanwhile, clearing out the hall was all that mattered.

"Glad you could make it out," Julian said, thanking an older couple he'd never seen before. "Your taking time out of an undoubtedly busy schedule means so much to me." He shook the husband's hand firmly, then hugged the wife, sending both off satisfied that their two-thousand-dollar contribution was well spent. "Yes, it is so good to see you," Julian greeted other couples likewise, while inconspicuously gesturing toward the door afterward.

With each firm shake, he stole another glace at his watch, wishing that the Rolex had been fashioned with a fast-forward button instead of all the bling. The last half hour drifted by like a dead log down a lazy stream. *The quiet before the storm.*

Julian turned his gaze in Kelly's direction and his brow shifted up a fraction.

Kelly inclined her head in understanding. She started toward Raja, but slowed her step when she saw the weasel, Natalie Huffman, snaking her way toward Victoria and Alex.

Panic hit. Kelly took one last look at Raja's seriously angry face and decided to play linebacker. Under any circumstance she would defend Julian, and she was by heading toward the enemy—Natalie Huffman.

She eased through the crowd and snagged Natalie's bejeweled wrist.

The woman sized up her hand first, then gave a curious grin to Kelly. "To what do I owe this unexpected pleasure?"

"I'm glad I caught you."

"I was on my way to meet the Nixons. He's planning to run for mayor. The Nixons radiate such energy. You feel it, I can tell."

"I don't feel anything." *Alex running for mayor? Late-breaking news.*

Natalie's knowing smile made Kelly realize she'd just been read.

"It's negative, and that makes them *very* interesting. The fact that you stopped me just as I was on my way to meet them puts them at the top of my list of people to get to know." She arched a brow. "Unless you have something you'd like to share."

Kelly had shifted in the crowd so that Natalie's back was to the Nixons. They headed up the stairs, but she didn't let on that they were leaving. "As a matter of fact, I wanted to talk to you about your column. I've read the stories that you've done on Julian, and I thought it was time to end your speculation about the councilman."

"And how would I do that?"

Kelly hesitated. "An exclusive interview."

Natalie's face creased, then brightened before her eyes narrowed. She started to turn, never forgetting that she'd been on her way somewhere when Kelly had stopped her.

Kelly hoped the Nixons had cleared the parking lot. She didn't know how much longer she could hold the nosy reporter.

"If you're not interested, *The New Yorker* called."

Never losing sight of Natalie, Kelly acted as if she were looking for someone else.

"Me or *The New Yorker*?" Natalie speculated. "Hmmm. No offense to me, but as Chris Rock said at the Oscars, why get him when you can get Denzel? Doesn't seem like much of a choice to me."

Kelly couldn't believe how difficult Natalie was being. She'd never shared more than a paragraph of words with the woman and now they were actually conversing.

This was a test, she realized. Natalie wanted to know how badly Kelly didn't want her to talk to the Nixons.

"It was nice talking to you," she said to Natalie, signaling the end of the game. Kelly pulled out her phone, dialed, and stepped away. She walked into the crowd only to have her arm ungraciously yanked.

"No need to refill your anxiety medication just yet." The woman closed her ringed fingers over each other. "I'll take that interview. At my office."

"Natalie, I'll have my assistant e-mail you the itinerary. And the meeting will be held in Julian's office."

"So he can kick me out? I don't think so."

Raja pushed her way toward Julian, and from her expression, she was far from happy.

"I'll call your office tomorrow, and we can iron out the details."

"Thank you, Natalie, but I'd better get back to work."

"You're such a pretty woman. My first question will be, why not you?"

The words stung as if a thousand bees had attacked. Kelly wanted to lash out and scratch the skin off Natalie's face, but she adopted her most regal stance and looked down her nose at the woman. "You will be massacred by the public for wasting a good opportunity to tell them something they really want to know. Who cares about a single man and his single publicist? I'd rethink my angle before there's rethinking at *The New York Weekly*. I'll be sure to get you ten minutes with Julian tonight before he leaves."

The crowd absorbed Kelly and this time, Natalie didn't stop her.

She didn't take the time she wanted to regroup. Raja was stalking around the narthex as if she were on the hunt.

"How's it going, girl?" Kelly asked, hoping this encounter would be easier.

"What the hell is going on?"

The vileness of her temper was unexpected. Raja usually reserved her show-out sessions for the white women at the bank.

"Watch your mouth, you're in church."

Raja's neck cranked back a few degrees. "Don't play me. Remember, I grew up in these hoods. I know rats when I see them. Now what's the deal? I'm Julian's date, but every time I look up, you're on his arm, by his side, in his face." Raja bared her teeth for the benefit of the men who edged by on the way to talk to the deputy district attorney.

"Raja, this isn't about you. Julian is at work, get it? If you want to be part of his world, you have to be willing to work too. He's got a meeting tonight, but he wanted me to ask you a favor. If you'd rather go home, Julian has already arranged for a limo to drop you off."

"How is he sending you to ask me something? Drop me off?" She scoffed. "I came with him, I'm leaving with him."

"Raja, don't be childish. He's going to be busy until the wee hours. It would help if the three of us could split up and take a segment of the crowd."

Kelly knew she almost had Raja where she wanted her with the little lie. "So . . . can you help out tonight? It would mean a lot to Julian." She put on her best PR smile.

"Sure," Raja agreed readily. "Anything."

Kelly lowered her voice. "Your sorors have money. Julian needs it. They came here under the auspices of wanting to donate to his campaign, but we haven't received a single check. Donations can be accepted up to two thousand dollars. Julian needs your help to secure those funds."

Raja unconsciously rubbed her hands together. "That's my area of expertise."

Kelly could see that Raja's gaze had been lured by Julian's as he was saying good night to the lieutenant governor.

"I still think he should be taking me home." She licked her lips as she watched him approach.

"Julian will make it up to you. And there *is* that limo waiting for you," she reminded her.

"He's got a lot of kissing up to do, too." Raja cocked her hip to the side. "But the limo is a good start."

"There she is," Julian whispered in her ear, easing up beside her and placing a quick peck on Raja's cheek. "I would ask where you've been all evening, but I'd hate to appear jealous this early in our relationship." Raja stood back on her heels, smirking behind a labored smile.

"Ooh, is that what this is, a relationship?" she asked modestly. "I'll have to remember that the next time I'm on the sidelines wishing I had a chance to carry the ball too. Just kidding, but I know you're on a mission and I will be there if you happen to fumble, seeing as how I've just been informed that we're in a relationship now." When she looked up at Julian and batted her eyes at him, she knew she'd get over carrying a clipboard and keeping up with his stats, for the time being at least. "Oh, and another thing," Raja added, "It was a nice touch sending a driver to get me home safely. If a girl's got to go home alone, a limousine should ease the pain."

Julian disguised his confusion with a lingering embrace until his eye found Kelly giving him the "hurry up and dump Raja" glare.

"That's exactly what I was counting on when making the arrangements," he lied convincingly. "I'll call you after things are wrapped up here. I'm happy to have you on Team Blake."

"I'll give you a chance to prove that," she said, her voice husky with innuendo. She turned and walked away, heading in the direction of her first victim, putting a little something extra in her walk.

Kelly stepped up next to Julian and cleared her throat when she couldn't get his attention. "Uh-hmm! You've got way too much going on to be checking out what Raja's been rehearsing all of her life," she hissed.

"Kelly, if I didn't know better, I'd think you were hating on your girl," he suggested.

"Obviously, you don't know better because Raja's been practicing that patented walk of hers for years," Kelly informed him.

"Seems to me all that practicing paid off," Julian jested, to irritate Kelly like a big brother picking at a younger sibling.

"Well, too bad you didn't notice Natalie Huffman waiting in the wings for some quality time with, and I quote, 'the man.'"

He snatched a look to his right. There she was.

Julian rolled his head back, thinking the evening would never end. "First the limo and now a one-on-one with the barracuda. Last time I put you in charge," he grumbled. "Can't we put her off until later?"

"No can do. It was the only way I could stop her from going after our mystery guests. Look, I'm just as tired as you, maybe even more. I would love to have my behind soaking in a warm bubble bath, too, but the show must go on."

Kelly had taken over like a seasoned publicist should have by keeping the talent under control, then controlling when and where the media had access to the talent. Julian caught on to what she was up to once he calmed down.

"You're trying to handle me, Kelly?" he asked, taking a measured short step back away from her. "You're not that slick."

"Ten minutes is all Huffman has to feel you out, so keep a level head and it'll be over before you know. Oh yeah, I am that slick and yes, you've just been handled by the best." Kelly waved over the column writer from *The New York Weekly*. The rather plump but moderately attractive white woman approached Julian with her notepad and a pound of attitude. Her dark hair, flipped in the back, needed a trim but Kelly assumed that Natalie's short business skirt got her into places where a salon manicured coif couldn't.

"Miss Huffman, please meet the next mayor of New York—" Kelly hailed as she extended her hand toward Julian.

"Julian Blake, you're even more handsome in person," Natalie interrupted, no longer having a need for Kelly. "I am pleased to finally meet the man who can certainly get a girl's circulation up."

Kelly held her tongue when she wanted to verbally slap Natalie for even thinking that she could come on to Julian like that. *How dare she?* Instead she reserved her comments for a more appropriate

time and place. "Ten minutes. Tops," she told Natalie before darting off to see if there were any other fires to put out.

"Miss Huffman, I feel that it's only fair we should meet face-to-
face," Julian said, sizing up the woman he was determined to be-
friend and then manipulate to prop him up in the media. "Yes,
seeing as how you've had mine plastered all over the city."

"If you're asking me to apologize for selling the sizzle, I won't."
Natalie was doing a bit of sizing up as well. "I have a nose for news
and you, Julian Blake, are news fit to print."

"All right, you're here and I'm here," Julian acquiesced finally.
"What is it that you'd really like to know, my political views on the
homeless? No?" When she didn't bite he resorted to easing the
tension by making her laugh. "How about free trade with Canada,
Cuba, or New Jersey?"

"Cute, Councilman Blake. Cute." Natalie glanced at her notes,
then back up and into Julian's dark eyes. "I may as well cut to the
chase. Sometimes I like to let the story *come to me*, and it's quite interesting how one story seems to crop up behind the next when
you're involved."

"Oh?"

"Exactly," she answered. "So, are you going to come clean on
what that look was about between you and Alex Nixon? It was almost as pensive as the look Mrs. Nixon shot at you. Made me think
that maybe you two knew each other." She let her comment hang
in the air.

Julian contemplated several quick nonincriminating answers but
decided instead to take it easy. "Well, first of all, the *oh* was a reaction to your mixed metaphors concerning your interviewing style.
Let's cut to the chase. Want to know what I think, Miss Huffman?"
Her body shifted, softened. "I think you came here for something
that might stick to page six but didn't find it, so now you're on a
fishing expedition hoping to land a big one. Now, Natalie, I'll toss
you a bone to sink your teeth into, off the record of course."

Her eyes sparkled with respect as she turned off the tiny voice
recorder buzzing her purse. "You heard it humming, huh?"

"Uh-huh."

She muttered a curse. "Okay, give me something I can use, off the record," she agreed, gazing at him intently without a clue where he was headed.

"The best scoop I can give you is the truth, which is I believe that you're much too attractive to get your shoes dirty digging around in someone else's trash."

Natalie was just about to toss out a retort when Kelly returned, in a manufactured huff, nine minutes and fifty-nine seconds after they'd begun the so-called interview.

"Where has the time gone? I hope we're all done here, Julian, it's getting late." Kelly turned toward the sneaky snoop, who was looking at Julian sideways. "Miss Huffman, it was truly an interesting experience meeting you. Thanks for coming out, bye-bye."

"It was very different meeting you as well, *Miss* Taylor," she replied, emphasizing the fact that Kelly was just as unmarried as she was.

Kelly forced a smile. "Be sure to call my office in the morning so that we can arrange for the exclusive." She took Julian's arm. "Let's go. Folks are waiting." She quickly ushered him toward the exit, spotted Raja doing her thing, waved, and kept walking when it looked like Raja was heading their way.

Once they filed out into the parking lot, Julian handed Kelly the car keys. "I sure hope you don't mind driving."

"Driving!" Kelly snapped. "Raja gets a driver and I get car keys. What kinda—"

"Kelly, let's not fight, I'm beat."

"You're beat! I'd like to beat that snotty Natalie Huffman into critical condition," she spat, with her arms crossed tightly. "That's what I'd like to do. How'd she fix her mouth to get into *my* personal business?"

"Could you unlock the door while you're hastening to a conclusion?"

She pressed the alarm remote. Two crisp chirps later, they were both comfortably seated in Julian's ultimate driving machine.

"Uh-uh, ole girl had some nerve," Kelly continued to rant. "Just because I don't have a husband doesn't warrant her reminding me of it on the sly like that. *Miss* Taylor," she mimicked. "If she was half the newshound she pretends to be, she would have been all up on you about Alex and Victoria Nixon. Even I could see there were some seriously unresolved issues circulating among the three of you."

Julian stared directly ahead as Kelly guided the Beemer down the avenue. "Was it that obvious?"

"Does a fat man wear big pants?"

"Wow, that's pretty obvious." He closed his eyes, replaying the whole scenario in his mind, thinking how the Nixons had materialized out of nowhere, sufficiently turned his life upside down, and then vanished into the crowd like apparitions in the dusk. "I haven't seen her in years, you know," he said in a tired voice. "It was like one of those scenes from a black-and-white movie where the old girlfriend turns up to wish the male lead good luck."

"You got the black-and-white part right, but what I don't get is why it seemed to throw you for a loop. Was it that her taste for soul food and dark meat might have been a problem for her husband?"

"If only it were that simple," he sighed wearily, while loosening his silk necktie.

"Then you've got some explaining to do. I put in work tonight sending Raja away and running interference with Natalie Huffman. Julian, you need to come on out with it before I stop this car right here."

Julian hadn't made a habit of concealing things from Kelly, so he knew her woman's intuition was being kicked into overdrive by his evasivness.

"Okay, you wanted it so here goes." Julian leaned forward. "It's time for you to earn your money."

Kelly drew back. "What the hell are you talking about?"

"Every politician has his ghosts." Julian's eyes fluttered as if he were trying to clear his head. "Victoria and I have had an arrangement all these years, not physical but financial."

"Money?" Kelly asked, her voice raising an octave. "She's got you all twisted over money? For what, a blackmail scheme?"

"No. Child support."

"What?"

"For our daughter, Brittany."

Julian could see that his confession took the wind out of Kelly's sails. She was so obviously shaken that no immediate words were forthcoming. He needed her to say something, anything, but then he remembered how speechless he was after laying eyes on Victoria again.

They had both been law students, spending long hours together studying and preparing for mock trials. Too much time together led to something neither of them planned on, a heated affair and a daughter he had yet to meet. Victoria's father, Atlanta's definition of power and old money, Haltom Hayes, wasn't having his pride and joy gallivanting around his friends with some ghetto homeboy. He'd sworn a lifetime of heartache would come to Julian if he ever touched Victoria again.

Oddly enough, Julian's feelings stirred a bit more than he cared to admit when Victoria stood merely inches from his face, considering how they were once secretly inseparable. Her presence conjured up old memories Julian thought to be long since forgotten, out of necessity and self-preservation because he vehemently believed her father's vile threats of bodily harm. Throughout the years, Julian sent sizable child support checks on time and without fail, resigning himself to the fact that that would be the full extent of his parental duties. Seeing as how he and Victoria had nothing else between them, except for those memories and the nights they had fallen asleep in the same bed after letting their carnal desires overrun their common sense. Now it appeared he might be facing threats of reporting his paternity to the world, one newspaper at a time.

A mere eighteen hours ago, he was a city councilman with his head in the clouds and his name in the hat for one of the country's most prestigious positions, the mayor of New York. As he stared into a mountainous haze of uncertainty less than a day later, he was already sorry.

"What are we going to do?" Kelly was finally able to say in a voice so strained it came out in a whisper.

"I don't know. That all depends on what she wants."

Seven

Raja leaned back in the limo with her arms crossed. The tough urban neighborhoods were flashing past outside her window, but Raja had been brought up on streets like these and wouldn't mind forgetting them if she could. Carefully selected memories of the evening's events played back on the recorder of her mind. No matter which way she viewed the situation at hand, or which variables she made allowances for, the nitty-gritty kept adding up to the nitty-gritty and the bottom line never wavered.

Kelly was trying to play her.

All that making nice and running around trying to put out fires for Julian had been an act. And not even a cleverly disguised act at that. Raja couldn't count the number of times she'd busted her so-called friend gazing across the room at Julian as if he were the last plate on a buffet line. The whispering that had gone on between the two of them, and the secret looks they shared when they thought nobody was looking. She didn't even want to think about that nonsense Kelly had tried to sell her about needing her to pitch in and help with Julian's campaign. Raja had seen past that slick attempt of appeasement with a quickness.

Kelly had better recognize.

She must have forgotten which streets Raja had come from. East

New York was in Raja's blood, and her instinct and intuition was as sharp as it had ever been.

But Raja was interested in seeing exactly what Kelly's motives were, so she'd gone along with the program and played Kelly's little game. Raja was street-bred and street-smart, and she kept her enemies close. She pretended to be flattered at the thought of helping Julian's fund-raising efforts, and even pouted as appropriate when she found herself being dismissed by the disheveled little heffah who was supposed to be her girl. But all the while Raja had been taking things in. Observing. Analyzing. Calculating her next move. Playing the role of the cast-off empty-headed little girlfriend when she was really steaming inside that Kelly, obviously, had never learned the girlfriend rules.

Sure, Raja herself was considered devious and manipulative, and yep, she'd snatched more than one man from the grasp of a woman caught sleeping on her game. But never had she chased the man of a friend, or a man who had even shown interest in a friend. Doing so was simply foul and low-down, and as much as Raja believed in pursuing her desires with vigor, there was such a thing as principle in friendships, and that was one line she had never crossed for any man.

But while she felt it was pretty underhanded for Kelly to be catching vapors from a man she'd insisted Raja meet and had even encouraged her to date, at this point that was neither here nor there. Women would be women, Raja knew, and even those you considered good friends could be shady where a high-powered good-looking man was concerned. No, for Raja, the prevailing issues were far more complicated than scolding Kelly or shaming her for salivating like a hot bitch over someone she'd hooked up with Raja. What needed to be determined now was what kind of vapors, if any, Julian was catching for Kelly.

Raja frowned at that thought. Any man who would be attracted to Kelly in that way was certainly not the man for her. Really now . . . educationally, culturally, physically . . . she had Kelly beat in every category and coming and going in every direction, and only a foolish man would risk losing a woman like Raja to a thrown-together substitute like Kelly.

"Turn here!" Raja directed the limousine driver out of the blue. Suddenly the solitude of her apartment had lost its appeal. She was not in an uptown state of mind. At times like these she needed the comfort and grounding that only her very best friend, Justine Williams, could provide, and as Raja gave the driver directions to the apartment that Justine shared with her husband and three young children, she was already anticipating the relief that letting her guard down and being her true self would bring. Sometimes a sister needed to go where everybody knew her name, and with Justine and her family, much more than Raja's name was known. They also knew her heart.

"Thanks," Raja said, stepping from the limo and reaching back to hand the driver a twenty-dollar tip. With her purse slung over her shoulder she sashayed across the pavement toward Justine's apartment building.

It was Sunday night in East New York, and after coming home from church and eating Sunday dinner, folks were sitting around looking fat and happy. A spattering of young adults and teens were hanging out on porches and stoops, others were silhouettes visible in open windows, and children who should have been in bed hours ago were still outside playing hopscotch and "Mother, May I?" under the glow of city streetlights. Raja smirked. If more of these people were employed they'd be inside getting their loud behinds ready for work on Monday morning.

The night air was semicool, but the residual smells of fried chicken and cabbage were still drifting from windows and out into the streets. Raja was at once both repelled and comforted by the sights and smells of her old neighborhood. Memories resurfaced and as usual she shoved them back down into her subconsciousness. Childhood could be tough in communities like these, and not only had Raja learned how to fight and scrape for what she wanted, on those rare occasions when she went after something and couldn't get it . . . she'd learned to adjust her desires and make a dollar out of fifty-nine cents.

All eyes were on her as she approached the tenement with her designer heels clicking across the concrete pavement. It wasn't every day that a stretch limo pulled up in this neighborhood bearing a beautiful, well-put-together sister, but these were Raja's people and as usual they were glad to see her.

"Hey, Miss Thang," a young woman called from a second-floor window. "Girl, that was a sharp ride you just rolled up outta! You shoulda took us for a lil' spin-spin before you let him go, though."

Raja kissed the forehead of a sleepy toddler who was bouncing in his sister's arms, then looked up and grinned. "Maybe next time," she said, enunciating her words carefully. "But how are you, Tanisha? You're looking well, I must say."

Raja deliberately missed the sly smirk and Tanisha's rolling eyes as she moved into the foyer of the building. These people could speak the same guttural language of old if they chose to, but Raja hadn't crawled up out of the barrel just to let those crabs scuttling around on the bottom make her revert to her old ways.

The rickety elevator was broken, as usual, so Raja pulled a Kleenex from her purse and used it to turn the knob to enter the stairwell. Using her other hand, she pinched her nostrils closed, then raced up the two flights of stairs in her two-hundred-dollar designer shoes, dodging urine puddles and stray piles of trash that littered the steps.

Justine needed to do better, she said to herself for the one millionth time. If she didn't love her friend so much Raja would never even think about setting foot in a monstrosity such as this building, and just the thought of touching the handrail or the doorknob, or even brushing up against the hallway walls, was repulsive.

Raja exited the stairwell and moments later she was standing outside Justine's apartment ringing the bell. Whereas the stairwell should have been fumigated, delicious aromas were seeping from the cracks surrounding Justine's door.

Ghetto food, Raja thought as she waited for the door to be answered. And late-night ghetto food at that. Her nose was calibrated and easily separated the scents and assigned them to their food groups. Fried catfish, collard greens and ham-hocks, and sweet corn bread. Her stomach growled so loud it was embarrassing. She'd eaten little more than two lettuce leaves while dining with Julian earlier in the evening, and if Justine didn't hurry up and open the door Raja could easily see herself kicking it down to get inside and snatch up a leftover plate.

"Girl!" Justine exclaimed, ushering Raja inside the tiny apartment. "What are you doing on this side of town at this time of night?"

Raja grinned. "I just felt like coming home," she said, and for the first time that day she felt totally at ease and ready to let her hair down.

"Well, come on in," Justine said, pointing to a hall closet. "We just got back from a gospel revival and I'm almost finished cooking. You hungry?"

Raja nodded, kicking off her shoes and retrieving a pair of comfortable house shoes she kept at Justine's for times like these. She slipped them on her feet and placed her pumps in their place. "You frying fish this time of night?"

Justine turned, a checkered apron fitting snuggly around her wide waist. "What? You can smell it? Is it too fishy in here?"

Raja shook her head. "No. No, not at all. It smells delicious," she said, even though she knew her hair and clothes would be reeking by the time she left. "Actually, it smells perfect."

Justine smiled. "Well, come on in the kitchen then. Dennis got the kids in the tub and by the time they get out the fish will be coming out of the pan."

While Raja hated the environment in which Justine lived, she enjoyed Justine and her family immensely and felt as though she never spent enough time with them. Justine was an excellent cook, and had served them deep-fried catfish hot out of the pan, just the way Raja liked it. Even though she seldom ate anything past 6:00 p.m., and she couldn't remember the last time she'd had anything fried, Raja had asked for a second helping after making sure everyone else had had their fill, and she'd picked the bit of ham-hock in her greens down to the fat meat, even sucking on the salty skin like she used to do when she was a kid. In fact, she'd tossed all those nightly salads with no dressing to the wind and slathered whipped butter on a thick slice of steaming corn bread and ate every crumb, including those that had fallen onto her napkin. She'd have to pull double duty in the gym the next day, but gritting back like this was worth it.

When dinner was over Justine's husband, Dennis, a sporadically employed housepainter, but wonderfully active father, shepherded his sleepy children to their rooms and prepared them for bed. Raja helped Justine in the kitchen as she always did during times like these, washing pots, pans, and plates as Justine dried them and put them away.

As they worked together in rhythm Raja found herself telling Justine all about Julian and her recent concerns over Kelly's friend-ship and true motives.

"Well," Justine remarked, keeping it real as she bent over to slide a glass pan in a low cabinet. "It really doesn't sound like you have any proof that Kelly's doing anything wrong. Hell, she works for the man. Just because you caught her looking at him doesn't mean anything. What is she supposed to do? Talk to the man with her eyes closed?"

Raja sighed, then narrowed her eyes at the sight of Justine's hefty thighs and endless hips. Justine had gotten huge, she realized. Too huge. All those horrible carbs and late-night meals had blown her up like somebody's hot balloon, but her friend didn't seem to care. She walked around in her Daisy Dukes and skimpy tops as if she weighed a measly 110 pounds. Her husband, Dennis, still gazed at her as if she were a shapely little brick house too.

"Don't get cute," Raja said, losing her carefully constructed di-alect and reverting to her Brooklynese. "You know damn well a woman can tell when another woman is clocking for her man. The bad part is, I'm perfect for Julian and Kelly is all wrong. I think on some level she knows that too."

Justine shrugged. "I don't think you should worry about being perfect for Julian or any other man. It's much better to find a brother who is perfect for you."

"Justine, please," Raja said, squirting dish liquid in the sink and scrubbing it down with a Brillo pad. "That man's got it going on. He's perfect for me in every area, and I do mean perfect. He's fine, educated, fine, cultured, fine, financially stable, fine, attentive, fine, polished, fine, a public figure . . . Did I mention the brother is fine?"

Justine laughed. "Yeah, I think you did. But if you think Julian's all that and a brand-new Porsche, what makes you think other women, including Kelly, won't feel the same way?"

It was Raja's turn to shrug. "It doesn't matter. Kelly should know when she's outclassed. But be that as it may, I'm not concerned about her, because as transparent as her behavior was, she's absolutely no competition. She's so far from being the kind of sister that Julian needs on his arm that it's not even funny."

"Does Julian know that?"

Raja stared at her friend. She was Raja Monet Jackson. If Julian didn't know, then shame on him. "Yeah." She nodded. "Yeah, I think so. And if he don't know . . ." A devious twinkle crept into her eyes as she schemed and planned. "Then he'd better ask somebody!"

Eight

Kelly let the name of Julian's child linger in her mind, a part of her still rejecting the fact that the two were interconnected.

Julian's child. Kelly was speechless.

As it was, she'd been on the treadmill for over an hour and her legs had gone beyond aching and had rounded out the last fifteen minutes at numb. Now they felt like spaghetti.

Ever since the rape, she no longer ran from her problems, but right now she had to simulate the act of escaping, or betrayal would kick her in the teeth and make her do things she no longer thought herself capable of, like crying because her feelings were hurt.

Instead, her body wept from every pore.

Perspiration flew from her skin, pelting the machine, and her legs begged to know why they were still trying to take her somewhere she wasn't really going. Kelly finally hit the stop button, but the more the machine slowed, the louder her thoughts became. How could Julian do this? How could he screw Victoria, a white woman, when all of his life he'd had his pick of the ebony satin litter?

Kelly stepped off the machine and grabbed the rail for support, her wobbling legs no longer obeying instructions from her brain.

She forced herself to walk around the gym, the left side of her brain telling the right to accept that Julian had a child.

Why didn't he tell me?

The question surfaced like a dead fish in a stream.

They'd been best friends for years and had shared their deepest, darkest secrets and fears, hopes, and dreams. They'd shared everything—except this. Maybe they weren't the friends she'd thought. Obviously not. Who could hide a living secret for the past fifteen years?

Julian could.

Kelly massaged her head with the heel of her hand, went to the water machine, and downed six cups before the icy water hit her stomach with a thud. She endured the belly freeze, her elbow on the blue water tank, as she bent over at the waist sucking wind.

All this time, she'd thought the strength of their friendship lay not just in their ability to deal with everyday bullshit but in the fact that nobody knew them better than the other.

Kelly stretched her body into yoga poses, feeling her fatigued muscles cry their last bit of pain before yielding to her will.

In two hours Julian was coming to pick her up, and she had to have her act together. Kelly stood in the downward dog position and caught her expression in the full-length wall mirror. Even upside down, she could tell that fury and confusion weren't good looks to mix. Did she think she was going to fool him into believing she was fine with his painful secret?

She walked to the mirror, her hands on her hips.

Get over it, she challenged, staring at herself.

Her gaze didn't waver as she touched the cold glass, letting the coolness seep into her hands and work into her bloodstream. Her forehead met the glass and she welcomed it as her breath came in long slow puffs.

Get over it. It's Julian's life.

But I'm his best friend and he should have told me.

The anger persisted, but logic peeked in.

As much as she hurt, she had to support Julian. He hadn't been with Victoria since college, and he hadn't ever seen his daughter.

Had it been any other man, she'd have raved about how messed up he was to have a kid and not be part of its life, but it was Julian.

And he had to have a good explanation. Then they'd figure out how he was going to deal with this intensely personal issue after the election.

Kelly peeled off her clothes on her way to the shower. She'd help him. But first, she had to know the enemy. Why were Victoria and Alex Nixon here in New York, besides to ruin the man the city loved?

She grabbed her robe and dialed her brother.

"Taylor and Associates," he answered.

"Hey boy, how you?"

Her little brother grunted, happy to hear from her. "Kell's Bells. What's up?"

Kelly thought about filling her brother's head with nonsense about how she was doing fine, but they'd never had to pretend with one another. "Ricky, I don't know."

"What happened?"

"I need you to do a background check on Alex and Victoria Nixon."

Kelly closed her eyes, hating the waver in her voice. She hoped Ricky didn't pick up on it, but he wasn't the most sought-after investigator by Washington insiders for nothing. He'd just opened an office in New York, and Kelly hadn't ever imaged that she'd be one of his first clients.

"I'll be over in fifteen minutes."

"Whoa," Kelly said to the boy she'd mothered after their mother's death when Ricky was seven and she was eleven. "I haven't even showered, and I have to wash my hair."

"You ran today?" he asked. He sounded calm, but Kelly knew Ricky. He was a lightning rod for her emotions.

"Yeah." She tried to laugh, and to her surprise, her eyes watered. What an idiot. "Six or seven miles."

"More like ten or eleven," he said, knowing her. "You can't out-run the wolves, baby. That's why you have brothers to beat them off for you," he said softly. "I'll have what you need in an hour, and I'll even dry your hair for you."

Her brother had played football for Syracuse University before blowing out his knee during his first season with the Tampa Bay Buchaneers. Nobody would believe Big Ricky Taylor would dry his big sister's hair. He was trying to comfort her, and he didn't need to.

"I'm goo—" she started to say, then stopped. "I'll be ready when you get here."

Julian's call flashed on the call-waiting, and Kelly let several beats pass before answering. "Hey, Julian. Are you wearing your blue Armani suit with the red tie? You have to look political, yet approachable."

"I know how to dress, but to answer your question, yes, I have on the blue suit. You didn't call me back last night.. We need to talk."

"I know," she said, rushing him. "But I've got to shower and get prettied up so we can kick butt with Natalie, and I have a meeting before I see you. I'll just meet you at your office."

"Kelly! You're trippin'," he said roughly. "We always ride together, and the fact that you're tryin' to ditch me is pissing me off. So I'm coming over, and we're going to deal with this issue about Victoria and—"

"Brittany," Kelly finished for him.

"Right, Brittany," he said softly. His voiced caressed his daughter's name. Julian had no idea what he was doing to Kelly's heart. His shoes were leaving scars. "We need to clear the air." He huffed, then paused. "Don't get quiet on me."

Kelly turned on the shower. "I'm naked."

Julian chuckled then sighed. "And you're telling me that because?"

"I have to shower and do my hair," she said, knowing she'd hear him out and help him through this. But she needed the whole two hours to get her game face together. "Meet me at the office. After Natalie, I promise, we'll talk."

She disconnected before he could say anything else and stepped into the shower. Before tossing the phone onto the woven basket of rolled towels, she caught her reflection.

How would she look pregnant with Julian's baby?

Kelly's mouth filled with tangy saliva and her chest felt as if someone had sucked all the air from her lungs.

Fantasies hurt almost as much as reality, she thought, squeezing shampoo onto her black- and mahogany-colored tresses.

But this was one fantasy that would never know a moment of truth. Julian and Raja were the *it* couple, and since Kelly had brought them together, she wouldn't be the one to break them up.

Kelly scrubbed herself and then got out, drying her hair before going into the wig section of her closet and choosing a human-hair ponytail that would look elegant once she made the necessary adjustments to her natural tresses.

Dressing minimally, she flat-ironed her hair, replaying the moment when she and Victoria's eyes met. The woman was smart and strong, and her gaze conveyed that she wasn't going to back down. No, Victoria Nixon was nobody's arm candy.

Their whole entrance had been staged. They'd wanted to upset Julian. Possibly destroy him.

Kelly's heart raced.

She finished her hair, then started on her make-up when the doorbell rang. Hurrying, she let her brother in.

"You finished already?" he asked.

"I've been doing this hair and taking care of this body for years. I know how to get ready in an hour, I don't like to, but I wanted to give us enough time."

Ricky walked into her condo, looking around. "Place looks good. I like the art." He referred to the portrait by Tom Feelings that Julian had given her about a month ago.

Pulling a presentation folder from his briefcase, Ricky walked into the dining room and laid it on the table. "Want to tell me why Julian's been sending Mrs. Victoria Nixon three thousand dollars a month? Or why the blood type of Mr. and Mrs. Nixon is O positive while their child's is AB negative?"

"Do you have a picture of the child?" Kelly said softly.

"I do."

Ricky wasn't the best for no reason.

"Please put it away."

He inserted the five-by-seven into the envelope and slid the remainder of the report to his sister.

Kelly didn't want to see Julian's child before he did. "That's Julian's daughter."

Ricky nodded. "I figured as much."

Silence filled the space between brother and sister. Ricky was waiting for her and Kelly accepted the truth. Julian was a father. And this was old baby mama drama.

"The Nixons showed up at his fundraiser, and Alex announced his intention to run for mayor. I get the feeling nothing about this is coincidence. However, I have no idea what their plan of attack is. Are they going to sacrifice their daughter just to embarrass Julian? But how does that make them look to the voters?" Kelly paced.

"He's going to lose votes. There are people who are going to be furious because he slept with a white woman."

"What about you?"

"Me?"

Ricky's knowing gaze wouldn't let her play off her pain. "I don't care if he slept with her." She paused because she couldn't go on with the lie. "Okay, I'm lying. We were friends then, better friends now. But Victoria Nixon? Why her? Why not—"

Ricky's brows slid up slowly. "I've said it before, I'll say it again. You've always been in love with him."

"There you're wrong."

"Why not you? That's what you were going to say, right?"

"Julian can't love me. I can't give him what he needs, which is someone polished, pretty, and professional."

"Kell, you're her. But that figment you're trying to project onto him isn't going to happen because she isn't real. I think you're shortchanging yourself."

Kelly stood up. "I make my money knowing people and knowing what's best for them. I'm not what's best. People start digging around in my private life and the skeletons will come out shaking hands. I'm a distraction; that's why staying on the periphery is where I need to be."

"You been there fifteen years. When's it going to be your turn?"

Kelly smiled at her baby brother. "My life is good, thank you very much."

"Then why the call to me? You were upset."

"Yes, I was. Julian and I are best friends and he didn't tell me he had a daughter."

"Okay. So now you know. How are you gong to deal?" Ricky walked into the kitchen and came out with an apple.

"I want to know why the Nixons are here. What are their motives? If they're trying to hurt Julian, I need to do damage control. He's the right candidate for mayor of New York. He should have his chance."

"But you're worried."

"Yes." Kelly contemplated for a while. "This could turn ugly. Victoria could make accusations, her husband could be a vicious jerk, and the public would turn on Julian and I can't have that. He deserves this."

Kelly realized she'd said more than she intended and grabbed her brother's hand. "I've got to go earn my paycheck. Thank you for everything." At the door she turned to him. "I'm going to be fine."

Ricky nodded and pressed a kiss on her forehead. "Be honest with him before things go a step further. What do you have to lose?"

"I've never been anything but honest with Julian and with myself. He was there for me when I was at my lowest. I see the hurricane of trouble approaching him. My job is to steer him out of harm's way."

"Good luck, sis. Read the clipped pages. I'll leave it at that."

Ricky closed the door softly and Kelly took the folder to her bedroom where she grabbed her cell phone, purse, and briefcase.

Her phone slipped, and as she bent to catch it, the folder hit the floor.

E-mails Victoria Nixon had written to someone slipped onto the rug.

Kelly lifted them.

I think my marriage to Alex is over because I still love Julian. It's only right that I try to make things right with my daughter's father. I have to give us a chance. For Brittany's happiness as well as mine, I'll do whatever it takes.

Damnit. This was worse than she thought.

Kelly read every word of the e-mails, noting the new private cell phone number Victoria had written to Lacy, her sister.

Before she stopped herself, Kelly dialed. "Victoria, my name is Kelly Taylor, and I'm an associate of Julian's. We met briefly at the church. I'd like to buy you a cup of coffee."

"Kelly." Victoria said her name as if she knew her well. "This isn't a good time for me. My husband and I are on our way to a fundraiser. Perhaps another time."

"Wait!" No she wasn't running scared. The e-mails in Kelly's hands were from a woman who wasn't a stranger to controversy. Meeting Kelly should be a walk in the park.

"This is very important. It seems several e-mails have come into my possession regarding your plans while you're in New York. I wanted to discuss those plans with you."

A sharp intake of breath filled Kelly's ear. "How could that have happened? I'm very careful."

"All security has a weakness."

"Yes, darling, I'm ready," Victoria said clearly, then spoke in a hushed voice to Kelly. "Coffee tomorrow at the corner of Park and East Fifty-fourth Street. It's a private spa. Give your name at the front desk and you'll be brought to me. And Kelly?"

"Yes?"

"Don't ever call this number again."

Kelly didn't waste time being offended at Victoria's condescending tone. "I'll be there."

Suddenly, an interview with Julian and Natalie Huffman was welcome.

Nine

The noonday sun had burned off the hazy morning exhaust from the city's skyline by the time Natalie made it around to Julian's office for the interview he'd previously agreed to do. Kelly's insistent prodding left him no way out. In order to get Natalie Huffman off Alex and Victoria Nixon's trail at the fund-raiser, Julian made time for an impromptu face-to-face with the gossip columnist so that the Nixons wouldn't get dragged into the reporter's nasty little world of who's doing who.

When Julian's executive assistant, Grace, tapped at his door to announce that Natalie had arrived, Kelly sighed deeply and rose to her feet. "Thank you, Grace," Julian replied, with his gaze trained on Kelly's folded arms and rigid jawline. "Please give us a minute." The secretary ducked out as quickly as she had entered. Considering the dense atmosphere inside that office, she was eager to be dismissed. "Kelly, I don't see why you're so bothered by Natalie Huffman coming here to see if she can rattle a few cages. That's what she gets paid to do and if I remember correctly, you did orchestrate this interview." Kelly's back was turned toward him, purposely, it seemed to Julian. There was something different about her, something different from the thousands of other times he'd seen her. Unfortunately, the vibes reverberating about his spacious office were not pleasant ones. *Perhaps Kelly's simply having a bad day,* he thought. *Hell, she's a woman, so there could be one of a million things on her mind.* "Kelly Taylor!" he called out, voice rising to get her attention. When his words penetrated her wall of contemplation, she jumped.

"I'm . . . I'm sorry, Julian. What was it you were saying?"

"There's something missing but I don't have time to get to the bottom of it right this minute. No doubt that Natalie Huffman's outside sharpening her claws. You staying around to watch?" Uncharacteristically, Kelly nodded in the place of actually answering him that she would.

Julian was worried about Kelly, but that would have to wait. His immediate concern was dealing with his eager visitor and what she might throw at him. After pressing his intercom button, Julian straightened his necktie and glanced down at his timepiece. "Grace, please send Miss Huffman in."

"Yes, sir," Grace responded.

No sooner had he stood from his broad executive-styled desk than the office door opened. Natalie stepped inside and closed it behind her. "Wow, nice digs, Councilman. This is quite a setup." She scanned the room, noting fine brass and crystal amenities, more space than any one person should ever need, and a personal attaché standing guard at the window. "Miss Taylor," Natalie announced, somewhat perturbed that she couldn't get at Julian alone and unencumbered.

As Julian strode toward the newspaperwoman, Kelly awoke from her daydream. "Natalie, it's always a treat," Julian offered, shaking her hand.

"Yes, always," Kelly suggested, with an ounce of apprehension.

"Please have a seat and make yourself comfortable. Is there anything I can get you?" Julian shot a "lighten up" expression in Kelly's direction.

"Yes, I'd love a bottle of Perrier, if you could manage it."

"I'm sure we can make that accommodation possible. Kelly, please see to it that Grace gets what Miss Huffman needs."

Kelly froze on the spot. She wasn't one to fetch or roll over, but she suspected that Julian had ulterior motives for sending her away.

"No problem," she answered, behind the best fake smile she could manage. "Will there be anything else while I'm out?"

"I don't think so," he said, gesturing toward Natalie.

"That'll be sufficient. Thank you."

The way Julian clocked Kelly's exit didn't slip by Natalie's roving eye. "Is there trouble in paradise already?"

"I'm afraid not. It's just that Miss Taylor's plate is full, with the demands of organizing a mayoral campaign and managing the difficult tasks associated with it. You know, control issues."

"What woman doesn't have a load of those?"

"Remember, those were your words, not mine." Julian grinned at her as she scribbled in her notebook. "I'd hate to read tomorrow's exclusive suggesting that Julian Blake was a dyed-in-the-wool misogynist who minimizes all women's woes down to mere estrogen-initiated nonsense. You would have half the voters in New York ready to run me out of town."

"Calm down, Julian. That's not why I'm here. Actually, I'm rather surprised that you kept this appointment, although that estrogen comment has a nice ring to it. Can I quote you on that?"

"I'm not going to answer that as I'm certain we both can assume the overblown ramifications if statements like that happen to make the paper without a hint of legitimacy. However, I had no intentions of going back on my word to meet with you on a private basis. I'm a man of my word and yes, you may quote me on that."

"I'm sure that you are nothing less," she complimented, while preparing her mouth for the next question to come rolling out of it. "It's also quite obvious that your female voters have developed a fondness for your public accessibility. Now that you've thrown your name into the ring, will you continue to log late hours getting to know more of them on a personal basis? That could be a job all in itself, seeing to the needs of the single women of New York." Natalie blushed after she'd made the ridiculous comment.

"I had no idea you were so talented," he jested behind a wide grin. "So, you write columns and comic scripts? I hope you're getting compensated properly."

"Okay, okay." Natalie was giddy and just this side of flirting when Kelly returned with a small serving tray. "I was out of line but the question holds a great deal of merit. The city is well known for its nightlife as well as its propensity for enticing powerful politicians and beautiful babes."

Kelly glared at the back of Natalie's head as if she'd walked in on the woman and her man involved in a lot more than simply sharing a laugh between them. "Here you go, Miss Huffman." Suddenly, using the woman's common name didn't appeal to Kelly. She was determined to be all business all the way. As she presented the bottle and cup of ice with a napkin setup, the thought of pouring it on Natalie's lap crossed her mind, though only briefly.

"Thanks, Miss Taylor," she remarked quickly without losing her momentum. "Oh, Julian, all I'm saying is not so many of your admirers are willing to trade in your man-about-town image for a stuffed-shirt facsimile. Goodness, we have enough of those already to populate a small country."

"While I'm interested in the physical, financial, and social well-being of my future constituents, I'm more than certain that the other half of the voting public would be more than willing to accommodate their need to blow off some steam from time to time. No pun intended."

Natalie stopped writing when his words caught up with her pen. She smiled and then went back to formulating her article. Kelly was standing at the window again, fuming over Julian's attempt to keep the mood lighthearted but peppering it with saucy innuendo, also fit to print. Of course he'd deny it later or insist that he was quoted out of context, but it would be newsworthy, discussed and debated in the tabloids. When Natalie neglected to put away her notebook, Julian knew he hadn't begun to satisfy her appetite for sex in the city.

"That brings me to a very important question, Julian. Who was the young lady you were photographed with and seen escorting later at the fund-raiser?"

"Ahhh, the *unnamed beauty* from your article?" Julian surmised correctly.

Kelly glanced over her shoulder to note Julian's reaction. When his face lit up at the mere mention of the latest love-to-be in his life, Kelly thought she'd lose her breath.

"Her name is Raja Jackson, a lovely friend and companion," he answered eventually.

That wasn't so bad after all, Kelly thought, once oxygen had returned to her brain.

"Natalie, I thought this interview was supposed to cover my public political policy, not my personal private life."

"Ha-ha, yes, it was at that. I was just checking to see if you were still paying attention." She wanted to steal a look at Kelly but couldn't take a chance at having her shut down the interview like she'd done the time before. "Councilman, political pundits around the state have you picked as a favorite for the Democratic ticket. Tell me what you think about Alex Nixon sliding into the race just under the wire." The announcement hit the news that morning. Julian was still reeling from the shock, but played it off.

"I feel that anyone who is qualified and serious about helping the people of New York belongs in this race, last-minute entries included." Julian knew what was coming next and welcomed it.

"Do you think that Alex Nixon has any chance at all to beat you for the Democratic nod, considering that he and *his wife* have only lived in the city for the necessary twelve months before seeking office here?"

Julian's eyes widened before he had the presence of mind to look away. Kelly clenched her mouth tightly, not sure when to step in and shut this atrocity down for good.

Patiently, Natalie waited for Julian to face her again. "Julian, I couldn't help but notice your reaction to my inferences regarding the Nixons. Was it something politically motivated or is there something else, something more, that your constituents need to be made aware of before heading to the polling booths?"

"Natalie, it would be nice to say that I'm surprised at you, but that would be a lie and not a very good one. Well, I'm afraid that we've been down this road before and I hate repeating myself, but for the sake of setting the record straight . . . for the very last time, the only interest I have in the Nixons is their role in the campaign and my beating out Alex and the other Democratic candidates for the party's nod. There's nothing more, nothing less, nothing else. That's it." The moment of truth was staring Julian in the face and he blinked. Since he hadn't fully faced it for himself, he wasn't ready to drop a bomb in the Nixons' laps, or on the front pages for that matter.

"Yes, I understand but—" Natalie started in again until Kelly slammed the door shut. She stepped between them and all but helped the reporter from her chair.

"Natalie, I'm sorry. We've run out of time," Kelly lied, very well in fact. "Julian, you're going to be late for your two o'clock if we don't get a move on. Natalie, thanks for stopping by. We really appreciate your taking the time to meet us here. Grace will validate your parking pass on the way out."

Natalie got the message loud and clear. She collected her things and made herself scarce, just as Kelly had demanded and Julian instructed beforehand. Natalie had to give Kelly her props though. She'd never seen such a precise blocking exhibition off the football field. Kelly handled the situation just right, but handling her own was another matter entirely.

"Thanks for stepping in," said Julian, loosening his tie. "It was about to get ugly."

"No, it's way past that already. Only, no one knows about it except you and the Nixons." Kelly was noticeably shaken but Julian had no idea why.

"I've stood up to tougher things than this, Kelly. You remember the Senate committee for—"

She cut him off. "No, you haven't, Julian. Nothing you've had to overcome is anywhere close to this. You have a child, one that I had no knowledge of, and we're as close as friends can get. Well, without, you know . . ."

Julian walked closer to Kelly. He could see that she was bothered by not having been previously made aware of such a big part of his life, so he decided to begin at the beginning.

"I'm sorry for keeping this from you, but there was nothing you or anyone else could do about it. I met Victoria at the library, one evening, and shared a table. We ran into each other again on campus and began sharing a lot more, but neither of us thought it would amount to much. We were headed in two different directions. I was finishing my last year of graduate school and Victoria was completing undergraduate studies."

Kelly listened attentively but couldn't find it in herself to look at him while he recounted a story he should have told her years ago.

"I don't expect you to understand how it was back then. I'm not so sure I do myself. Times were different, a lot different. Victoria's father was a very powerful figure in Georgia politics and I was a nobody. He told me that he'd kill me if I ever tried to contact her and I had no reason to think that he was bluffing." Julian's eyes floated toward the floor when he realized how weak that sounded. He often regretted leaving town despite how much he cared for her. "It wasn't until I had received a letter from Victoria over a year later when it all became clearer. She sent word that she'd gotten married and had a daughter, named Brittany. I thought it seemed odd because Brittany was the name I'd chosen for my first daughter. I did the math and concluded that her child was mine. Victoria didn't have the heart to come right out and say it, but I knew. In my gut, I knew."

Kelly perked up when a random thought occurred to her out of nowhere. "Julian, so you don't really know if it's yours?" She began to pace as she considered the possibilities of the child not being his. "There is a chance that Victoria was sharing quite a bit more than a library table with at least one other student."

"No, it's not possible. If you knew her then, you'd know how impossible that is. Victoria wanted to run away together and get married, but I couldn't, didn't want to put our lives at risk. She was always strong that way. Defiant. If she kept Brittany a secret all this time, it was because of the child's best interest." With Kelly fighting against the idea of Julian's life becoming a powder keg, he had to ensure that nothing happened to hurt his child. "Kelly, you might find it difficult to believe but Victoria's and my situation is real, Brittany is real, and making sure that this never gets out is paramount. I can't imagine how much damage would come from this getting out. It would ruin an innocent young girl's life and I can't let that happen." Julian approached Kelly, whose eyes were misting up, and placed his hands on her shoulders. "I'm sorry to keep secrets from you but that's water under the bridge now. I need you to be okay with it and on board with moving forward. Can I count on you like always to do whatever needs to be done?"

"Like always, Julian," she answered softly. "Like always."

"Thank you, Kelly."

Julian held her closely, like a sister he'd done something to hurt. He had no idea there was another explanation for her pain.

Ten

Kelly entered Swathmore Day Spa through smoky gray doors. The woman behind the granite desk walked toward her with a smile.

Kelly extended her hand. "I'm Kelly Taylor."

"Good morning, Ms. Taylor, I'm Lily. I'll be your escort. This way, please."

Kelly followed dutifully, the opulence of the facility capturing her attention. Gentle music played through ceiling speakers as they rode up an escalator one level.

"What's on this floor, Lily?"

"Workout rooms. Clients work with their personal instructors in Pilates and yoga. Then they shower, tan, or have a massage."

Kelly gazed up at the chandelier that stretched ten feet across the ceiling, then cascaded down in tiers. "What's a membership cost?"

Lily smiled demurely. "That's confidential and you have to be invited to join."

Kelly's back straightened as they exited the moving staircase. She was led to double doors, which Lily opened in one smooth gesture.

The fourth floor smelled faintly of rare and expensive perfume, with beverages served by white-gloved waiters who floated by on silent shoes. Comfortable overstuffed chairs, sheer tinted glass lamps, and couches fashioned into groupings to emulate ten different living room settings dotting the shiny hardwood floor.

This was Manhattan's old money's best-kept secret.

What was Victoria Nixon doing here? She'd been back in New York for a hot minute and she was already in the mix? The woman had secrets, and Kelly was going to get to the bottom of some of them right now.

She followed Lily to where Victoria sat, pretending to read a magazine.

"Mrs. Nixon, your guest has arrived."

Victoria stood, clad in a pink workout outfit that cost a grand the last time Kelly had eyed it in Saks. The forgotten magazine hit the floor.

Lily bent to pick it up and handed it to Victoria. "Coffee, Ms. Taylor?"

Kelly walked to the chair opposite Victoria's. "I'll have the same as Mrs. Nixon."

As Lily glided away, both women waited until their coffee was delivered before beginning their discussion. Lily was back in less than a minute with a full silver service.

Kelly indulged in a little introspection. The entire way over, she'd thought of a million questions, but now that she was facing the woman from Julian's past, only one question pressed ahead of the rest. "Are you here to destroy Julian?"

"Are you his self-appointed bodyguard?"

"No, but I've found that women from the past appear at pivotal times in a man's life for one of two reasons. They want something or they want to destroy something. Which is it for you?"

A nostalgic smile dusted Victoria's face. "It's definitely not the latter."

"Then what is it?"

Her head tipped to the side and Kelly tried not to react. Victoria was a beautiful woman. Blond and tanned just enough, fit, but somewhat uncomfortable. "Before I lay my heart on the table, Ms. Taylor, I'd like to know the extent of your relationship with Julian."

"We're friends."

Victoria let the words hang between them as she sipped her coffee. "I remember you from undergrad, Kelly. You were rough back then. Bold and confrontational, outspoken and righteous. You were from the streets and didn't mind showing it when you needed to. I remember thinking how much I wanted to be like you. I admired you then for your brutal honesty. I hope the years haven't taken away all those good qualities."

Kelly leaned in, cognizant of the women in the living room a few feet away. "Let me tell you something, Victoria. I can't be manipulated. I'm not the person with a child with Julian, who's suddenly come back into his life, married, professing to love her baby's father. I asked you a question and I want an answer. What do you want?"

"If you two are only friends, I don't see how the nature of my relationship with him is any of your business."

Frustrated, Kelly set her cup on the delicate saucer. She and Victoria could talk in circles for the next twenty years, but time was of the essence. Victoria was hesitating for a reason. And Kelly knew that she'd have to give up a little to get a little in return.

"When we were in college, Julian and I became friends. After we graduated, I moved back here to start work in public relations and he worked as a lobbyist. We kept in touch, and to make a long and otherwise boring story short, we stayed friends. Never anything more."

"Why?"

A battle within her ensued as to how much she should reveal, but like a baseball player on base with one out, Kelly played it safe. "I'm not the woman for him."

Victoria clasped her hands together and shook her head. "Why is it that black women love to be martyrs? It's so . . . boring. You didn't say you didn't love him or that you're involved in another relationship. You didn't say that you two tried it and it didn't work. No, you said you weren't the woman for him. You love him," she said and sighed. "I could never be you."

Loving Julian wasn't an option, Kelly thought, but the subject had arisen three times in less than twenty-four hours. Ricky, Natalie, and now Victoria had all posed the same question. Kelly decided to do a mental checkup. Obviously she was emitting signals that had been misinterpreted. She and Julian were best friends and colleagues, that was all. He and Raja were meant to be together, and Kelly would make sure that their relationship was given a chance. As for herself, she needed a boyfriend.

"You're wrong," Kelly said evenly, standing up to Victoria's piercing assessment. "But this isn't about me. For some reason you've chosen now to pursue Julian, and frankly, I'm baffled as to why. You already have Alex, who stated in every interview of his I've located over the past few weeks how much he loves you and your daughter. Are you pursuing Julian because of spite or regret?"

"I never regretted pursuing him," she said with a quiet sternness. "I never regretted a moment of the time we shared."

"Yes, you have."

Victoria's perfectly arched brow shot up. "What?"

"You have his child, and according to Julian nobody but the two of you know the truth. You regret the breakup, dont you?"

Victoria's gaze wandered out over the Manhattan skyline. "I wasn't as strong then as I am now. My father was very firm in his beliefs, including those where the races didn't mix. I needed Daddy's money to get my education, and I thought I couldn't live without the life I'd become accustomed to."

"So you took his unborn baby and left."

"I didn't know that I was pregnant at the time, but when I found out, I contacted Julian and we agreed to meet, but he didn't show. After I got married, Julian later explained that on the night of our meeting, you'd been in some kind of accident and he'd gone to see about you."

Kelly froze, her eyes closing briefly to mask a remnant of pain. She'd been in the hospital when Julian had rushed in. Despite admonishment from the nurses, he'd taken her into his arms and held her while she'd cried her pain into his chest.

He'd been there for three days, and when she'd been discharged, he'd helped her restart her life. The attack itself was a blur, a jumble of moving gray matter that ended up changing her life. But Julian and her recovery, she remembered.

"I'm sure had you told him the nature of your meeting, he'd have come. Julian was and still is honorable. Does he not take care of your daughter?"

"He does." Victoria's head dropped briefly. "He's a great man. Never once have I ever wondered how she'd make it if I weren't in her life. All the money Julian's given has been put in a trust for Brittany."

"Why are you telling me this?"

"Because I want you to know why I'm here."

"Do you realize what your presence in New York can do to Julian?"

"As far as everyone knows, I'm here to support my husband."

"A man you stated in your e-mail you don't love. If my investigator could get his hands on that information, others can. You're playing a dangerous game."

"Maybe I'm tired of playing games, Kelly," she said between clenched teeth. "Maybe I'm ready to finally be honest with myself and him."

Chills ran up Kelly's body. "That will destroy everything Julian's worked his entire adult life for. Do you think you can build love after you've destroyed his dream?"

"He loved me once and now there's nothing to stop him from finally having me. And his daughter."

Kelly shook her head and bit her lips.

Not a hair moved on Victoria's perfectly coifed head, but weakness in her otherwise faultless chain reflected from her eyes. "But then there's you. Again. The difference is, this time I won't be deterred."

There was no appropriate response that Kelly could offer that would satisfy Victoria. The woman was on a one-way street that would end at one destination.

"I'd think you'd be more concerned with the man you married than a woman you're seeing again after fifteen years."

Guilt brought a shadow of remorse across her face. "Alex and I will figure out the best course for us. We'll work it out."

"Victoria, you're dreaming. He's loved Brittany as his daughter her entire life. They will be crushed. You act as if you and Julian have been having a secret affair. Has Julian ever given you any indication that he has the same feelings for you?"

The question for Kelly was like rolling loaded dice. She knew what she'd read about Victoria. She was a community icon. A civic-minded, churchgoing woman who had a lot to lose. She was acting impetuous and reckless. Kelly looked at her closely. "Victoria, has he ever—"

"Yes, he has."

Kelly had raised her cup and now burned her leg when coffee sloshed over the side. She dabbed at her lap, her hands shaking. Waving off Lily, Kelly leaned close to Victoria. "I don't believe you."

"You don't want to."

"How has he encouraged this notion of you two spending your lives together?"

"He wants to get to know his daughter, he told me so. He said he loved me for taking such good care of her. To me it isn't such a stretch for him to fall back in love with me. I'm willing to risk everything for us to be together."

Kelly felt as if her chest would explode. Victoria looked vulnerable and determined and not at all misguided. She looked like a woman who was searching for herself in her past.

"Why didn't you stay with him in college?" Kelly asked.

Color rose above Victoria's almond-bean tan. "Unlike you, Kelly, I didn't know who I was back then. I was still Daddy's little girl. The thought of being cut off scared me to death. I did what I had to do and now I'm going to pursue what I let go of fifteen years ago."

Kelly picked up her purse, but remained seated. "Do you have a picture of your daughter?"

Victoria's gaze met hers head-on. "Of course."

"May I see it?"

Kelly didn't really want to look at their child. Seeing the young lady would link their old life with the present in a way memories couldn't.

Kelly took the extended picture and her breath caught.

The sweet-faced teenager was flawlessly beautiful, and looked just like her mother, down to the tips of bone-straight blond hair. Julian and Victoria's daughter was white.

"She believes Alex is her father. Doesn't she?" Kelly breathed the words in shock.

"I'll tell her before it becomes public. She's old enough to handle the truth."

Kelly gazed up at the woman in disbelief. "You're selfish. You'll destroy Julian's, your husband's, and your daughter's lives and you don't care."

With delicate fingers, Victoria touched the bridge of her nose. "Alex decided to uproot our family to run for mayor of New York. For his own selfish endeavors. In two years my little girl will go off to college and begin her life. Don't I deserve happiness?"

Kelly set the picture on the table. "You let Julian go when you had his heart in the palm of your hand. You married and began a family. Now that they have other interests, you decide it's time for Victoria to get hers. You're selfish."

"You've got it all wrong. I love Julian. I always have. And you being in love with him doesn't scare me. Losing an empty life doesn't either. I'm just wondering if you are going to become a source of aggravation for me."

Kelly rose. "I'm not your problem. I know my place in Julian's life. We've always been and will continue to be friends." Kelly looked around the room. "I know you can afford this level of luxury, but I promise you that if you hurt Julian, you won't have another comfortable day for a long time."

Kelly had started away when Victoria grabbed her hand.

"You may have Julian's ear, and maybe his heart, but I have his daughter and there's nothing that you can do to change that. He'll do right by his family, and like it or not, I am family."

Victoria smiled in true southern belle fashion, leaving Kelly cold and afraid for Julian's future.

Eleven

Raja spent the late afternoon pampering herself.

An impromptu telephone call to Julian's office led to one of the most sensual conversations they'd had to date, and during the conversation Raja slipped in an invitation to dinner at her place that Julian had readily accepted. Raja had hung up the phone in a state of euphoria, and anxious to prepare herself for their evening rendezvous, she laid out her plan of seduction, or rather her plan of attack, depending on how you looked at it.

Julian had sounded so glad to hear her voice when she called that she was almost taken aback. She'd known he was charmed by her style and intellect, but the warm rush of affection he'd displayed the moment she said his name had given her a boost of confidence in their relationship that she sorely needed.

Raja swung by her favorite nail salon for a fresh manicure and pedicure. She had her toes and her fingers polished in a hot cinnamon hue that matched both the stunning dress she planned to wear that evening, and the bodacious Victoria's Secret ensemble that would be hugging her curved brown body beneath it.

Mozelle's was too far away to just drop in for a wash and wrap, so she did the next best thing and shampooed her own hair, then sprayed it with a bit of wrap lotion and blow-dried it to perfection, marveling at the amazing cut that settled on her shoulders like magic.

Ten minutes before Julian was scheduled to arrive everything was set. Raja's stylish apartment was sparkling, the lights were dimmed low, the table was set for two, the Thai dinner had been delivered and was waiting in the kitchen in insulated containers, and Raja herself was looking and smelling good enough to eat.

"Hi," she greeted Julian at the door.

He looked wonderful standing there in a modest designer suit and holding the most exquisite arrangement of lilacs and baby's breath she'd ever seen.

"Hi yourself," he said, smiling and offering her the bouquet. "These are for you." He leaned down and kissed her, his lips lingering on hers for several intimate seconds.

"Thank you." Raja grinned, dimples flashing in her pretty face. She accepted the flowers and briefly pressed her nose to them, inhaling appreciatively before glancing up to smile at him again. "These are wonderful," she said, leading him into her living room. "Just wonderful."

"As are you," Julian said, entering the room behind her.

Raja noted him checking out the layout and the décor with an impressed, approving look on his face. She swelled inside like a lioness who was proud of her lair. It had taken quite a bit of effort and an eye for detail to select the solid, quality pieces of black art and sculpture she had on display, and she was glad Julian's cultured eye had acknowledged this.

Raja had intended to serve dinner right away, or at the least the edible version of dinner, but the way Julian looked as he relaxed on her sofa drew her to him.

"Hard day?" she asked, sidling next to him until their thighs were touching.

He sighed, then reached for her, draping his arm around her shoulder and encouraging her to snuggle closer. "Yes," he said evenly. "Very hard."

"Hmmm," Raja mused. She knew better than to ask for details. If a man like Julian wanted to share his professional dilemmas, then he would, but Raja's intuition told her that Julian was in need of something more than a sounding board tonight. If the pensive set to his shoulders was any indication of his mood, then it was comfort that he needed. Not counseling.

She sat beside him as they made small talk, mesmerized by the way Julian's fingers absentmindedly stroked hers as they chatted. They were at a stage in their relationship that most people might find awkward, but was a welcome challenge to Raja. They'd had some pretty revealing late-night conversations and had shared a few breathtaking kisses, but they'd not yet crossed that line of intimacy, and before things went "there" Raja had to make sure that what she was feeling for Julian was being reciprocated on more than just a physical level.

"You look beautiful," Julian said during a brief pause in their conversation. He pressed his nose to her hair and moaned. "Yum . . . you smell great too."

Raja smiled with confidence. She smelled good on purpose. Unbeknownst to some women, a man's nose was one of his most sensual organs, and Raja planned to tease and please Julian's at every opportunity. He didn't have to worry about a trace of Blue Magic grease rubbing off her tresses to stain his shirt, or the slightest scent of Sulfur-Eight to sting his nose either. Those ghettofied days were long over, and as Raja lifted her chin and exposed her sleek neck to his hot kisses she found herself getting lost in Julian's scent as well, and it took considerable control on her part to break the embrace and stand up from the sofa.

"Wow," she said, standing before him in her dynamite dress. She knew how scrumptious she looked, and the smoldering embers in Julian's eyes and the rising bulge in his pants confirmed it. "You almost made me forget about dinner. Are you hungry?"

Julian nodded slowly, never taking his eyes off her.

"Okay, then!" Raja said brightly. He was hungry all right, she mused. And it damn sure wasn't for Thai food. She turned to walk into the kitchen and felt his eyes on her sisterly hips. They were in perfect proportion and Raja knew it was a blessing to look devastating whether she was coming or going.

They ate dinner by candlelight, sitting side by side at her dining room table. Julian was the perfect gentleman, serving Raja and spreading her napkin in her lap, then taking her hand and leading her in a blessing of the food that would have pleased anybody's grandmother.

Raja played it cool. She'd dated lots of men and she knew what most of them wanted. Experience had taught her that no matter how smart she was, how savvy or how personable, there were some men out there who were looking for one thing and one thing only.

Her body.

Raja enjoyed sex immensely, but only on her own terms. It wasn't about giving a man what he wanted when he wanted it. Especially a man like Julian. He already possessed a sense of entitlement that was part of the persona of most powerful men. She refused to be just one of his convenient sack mates to be tossed to the side when the moment was over.

Raja enjoyed the flow of their conversation. She was sweet and charming and her interest in Julian and his ideals was genuine and sincere. She loved his wit, his style, and his soul, and for the one thousandth time she prayed to herself that he was being real with her and that his interest in her extended further than being seen out together on the town with hopes of ending up with a quick romp in the sheets.

But of course she had to test him.

"Wow," Raja said, steering the conversation in the direction of her choosing. Julian had been outright flirting with her over dinner. Making sexy little comments and staring into her eyes with unmistakable longing. "We always seem to have such a good time together, Julian. It was wonderful of Kelly to bring us to each other. Don't you think we should find a way to thank her?"

She watched him carefully but he was smooth as butter.

"Absolutely," Julian said, taking her hand in his and lifting it to his lips. "I'm really digging you, Raja. You're sweet and you're special. A real gift. Kelly did me a big favor by bringing you into my life, and I look forward to building on this relationship in the future."

Raja beamed inside, but accepted the compliment with outward calm. It was just what she'd needed to hear. He dug her. She was special. A gift. He was anticipating a future that had her in it. Finally, a man who understood her worth and recognized the gem that she was. Of course, Raja had heard it all before, from the mouths of many other men, but this time was different. Julian was a man of honor. His integrity was of the highest caliber and his spirit was honest. She believed him because she knew he was believable and had no reason to lie to her. There were scores of hot honeys anxious to be on his arm and in his bed, and he could take his pick. The fact that the wonderful, powerful Julian Blake had chosen her was a testament that one did not have to stay ensnared in one's humble, horrid roots. The person that Raja had once been was not the person she had worked so hard on becoming. The ugly buck-toothed little girl from the projects was now wanted and desired by one of the most important men in New York City politics, and not only was she perfect for Julian, Julian was perfect for her.

They didn't bother to tidy up after dinner.

In fact, they made more of a mess in the kitchen than either of them could have anticipated. One moment Raja was scraping their plates down the garbage disposal, and the next instant Julian was behind her, insistent. Still hungry.

"I want you . . ." he whispered in her ear as he planted greedy kisses along the nape of her neck. Raja dropped the plate as electricity surged throughout her body, the unmistakable heat of Julian's arousal pressing into her from behind. "I want to be with you."

She fought the feeling, knowing full well that want wasn't good enough. No, if she gave herself to Julian it wouldn't be simply because he wanted her. He could get what he wanted anywhere. It had to go deeper than that.

She reached back with one hand and ran her fingers through his hair. His hands were cupping her hips as his tongue found her ear and sucked gently on the lobe.

"Oooh." A moan slipped from Raja's mouth before she could bite it back.

Julian urged her around to face him, and when she did there was no mistaking what she saw in his eyes.

"Raja," he whispered, gathering her close to him. Her breasts were crushed against his chest as his hands found her small waist and wandered downward. "I need you . . ."

Yes, Raja thought, finally satisfied. Yes, he needed her. And she needed him too. She arched her back as his lips slid across her throat and left a hot streak on her chin. And then his tongue went to work, sucking her lips and probing her mouth as though the secrets of the universe lay just within its borders.

It had been such a long time since she'd been made love to by a man who had her heart, but Raja was no amateur and knew better than to let herself get swept away. *No*, she thought as Julian slid the thin straps down her shoulders and exposed the mounds of her breasts. She wouldn't allow her passion to make her fall overboard. Instead, Raja thought, panting as Julian buried his face in the lush valley of her flesh, guiding one erect nipple to his mouth as she tried not to scream with pleasure, she would work her magic on him so well that there'd be no room left in his imagination for any other woman. Especially Kelly.

Raja regained control of herself and turned Julian's passion back on him full force. She lifted his face from her breasts, and now it was she who explored his mouth, her tongue darting expertly, nibbling and tickling and kissing him with such erotic passion that his moans filled the air.

Meanwhile, she unbuttoned his shirt without him even realizing it, and moments later her head was lowered, her lips locked on his nipple, her teeth biting gently, her tongue swirling wet circles as he panted and surrendered and urged her on.

In minutes they were both naked and gazing at each other appreciatively. The candles flickered sensuously, and Raja realized that even if the lights had been on, that would have been fine too. Neither of them had a thing to be ashamed of as both of their bodies were in prime condition.

"Damn," Julian muttered, staring at her in amazement. "Girl," he whispered thickly. "You got it."

Raja was staring too. At the delicious sight of Julian's organ as it rose from his body and stood at attention against his muscular stomach. She wasted no time getting to know it. Thoroughly. Cupping its weight in her hands and showering it with rapt attention until Julian's whole body began to tremble, his knees weak with need.

"Come here." He beckoned her, pulling her up and moaning as their naked bodies met. Holding her under the arms, he lifted her easily onto the kitchen counter and pushed her knees back until her womanhood was fully exposed.

Julian's breath caught in his throat at the sight. "You look like a flower, baby," he told her, moving toward her like a honeybee. "A beautiful, blossoming flower."

Never had Raja experienced such pleasure, and even in the throes of the passion his tongue was creating she understood that it was her feelings for Julian that made the act so very good. She arched her back and gave in as he delved into her moistness, savoring her taste and her aroma far more than he had savored his dinner meal.

The first time was good, but they were both starved.

By the second time they'd made their way into Raja's bedroom and rode each other to multiple climaxes in the comfort of her fresh, scented sheets. *Careful,* Raja had warned herself more than once. Julian was giving it just as good as he got it. She felt so good and so right in this man's arms, under his body, shivering at his touch, that it was easy to forget who was supposed to be whipping who. Raja was adventurous and totally uninhibited with a lover who had her heart, so the third time was slower, but no less passionate, with Julian whispering sweet words of love in her ear while she pleased him in ways that were apparently beyond his experiences.

By the time she had coaxed the very last drop of love from his body, Raja knew the intimacy they'd just shared and the passion they'd enjoyed was more special than anything she'd ever experienced. She closed her eyes and rested her head on his stomach as his hands gently stroked her hair and massaged her shoulders.

They slept this way, for several hours, and during the night when the room became chilled Julian gathered her in his arms and wrapped the blanket around her, taking great care to cover her shoulders and make sure she was warm and snug.

Some time before dawn Raja awakened and extricated herself from Julian's protective arms. She walked into the bathroom naked and lit her row of candles, then ran her bath, going light on the scented oils. She stood in the mirror gazing at her naked, sated body and recited her affirmations from memory.

> *Raja Monet Jackson, you are great.*
> *Nothing can stop you from achieving your goals.*
> *No one but God is more glorious than you.*
> *You have the power to do amazing things.*
> *Whatever you pursue with all your might, you conquer.*
> *You are black and beautiful and female, the envy of the world.*

And then for the first time ever, she added a few extra affirming lines.

> *Raja Monet Jackson, you are worthy and valuable.*
> *No more buck teeth, crusty skin, or nappy hair to diminish your true worth.*
> *You deserve the love of a powerful man.*
> *The love of this man.*
> *And he deserves you too.*

No sooner were the words out of her mouth than Raja saw Julian standing in the doorway behind her. He stared at her with quiet intensity, and it was hard to read what was in his eyes. For a moment Raja felt coy. Shy even. Who had actually captured who last night? The moment passed and Raja beamed as Julian bent to kiss her lips, the scent of their sex rising from his skin. He gazed around the bathroom in quiet approval, then took her hand and led her over to the sunken tub.

He allowed her to climb in first, steadying her with his touch. And then he joined her, sinking down into the scorching heat of the water without blinking his eyes. Julian pulled Raja down on top of him until she rested between his legs with her head against her chest. She sighed as Julian cupped her breasts, holding onto them for comfort. Yeah, the sky was breaking into bright colors and pretty soon he'd leave her and return to his own apartment to ready himself for the day ahead, but right now he was all hers, and Raja closed her eyes and placed her hands on his and waited for the sunrise.

Twelve

"First American Bank, this is Raja Jackson speaking. How may I help you?"

The voice on the other end of the line was male and authoritative.

"Yes. You can help me by wiring funds from my Cornerstone Fund account to one of my secondary accounts. Grab a pen and prepare to copy down my account number."

Privileged white people! Raja had to stop herself from rolling her eyes.

"Sorry, sir. You've reached the international banking department. Wire transfers are handled by customer service. Please hold while I ring them for you." *Click.* Raja cut the man off before he could protest and end up working her last nerve.

Dealing with snooty clientele was to be expected when one was employed at a select service branch where the average daily account balance hovered in the five-figure range, but Raja had come a long way since those bank teller and customer service days. The banking industry was notorious for the glass ceiling that hovered above women of all races, but for black women that ceiling was low enough to bump your head on. When it came time to climb the corporate ladder, rungs seemed to break off and disappear when minorities approached.

Raja sat back and exhaled. She'd been jumpy and on edge all morning, which was quite disturbing considering what kind of night she'd had. Just the memory of those horizontal gymnastics she and Julian had played sent heat spreading throughout her body. She'd performed like a champ and had mentally thrown her fist in the air in triumph as she rocked Julian's body in ways he'd never even dreamed of.

As her mind replayed their lovemaking Raja's nostrils were filled with his scent, her skin tingled at the way his hands had roamed and kneaded her curved, firm flesh. They'd bonded physically and emotionally last night with Julian whispering all the right things in her ear as they pleased each other to the max. But it wasn't the physical aftermath of their coupling that had Raja staring dreamily at the wall when there were high-profile accounts that needed to be serviced. No, her little heartstrings had been plucked too, and that was a first for her.

"Good morning!"

Raja jumped so hard her hand struck her coffee cup, nearly sweeping it from the desk. "Sh—" She almost cursed out loud, then caught herself as she looked up to see Phinius Morgan standing in her doorway with one eyebrow raised.

"Well!" Phinius exclaimed in her sweet white-bread voice. A classic spoiled little rich girl, she and Raja had grown to despise each other and were long past hiding it. Workplace etiquette dictated they behave civilly in public, but the gloves came off whenever they were alone

"Jumpy today, are we?" Phinius asked slyly. "You always try to appear so calm and collected. So in control. Is something wrong?"

Raja was busy mopping up her liquid mess with soggy paper towels, but she didn't miss the question, or the implication in Phinius's voice.

"No, but when you barge into someone's space and scream at them from the doorway, what do you expect? And for the record, I am calm. Now what do you want?"

Phinius giggled, her windswept bleached-blond hair fanning

around her shoulders. "Bob called a ten a.m. meeting. He wants
your last four spreadsheets on his desk by nine."

Raja nodded coolly. "Fine," she replied, her tone dismissive. "I'll
be there."

Phinius remained in the doorway. Posing in her two-thousand-
dollar designer dress. With a senator for a daddy and a trust fund
that wouldn't stop, the young white woman contrasted Raja in
every way, a fact that wasn't lost on either of them. Whereas Raja
had grown up poor and filled with a negative self-image, Phinius
had lived a privileged life and been assured from the moment she
took her first breath that she was worthy and beautiful and entitled
to the best the world had to offer. While Raja had scrimped and
scraped to get through college, Phinius had floated through like
school was just something to do. She'd been oblivious of the value
of an education because working for a living was not a requirement
for people like her. Where brothers had to be self-assured and pro-
black to date a strong sista like Raja, the average man fell all over
himself trying to get noticed by blue-eyed white girls like Phinius.
And Phinius certainly liked them black. The blacker the better, in
fact.

"You still here?" Raja looked up again. The only satisfaction she
got out of all of this was that Phinius's beautiful blond ass was in-
competent. She spent more time in the mirror than she did at her
desk, and no matter how prestigious her pedigree, First American
Bank wasn't about to put her in charge of their top international accounts. Raja was officially her boss, although both of them knew
that title was largely symbolic.

Phinius pursed her well-lined lips and narrowed one eye as
though she was thinking.

"Don't do that," Raja warned.

"Do what?"

"Think too hard. I can smell your brain frying."

Phinius scowled, then crossed her arms under her ten-thousand-
dollar implants. "Didn't I read something about you in *The New
York Weekly* a little while back? In that crude woman's column?
What is her name . . . Huffman? Natalie Huffman?"

Raja broke a few dried leaves from the stem of her desk plant and tossed them into her wastepaper basket before answering. "If I had known you could actually read I would have insisted you pull your own weight around here a long time ago. Can you count too?"

"Oh yes," Phinius mused, ignoring the jab. "I believe I did read something. Something about you and that gorgeous councilman. What's his name? Julian Blake? Now that's the kind of man who can get your juices flowing. I bet he's dangerous where it really counts."

Raja could have slain Phinius with just one Brooklyn glance, but instead she remained completely unruffled on the outside. She was sick of the way white women like Phinius threw themselves all over successful black men like Julian. If it wasn't the cultured cream of the black crop the white girls went after, it was the thugged-out entertainers or professional athletes who thought having a white woman on their arm signified some sort of status. And black men had so little self-love and were so easily misled and charmed by the forbidden European fruit illusion that it was pathetic. If you took those same successful brothers and stuck them back in the hood and dressed them in funky sweat suits and run-over sneakers, most white women would clutch their purses and cross to the other side of the street.

"Well, boss lady?" Phinius asked, leaning against the door frame with a devious twinkle in her eyes. "Are you seeing him or not?"

Raja's expression never changed, and neither did the tone of her voice. "None of your damned business. Now get out of my office. Unlike some people, I have work to do."

Phinius laughed good-naturedly. "All right then! I'll take that as a yes, which means he's probably working with something that I can use. Politicians are freaky, you know. I once slept with a black alderman. Incredible lover. So . . . um . . . well equipped, shall I say? You know that rumor about the black man's apparatus. I've usually found it to be quite true. Anywho, this particular political figure wanted me to bray like a donkey while he slapped me on the backside and yelled giddyup! I kept trying to explain to him that giddyup was a horse command, but he finally convinced me that horses and donkeys spoke the same language."

Phinius laughed again. As usual she was searching for Raja's hot button and little did she know how close she was to pushing it.

Calling up a genetic cool cultivated way back on the plantation, Raja yawned and looked bored. "You know, Phinnie," she said, using a nickname she knew her coworker detested, "if I didn't know any better I would swear you were born in a brothel. I guess all of that money your daddy spent on your fine upper-crust education went to waste, huh? Judging by your gutter antics, money is not the only thing your father wasted."

It took Phinius a moment to realize just how badly she'd been insulted, and when the scope of the insult finally sank in, anger flushed her face as she clenched her fists at her sides.

"That was mean, Raja!" she said, pouting. "Even for you!"

Raja smirked and, ignoring Phinius, began gathering the spreadsheets she'd need for her impromptu meeting. *This white chick can go to hell*, she thought. She hadn't climbed her few rungs of the corporate ladder without stepping on a few of their spineless backs, and Phinius may not have noticed it, but one or two of Raja's shoe prints had landed squarely between her shoulders.

But Phinius wasn't the only female employee at First American Bank who had it out for her. In fact, Raja was willing to bet that most of the white women at her job got together over lunch and schemed on how to sabotage her efforts and take some of the brightness out of her shine. She smirked again. When would they realize that they were no match for the great Raja Monet Jackson? Even with all the advantages they'd had in their lives, Raja had worked ten times harder than they could even imagine and none of them were good enough to hold a candle up to her or to even polish her fingernails. Their office politics and conniving antics disgusted her. Swooning and fainting whenever they didn't get their way. And she pitied those weak black men who fell prey to their pale skin and blue eyes. It was a good thing that men like Julian knew better. The way he had kissed and adored and savored her dark skin the night before let her know that he was a true brother who had genuine love for his black sisters.

Just the thought of him sent unfamiliar pangs of longing charging through her, causing her to take deep breaths to calm their intensity. Playing cat and mouse was all well and fine when everybody knew their roles, but exactly who had hooked who last night? Raja had to ask herself. And if she had to even consider the answer, that meant she was in trouble. And as usual, whenever she felt trouble looming Raja fled straight back to East New York. Pushing her spreadsheets aside, she picked up the telephone and dialed Justine.

Immediately after work Raja took the subway into Brooklyn, exiting the train at New Lots Avenue. She didn't relish the idea of walking to Justine's apartment building, but it wasn't far enough to flag down a cab and besides, throngs of people were walking from the train station and heading in her direction, so she had plenty of company.

She walked with her head up, conscious of the cracked sidewalks and the heavy pall of an overworked population. This was a trek that the people of this neighborhood made day in and day out, and most of them would die before they were able to work themselves out of this urban rut.

Outside Justine's apartment Raja couldn't resist. Setting her briefcase within arm's reach, she joined a group of little girls who were playing sidewalk hopscotch on a chalk-drawn grid.

"Gimme something," she said, holding out her hand for something to throw.

"Here," said one of the girls, a cute little brown-skinned wonder with gapped teeth and long braids. She passed Raja a piece of broken glass that had once been part of a liquor bottle, then stood back as Raja tossed the glass into the number-one box and hopped into it on one foot.

Raja was bent at the waist and tossing her glass into box eight when Justine called her from the window.

"Miss it!" Justine joked, wearing a wide grin.

"Don't even try to jinx me!" Raja yelled, and not only made the throw, but hopped up to box eight and successfully navigated a two-foot hop and turn as well.

Minutes later Raja was sitting in Justine's tiny kitchen eating a warmed-over potato knish that Justine had gotten from a pizza shop on Stanley Avenue.

"Okay," Justine said as Raja squeezed a bit of mustard on her plate and dipped the crusty edge of the knish in it. "We have about an hour until Dennis and the kids get home, so give it to me hot, quick, and nasty. Was it good?"

Raja laughed, throwing her head back and not caring that she hadn't even finished chewing what was in her mouth. "Was he good? Is the Hudson River funky?"

Justine squealed and Raja fanned herself.

"Girl, he bathed me."

"Bathed you?"

Raja exhaled, reliving his touch. "Yeah. He bathed me. Like I was a little baby. His baby. It was amazing. Just flippin' amazing. I mean, you know I played it cool as a cucumber and all, but I swear it was one of the hardest things I've ever had to do. Julian made me feel so good I wanted to whisper it in his ear and shout it from the rooftop. I even thought about asking him to call in sick so I could fix him breakfast and then show him how good I could work it on round two, but you know I couldn't play myself like that."

"Play yourself like what?" Justine asked, a grin of happiness for her friend still lingering on her lips.

Raja shrugged and took another bite of her knish. "Like I was so into him, you know? I would never let a man think I adored him one iota more than he adored me. I mean, Julian has already told me how deeply he cares for me and how much he wants me to be a huge part of his future, but nah. I'm always in control of my emotions. It just doesn't pay to go gaga over a man until he is at least gaga-gaga over you."

Justine waved her hand. "Raja, please. This is the new millennium, honey. Sisters these days go for what they want. All that playing it safe and cool and waiting around for a man to decide to make you his is over. If you really want Julian you need to hop all over him and let him know he's been chosen."

Raja frowned, and shook her head. "I do want him, Jus. I want him so bad I can taste him. But I can't just push up on him like all those other desperate hoochies do. He's probably used to aggressive black women chasing him down for a commitment and trying to convince him that they're the right one for him. No. Getting hooked up in a long-term relationship with me has to be Julian's idea. Or at least he has to think it is."

"Okay then." Justine shrugged, but the doubt was obvious in her voice. "You know most men ain't the smartest creatures out there. Sometimes they need sistas to help them along. Nah mean? You gotta motivate them suckers to do what's best in a lot of situations, and when it comes down to commitments and relationships they damn sure need a little help. You might want to do like I did with Dennis. He's a damn good black man and the best father my kids could have asked for, but that's only because I kept forgetting to take one of those little daily pills."

"Ooooh, heffah!" Raja exclaimed. "You mean you tricked him?"

Justine laughed. "Set his behind right up. And look how happy he is now. Marrying me was the best thing in the world for him."

Raja chewed her food pensively. On the one hand she loved the idea of Julian falling so in love with her that he asked for her hand in marriage and set her up for the rest of her life. But on the same note, there was something thrilling about the chase that she wasn't sure she could do without. Raja loved it when men pursued her and admired her and sought to satisfy her every whim. Sometimes all of that attention and admiration ended the moment they said, "I do." She glanced at Justine's ever-thickening girth. Forget what could happen once a woman had kids and got comfortable. The adoration usually went out the door.

No, she told herself. Even with all that Julian had to offer, she didn't want to lure him with anything except what she felt in her heart and could offer him in return. There would be no trickery, no birth control malfunctions, or manipulative games. If Julian meant all the things he'd said to her, and if he was half the black man he represented himself as, things would continue to click between them naturally. And when she found herself standing at the altar dressed in white and holding his hand, she would know in her heart that it was only love that had brought them there.

Thirteen

Kelly ran her fingers across the log of hours she planned to submit to Julian's accountant and wondered if trying to convince Victoria to leave Julian alone would be considered business or personal.

No one but her brother Ricky knew of the intense personal turmoil she'd endured delving into Victoria's life, but confronting her had been about saving Julian's life—professionally. Still, the encounter had left a bad taste in Kelly's mouth because Julian didn't know what she'd done.

For the fifth time she dragged the white-out brush across the numbers and calculated one last time before signing her name in blue ink.

Nothing could obliterate the two-hour encounter from her mind. Her time had been worth one hundred dollars an hour, but seeing Victoria drive out of Julian's life would be . . . priceless.

Glancing at the clock, she grabbed her purse and briefcase, changed her shoes, and shut down her desktop computer. Her laptop was already in the briefcase and Kelly stood, but didn't move. She was supposed to meet Julian at his apartment in thirty minutes, but she still hadn't fully adjusted her attitude to be all right with everything that had been thrown at her over the past two days.

Rubbing her forehead, Kelly gathered her things, vowing to take a vacation as soon as the election was over. She didn't need to die young because she cared about someone more than he cared about her.

She stopped abruptly. The admission snuck into her reality like smoke and choked the air in her throat. Kelly shook her head. She was definitely tripping. Victoria's presence had altered her universe, and now she had to act as if nothing were different. In the distance the elevator bell rang while the voices of the last employees leaving the floor faded behind the closed doors.

Kelly left her office and arrived at Julian's in a record thirteen minutes.

Knocking, she lowered her hand when the door was snatched open and she was pulled inside.

"Hey, where you been? I ordered dinner a long time ago."

"I had some things to take care of. I hope you ate. I'm not hungry."

Julian looked at Kelly, wiping his mouth with the cloth napkin. "Since when aren't you hungry for Sylvia's? Hey, what's up?" Julian had moved in close. "Who's been messing with you?"

Kelly tried to sidestep Julian's inquisitive look, but he was more agile.

"Will you stop? Goodness!" she exclaimed. "I don't want to eat. I'm sorry I'm late, but I'm here now, so let's get started. God!"

He folded the napkin into a precise square, then threw it in the air, shaking his head. "You're pissed that I was with Victoria and didn't tell you."

"I'm not pissed off, Julian. Can we get to work?"

"Don't lie to me," he said in her face. "All this time we've been friends and we've never lied to each other. I'm not about to start. So what the hell, I didn't tell you. Being with her was my business."

His words beat on Kelly's heart. Julian knew everything about her. Her private pain and the most intimate details of her life had been mulled over and rehashed time and again, and Kelly thought the sharing had been mutual.

She and Julian went so far back, they could recount stories from each other's childhood. They'd discussed everything, except Victoria.

He'd protected her, as if she was a precious gem, and Kelly wanted to know why. "What the hell, Julian? I thought we were tight."

"We are tight, there's no question about that, but I just didn't tell you."

"Why?"

"Because I didn't," he said, being evasive and defensive.

"Why, though? We're supposed to be best friends. At least I thought we were."

"Don't start trippin'. We aren't in high school."

Kelly laughed but didn't find anything funny. "So now I'm acting immature? You're the one with the white-woman-secret lover and love-child, and I'm the one who's acting childish? Please. You've got that whole corner covered."

"That's exactly why I didn't tell you."

"Why?" Kelly demanded. "Because she's white? So what, Julian? In case you hadn't noticed, interracial couples are everywhere."

"You trying to tell me you wouldn't have had a problem with me dating Victoria back then?"

Kelly aimed for nonchalant and failed. "Why would I have cared?"

"I know you better than that."

"Okay," she said, stalking around his circular living room, before coming to face him. "I would have cared, Julian. But not for the simple, almost inconsequential fact that she's white. Oh no. I would have cared because there were plenty of sisters around Howard for you to choose from.

"I would have cared that an intelligent, educated, good-looking man, who was surrounded by sisters day and night, who studied, prayed, and fought alongside you for the civil and every other right to be black, cast aside these sisters for a Barbie look-alike.

"I would have cared that sisters like me got to prop up your tired, dirty, tearstained, broken-down pride, but she got the tiny bit of goodness you had to offer."

"It wasn't like that, Kelly. Victoria and I just found each other. We were in a tort class together, and one thing led to another. Being with her was so easy. I could forget—"

At that moment, Kelly hated Julian. "There's the rub, Julian. We couldn't ever forget. Everything for us sisters was hard. Brothers were all we had and once you were gone, we were left with the crazed rapists—crap!"

"I get it, Kelly, that's why I didn't stay with her."

"You didn't stay with her because her father would have pulled a modern-day Emmitt Till on your ass."

Julian had flopped on the arm of the black leather armchair, staring up at her. "What the hell are you talking about?"

"Her family was rich. Her daddy wasn't having a black son-in-law come live at his Forsyth County, Georgia, home. You didn't leave because you wanted to. You left her alone because you had no choice."

"What do you know about what happened?"

Kelly realized she'd said too much and moved away from Julian. "Look, we don't need to rehash your private life. We're supposed to be strategizing."

"What do you know? Because it damn sure sounds to me like you have a whole lot more on your mind."

"I met Victoria yesterday. She told me what happened."

"The hell you say." The shock settled in and he walked around, a bewildered smirk on his face. "What are you doing digging around in my life?"

"I wasn't digging. From the moment you grabbed me at the church, you pulled me into this realm of your personal life. You told me not to leave your side and I haven't. As your PR consultant, my *job* has been to protect you and ward off the unexpected. That's what I was doing."

"Bullshit! Damn it, Kelly, that is my personal business and I don't want you or anybody else getting involved in it."

"You know what, while you're so busy protecting yourself," she said sarcastically, "Victoria is planning how to derail your career. She wants you, Julian. And she's going to ruin your political aspirations, her husband's and your daughter's existence just to get what she wants. She's selfish and she's going to take you down."

"You're lying. Victoria isn't anything like that. She and I have an understanding that's been in place fifteen years. I know why you're doing this. You're in love with me and you want me for yourself."

The moment of truth had arrived. Kelly understood this better than at any other pivotal moment in her life. She stared at her best friend and hated that the words he'd spoken sounded like an accusation. She did love him—enough to know that they didn't have a future as Mr. and Mrs.

But Julian didn't see that she wasn't the person about to drop a grenade into his life. "You insult me by acting like I wouldn't love you, but we know what kind of love that is. It's called friendship deeper than anything you've ever known with her or anyone else."

"You're right. We are friends, but that doesn't give you the right to delve into my personal life. You had no right to talk to her. I thought I could trust you."

Kelly walked past Julian into the foyer where he caught her by the arm. She tried to jerk away, but he held tight. "Don't give me the benefit of the doubt, Julian. That's not what I deserve. Give it to the woman who had your baby in secret and married another man. The same woman who hasn't told your daughter about you, or her husband who treats Brittany like his. The same woman who will ultimately destroy your dreams. She deserves your loyalty. As for me, you can go to hell."

Kelly pushed past Julian and walked out the front door, her purse over her arm. She stumbled to the elevator and stabbed the buttons, praying the tears rushing through her body wouldn't fall while she was still in his building.

She got outside and ran to the curb, hailing a taxi, but none immediately came, so she started walking.

Kelly moved to separate her bags, when she realized she'd forgotten her briefcase in his apartment. "Damn it!"

Tears flooded her eyes at the thought of facing Julian again. His words tore at her, the look in his eyes etched in his brain.

They were no longer cool. He was a different man. She'd heard that power changed people, but she'd never thought it'd happen to Julian.

What would happen now?

Walking home, Kelly knew one thing. Julian would have to figure out the rest of this campaign on his own.

She quit.

Fourteen

Visibly shaken after his confrontation with Kelly, Julian marched circles over the imported tile throughout his front foyer. He considered running out to catch her, but his anger warned against it. There's no telling what he would have said or done if he had managed to stop her from getting away. While pacing ferociously like a caged lion, Julian was seething in frustration. "Going behind my back!" he ranted loudly. "You went too damned far, Kelly!" he shouted as if she were still there to hear him. "What in the hell am I going to do now? Huh? Tell me that!"

Before Kelly walked in and told him how she'd met with Victoria clandestinely, all cloak-and-dagger like, Julian never would have imagined it happening. *Where did Kelly get off?* he reasoned. Kelly should have known better than to take it upon herself where Julian's most private business was concerned. He wanted to believe that she'd done it out of blind loyalty to him and his career aspirations, but there was something gnawing at him, something so out of place that he didn't recognize it. Julian's intuition was clouded by his fury or else he would have noticed what that annoying *something* was.

Severely overwhelmed, Julian tried to replay his discussion with Kelly, all the time wondering where it went wrong or if she had bated him and then deliberately pulled the chair out from under his ever-increasing troublesome world. To compound matters, not only did Julian feel betrayed by Kelly's perceived overzealousness but he also felt that she had made an inexcusable statement regarding his continued estrangement from his daughter. There was something very wrong with a black woman encouraging a black man to stay away from his own child. That very annoying *something* had reared its ugly head again. What kind of woman would fix her mouth to openly suggest that he blow off his only child? he asked himself several times before cursing the day that he no longer trusted Kelly implicitly. On the other hand, Kelly had actually met with Victoria. Even though they had exchanged harsh words in the process, the cat was already out of the bag and there was no stuffing it back inside. Julian shook his head in disbelief when it occurred to him that Kelly, after having met with Victoria, knew more about her and Brittany than he did. Having been told how things were playing out, albeit during a heated argument, left a stinging pain in his chest.

It had been a long time since Julian felt so alone. Alone, deceived, betrayed, and determined to give Victoria one hell of a fight if that's what she wanted. Oddly enough, the Victoria of today didn't resemble the kind and compassionate Victoria that he remembered. His Victoria wouldn't have stooped to plotting against him, but then again she hadn't been his Victoria for quite some time. She belonged to another man now, a man who was plotting to defeat him in the mayoral race. What if she had turned her back on Julian? he questioned. What if everything Kelly had told him about her was true? That cinched it, as far as he was concerned, he'd have to accept the place and time that Victoria proposed for a very special meet-and-greet of their own. Since there wasn't much to be done about it at that late hour, Julian poured himself a two-finger measure of Kentucky bourbon over ice, and then he chased that with another stiff portion while mulling over more damaging thoughts that could have gotten someone hurt, perhaps even killed.

After downing a very convincing four-fingered sedative, Julian finally calmed down long enough to relax. Unfortunately, his natural instincts took over where the tumultuous inner cognitive dissonance left him. As he tossed and turned in his bed, it appeared as if the clock on his bedroom nightstand slinked by slowly, mocking him. With no rest in sight, he contemplated other things he'd rather be doing at 1:00 a.m. Although it went against his better judgment, Julian had dialed up the one person he wanted, needed to see.

"Raja," he whispered, when she answered on the other end. Her voice was thick and creamy.

"Yeah, it's me and it's also very late," Raja replied, with one eye reading the green numbers on her digital clock-radio.

"I know, sweetheart, this is Julian."

"I knew that or I wouldn't have answered," she informed him, with both eyes closed. "You okay?"

Julian wanted to lie but saw no benefit in it. Actually it would have been counterproductive to try and minimize his emptiness. "No, not really," he said eventually. "I just needed," he started, then turned and headed back in the other direction. "You're right, it's late. I shouldn't have overstepped my boundaries. Why don't I call you back tomorrow?"

"No, that won't do now that I'm up. Why don't you tell Mama what's on your mind and give me a shot at fixing it?" Raja had propped up both of her goose-down pillows to support her head while she mapped out a guarantee to get Julian in her bed again and deeper under her spell. She was delighted that her charm had summoned him back so soon. "I wouldn't sleep at all knowing that you're lying awake with something so taxing that it won't let you rest. Tell you what. If you'd like, I'd love to see you as soon as you can get here," Raja offered, wearing an impish grin.

"Do you really mean that or are you just being kind to a complicated black man with a lot on his mind?"

"Is there another kind of black man, Julian, baby?" Raja sighed. "Don't make me beg to see you," she threw in to sweeten the pot and hasten his decision. Although she hadn't been the begging kind, Raja knew how to convey that it felt good being needed, if Julian was the one in need.

"I'm on my way," Julian confirmed swiftly, before ending the call. Raja grinned again, knowing that she was on her way to hooking Julian like the big fish that he was. She'd decided that the sky was the limit before it was all said and done. It wasn't an unreasonable assumption to think she would get anything she wanted from him, once he'd grown accustomed to sampling her bait. What she hadn't accounted for, when devising her devious diagram, was another woman dangling her bait in Julian's face at the same time.

During the ride to Raja's upscale apartment, Julian was plagued by Kelly's torn expression as she had bolted from his home. Her twisted lips and disgusted leer left an indelible impression on his heart. He couldn't help thinking how she'd taken the news about his daughter and the subsequent meeting with Victoria much harder than she should have. Kelly was a good friend but she was only his friend, he reasoned. Her over-the-top demands and outlandish accusations about Victoria were out of line and unsubstantiated, and neither did they warrant such a backlash of emotion. He rang Raja's bell while trying to chase away the look on Kelly's face in parting as well as the memory of her going about protecting him from his past and the ruthless manner she utilized to do it.

Raja met him at the door wearing nothing beneath a short, black, silk chemise that barely covered her best assets. She inched on her toes in order to throw her arms abound his neck. "It'll be all right, baby," she cooed, after pulling him inside. "I'll make it all right." Raja undressed Julian on the way to her bedroom. By the time they made it upstairs, Julian was naked and carrying Raja in his strong capable arms. Julian kissed her passionately, tasting her firm breasts with his moist tongue. Raja was lost in the heat of the moment. Julian was simply lost and questioning everything in his life, but it seemed that he was willing to search every inch of her body for answers.

He kept up his sensual strip search for hours until the weight of satisfying Raja's desires toppled him. Julian fell asleep just after the sixth time Raja exploded in unbridled ecstasy. The last thing he remembered was her screaming his name as if she were paid to do it.

Raja was honest in her cries of joy, but she was looking for compensation of another kind altogether. She had her heart set on taking home the grand prize, Julian's undying love and a rock the size of a small state. By morning she'd be wondering if either was within her grasp.

When the sun began to peek over the New York skyline, Julian awoke with a strange set of eyes locked on his. He recognized Raja immediately, but the glare she pierced him with was sharp enough to cut diamonds. He was in a difficult situation already. After he'd fallen asleep with Raja lying across his chest, Kelly's face tormented him throughout the rest of the night. If there was a poster boy for dazed and confused, Julian fit the bill precisely. "What, was I snoring?" he asked finally. "Sorry if I did, just tired."

"Tired, huh? Mind telling me what's got you so *tired*?" Raja didn't buy that explanation for a minute. He had called to say how much he needed her before he'd put in the kind of work to get him so tired. "Something's on you pretty bad and I'd like to help if you'll let me." Raja was fishing again, this time for something to gain more leverage with, something hiding beneath the surface, something to help build her future.

Julian sat up in bed, rubbed his eyes, then looked into Raja's a second time. Now they were gentle and inviting. She'd transformed, taking the steps to ease his woes so that she could learn all about them while doing it. Julian contemplated sharing all that had transpired between Kelly and Victoria but thought better of it. There was already one person close to him who seemed to have turned on him. He didn't need two of them.

"Nothing to speak of, really," he grumbled. "Just work stuff; it'll pass. I wish I could say the same for my headache. I'm getting too old to drink during the week and expect to be productive afterward. I could blame it on a lack of sleep, I guess." He glanced at Raja to see if she caught his inside joke, but she wasn't smiling anymore. Instead, she was looking him over, reading him as best she could before asking a very important question that begged to be answered.

"Speaking of that, Julian, I was wondering if you usually call Kelly's name in your sleep?"

"What?" Julian was too surprised to say anything else.

"Kelly, you called out her name several times after we made love. Now, is there something I should know, a reason we weren't alone in bed last night?"

"No, no. It was nothing like that," he assured her. "It was an unresolved issued we argued about. End of story."

"Obviously not, because I'm taking offense to my man pleading with another woman while in my bed, whether he's conscious or otherwise." Now it was Raja's turn to note Julian's reaction to stamping a *taken* tag on him.

"Well, believe me, if I said her name while I slept, it was a nightmare and nothing more." He leaned over to kiss her, then again and again. Before Raja knew what happened, she had her legs opened for another private invitation.

Thirty minutes later, Julian was putting on his clothes as Raja watched him from her bed with a single top sheet wrapped around her toga-style. "I really like the way you do that, you know."

"What's that?"

"The way you put on your clothes, even the wrinkled ones. It's as if each piece is important to you. That's the part I like."

Julian smiled *thank you* to her reflection in the dresser mirror. "I gotta go. Uh, don't get up. I'll call you later."

"Who said I was getting up?" she smarted back playfully. "I'm just shifting my weight so I can slide back under the covers. The way I feel, you've done enough getting up and staying up for the both of us."

Feeling guilty about the date he'd set to stop in and see Victoria at the hotel, Julian stood there choreographing his entire morning, which including getting home to shower and shave, then double-timing it to the office, before showing up at the Embassy Suites at two o'clock. After letting himself out, Julian trudged down to his car with the night's events behind him. It was kind of funny when the thought of taking out his frustrations on Raja's body passed through his mind, but the joke was on him because he didn't come out on the other end of that lengthy body-slapping escapade feeling any better than before he had rung her doorbell. Too bad no one was laughing, especially not Raja, who was perched in her bedroom window. Her contemptible leer had made a smashing return to the scene of a crime, the lie Julian told and thought he'd gotten away with.

Raja made a few on-the-fly recalculations as he drove away.

"A nightmare . . . hmph," she huffed. "You ain't seen a nightmare until I've served up one made to order."

Fifteen

Although Julian hadn't been in the office but a few hours, he made a mad dash down to the parking garage to keep his scheduled meeting with Victoria. He couldn't think of anything but her, well, what she used to mean to him, and the child they created together. As he zipped down the freeway toward the hotel, his palms sweated. What if Victoria had taken it upon herself to stage an introduction with Brittany? he feared. What would he say to her? How could he in good conscience explain not having been a part of her life in all those years past? It stood to reason that Julian had a lot to sweat about.

As he climbed out of his expensive luxury car in front of the Embassy Suites, the valet attendant dashed over to retrieve the keys. Julian nodded his thanks, glanced up at the massive hotel, and then exhaled a deep sigh of apprehension. "Don't put it away. I won't be long," he said to the attendant in passing.

Walking through the revolving door, he reached inside his suit coat for a handkerchief. After wiping perspiration from his hands and forehead, he returned it to his breast pocket and surveyed the vast lobby for any signs of Victoria. Suddenly, his cell phone buzzed. "This is Julian," he said, still peering over the first level of the hotel.

"I see you've made it safely," a woman's voice replied. "And, might I add, you're on time? But then you always were a stickler for punctuality."

"Victoria," he said, in a perplexed tone. "Where are you?"

"I'm in the lobby bar, near the gift shop." When she saw him looking in her direction, Victoria chuckled. "Yes, the one in the very back."

Julian was relieved, all but certain that she wouldn't have brought their teenaged child to some hotel lobby bar. Without offering so much as a closing salutation, he ended the call by shutting off the phone. He felt like a man walking the Green Mile, the death row march to uncertainty.

If Victoria didn't ask him there to facilitate a long-overdue family reunion, perhaps she went there to apprise him of her plans to do just that at a later date. What she actually had in mind was far from anything he had imagined when he agreed to the time and place.

As soon as he entered the quiet sitting area, he studied a small group of white businessmen ogling an attractive woman sitting all by her lonesome at the bar. He knew then that their casual business meeting had been derailed by Victoria's classic appearance. She eased off the chair as Julian approached her with a somber expression, no apparent pleasantries forthcoming.

"Victoria," he greeted cordially, noting that her short silk skirt and blouse appeared to be better suited for a woman ten years younger than her, but he didn't have time for lessons in appropriate attire for mothers with coming-of-age daughters. "Are you sure that *this* is a good idea?" Julian asked cautiously. He paused to steal a glance at the businessmen to see if their eyes were trained on him, now that he was in the company of the woman they were prepared to draw straws over with hopes of getting the first crack at her. Julian wasn't at all surprised when they sneered at him, considering how the strange black man caused Victoria's face to light up like a Christmas tree. "We seem to have an audience," he added curtly. "If we're going to talk, it needs to be more discreet. There's a park not far from here, we could—"

"I don't do parks," she corrected abruptly, "not any more than this," she added as an afterthought. Victoria handed the bartender more than enough money for the white wine spritzer she'd sipped from only once while waiting. "I agree, that's why I've taken the necessary precautions and arranged a place where we can converse, uninterrupted. I have a suite upstairs. There's enough room to relax and discuss matters comfortably without having to look over our shoulders the entire time." Before Julian had time to think over the possible repercussions of joining a white woman, an opposing candidate's wife, in her boudoir for a late afternoon *conversation*, Victoria picked up her small handbag from the bar top and headed in the other direction. "Seven-oh-six," she added, just above a whisper.

He had tried to turn his eyes away but couldn't. Victoria had accrued several years of practical experience manipulating men into compromising positions before they knew what hit them. Instead of spending the past five minutes nursing a gin and tonic, Julian should have better utilized it by racing through the lobby at top speed to wrestle the valet attendant for his car keys, but he didn't. He didn't fly through the lobby, he didn't leave, he didn't think. His better judgment failed him. Curiosity had him knocking softly on the door outside room 706. "Come in. It's open," he heard her call out from the inside. Julian was not in his right mind when he entered Victoria's den of deception. He was also a damned fool. Unfortunately, men have been swayed by the charms of beautiful women throughout the ages. On that very afternoon, Julian was counted among them.

Julian stood against the door, again expecting to see Brittany patiently waiting there to meet her father. However, he was proven wrong yet again. As the door opened wider, he strolled through it and stopped just on the other side. "Alex?" he asked, knowing that she'd understand his single-word query.

"Please, Julian. Come in and close the door," she asked politely. "Alex will be out of town for days. He has to close some real estate deal, out of state." Oddly enough, that was sufficient for Julian, so he did as she suggested. Up till then, he had done everything she had suggested, but he didn't look at it that way. Victoria had improved on her skills of persuasion since her undergraduate days. She was much, much craftier now.

"Wow, you haven't aged a day," she complimented him innocently. Victoria made a sweeping hand gesture, offering Julian to sit opposite the rectangular coffee table in the spacious common area of the suite. He obliged her and took a seat facing the door, not wanting to get caught with his guard down in the event someone came through it unexpectedly. Victoria grinned, knowing full well what he was concerned about. "No one knows I'm here. Relax. Can I get you another gin and tonic?" She motioned toward the stocked in-room wet bar. "I assume you had to order something while you were downstairs trying to look as if you weren't counting the seconds before following the pretty white lady up to her room."

"Some things never change," Julian said eventually. "Human nature, I mean."

"I'm afraid you'll have to explain, seeing as how I'm lost in your rhetoric." Victoria finally sat down across the table from him and crossed one leg over the other in a demure nonthreatening fashion, then carefully placed a glass of ice water near the edge.

"That's it in a nutshell. Take you for instance. I'm sure that you've never, for a moment in your life, been lost in someone's rhetoric or anywhere else. You're too smart, always have been from what I remember. Your whole day, planned out down to the nth detail by the time the sun comes up. Isn't that the way it was, is?" He had no idea how well she'd led him around by the nose from the very beginning, no idea.

Not at all bothered by Julian's frank opinion of her, Victoria defended herself without getting her feathers ruffled. "Should I apologize for acquiring sharper survival instincts than most?" Her eyes drifted up to rest on his.

"For starters, you can tell me why you've asked me here today."

Sighing deeply, Victoria clasped her hands, then placed them beneath her pointed chin as if she was searching her mind for the appropriate words, those which had been bottled up for far too long. When it appeared to Julian as if she was preparing to share them, Victoria made another broad gesture with her hands like before.

Just as she had designed it beforehand, the glass of ice water tumbled onto the floor. She knew that it wasn't in Julian to pass up assisting a woman in distress. As planned, he left his chair to collect all the ice cubes from the carpet, near Victoria's toned bare legs. She had premeditated every one of his moves and now was her chance to corner the king.

Victoria pretended to lend a helping hand. She slid forward in the chair, toward Julian. Her short silk skirt rode up her thighs just enough to expose what she wanted Julian to see. On cue his gaze landed between her legs, on her bare, freshly shaved pubis, where he had played in the dark too many times to forget.

"Ah yes," Victoria cooed seductively, her long legs still spread apart, just so. "Remember how you'd drive *her* crazy while I watched? She does. I often dream of those days, you doing those wicked things to me, as I watched." Her breathing became noticeably heavier, voice lowering an octave. "Those wicked things, Julian, do you . . . remember . . . how?"

Of course, he remembered. Staring at her naked crotch had his memory doing back-flips. Flashes of Victoria's insatiable sexual appetite had him shaken and stirred, both equally so. Suddenly, Julian pounced up from his kneeling position on the floor. He swallowed hard when he felt the noose tightening around his neck. "Shit!" he barked. "How could I have been so damned gullible?" Weak-kneed as the tension mounted, Julian felt his head spinning. "What, Victoria, you called me here for a quick push and pull while Alex is out of town?"

Displaying no shame in her game, Victoria began rubbing her legs, one against the other, in a slow sensual manner. "As I recall, there was hardly anything quick about the way you *pushed and pulled*. Did I say that right?" She flashed a devilish grin when she discovered an unmistakable bulge in his slacks. If she played her cards right, Victoria reasoned, she might get a chance to ride that monstrous bulge in his pants. "Julian, calm down," she pleaded tenderly, standing to inch nearer to his rock-hard penis. "I didn't plan on any of this happening. All I wanted was to see you and talk without some nosy reporter getting wind of it." She sauntered up to him, dangerously close. She could smell the excitement boiling within him. "But we are here and it's obvious that you want to do more than talk." Victoria reached down toward Julian's erection to massage the tension away, but he stopped her advances with the palm of his hand.

"You must be crazy or think I am," he spat viciously. "Tell you what I want. I want to see my daughter."

"I think that's a great idea as well, but the timing has to be right or all of our lives will be irrevocably damaged." For the first time since Julian had wandered into that hotel room, Victoria appeared genuinely concerned for someone other than herself. She turned her back to Julian. "It's just been so damned difficult living the lie. Our daughter suspects something is different about her, but she hasn't a clue that she's a black girl masquerading as a white one. If it isn't handled correctly, it could ruin her." Victoria's damsel-in-distress routine was still in full effect and working overtime.

Taken in once again, Julian nibbled at the bait until he bit down on the hook. "Victoria, listen. I wouldn't intentionally hurt her, you know that. I'm just tired of getting caught in the middle of a wedge I don't fully understand."

Sensing that he was close enough to touch, Victoria leaned her back against his chest. Reluctantly, Julian held her with his strong arms wrapped around her shoulders.

"See how nice that feels?" she moaned. "Oh, how I've missed you." Victoria spun on her heels to kiss him.

Julian stared into her eyes the way he had allowed himself to gawk between her legs just moments ago. Only now, he recognized undeniable glints of deceit.

"I see. I thought that today was supposed to be about Brittany, not us?" he asked, pushing her away. As he made a path toward the door, Victoria dashed in front of him.

"Today is about all of us, Julian. I can't help it that I'm still drawn to you."

"You're pitiful, using your own child to lure a man into bed with you. Why am I surprised? Your daddy taught you well."

As he opened the door to leave, Victoria screamed after him, "What about Brittany!"

"Don't fool yourself, this was never about Brittany, but from now on I'll make damn well sure that it will be." Julian was fuming. He stomped out of the hotel lobby, snatched his car keys, and darted out of the parking lot. He hated admitting to himself that Kelly was right about Victoria being up to no good. Since she was right about that, what else could Kelly have assessed correctly about her?

That thought stayed with Julian for the remainder of the day. He couldn't shake the desire to push the envelope even though it could have meant the end of his political career. Rest was what he needed, rest and discernment. Neither would come by morning.

After falling asleep, utterly exhausted, Julian awoke with tired eyes and a throbbing head. He popped four aspirins in his mouth and chased them with apple juice. While waiting on the medicine to relieve his pain, he retrieved the newspaper from the front porch. The article Julian read as his car warmed outside his brownstone caused his head to hurt all over again, but much worse than before.

SPOTLIGHT
By Natalie Huffman

The old town was hot last night as our man of the hour and candidate for mayor of New York City, Mr. Julian Blake, was seen easing out of the Embassy Suites Hotel early yesterday evening. Blake, known for his style as much as his passion for politics, was quick to dash into his trademark BMW and speed away before we had the chance to ask what everyone wants to know: What were you doing at the hotel, Mr. Blake, better yet, with whom?

I did get a chance to have a one-on-one with the dashing councilman earlier this week, and I must admit even I was impressed with his zeal. (See the full interview in a special edition next week.) He has a clear vision and a solid platform for reforming and redefining this city. There is something about Julian Blake that makes you want to believe whatever he tells you. Is it real or is he simply a masterful politician? I say a combination of both, and whoever the lucky individual was who shared several hours of his time at the Embassy last evening . . . well, let's just stop right there . . .

Julian was so pissed that his jaw locked after he painstakingly read every word, twice. Fear caused another reaction. His chest constricted and his breathing became labored. "I can't let them kill me," he grunted, yanking angrily to loosen his necktie. He powered up his cell phone, then hit Voice-Activate. "Kelly," he requested. "Kelly Taylor." The phone rang until her voice message clicked on. "Kelly, this is me, pick up. Okay, call me when you get to the phone." He continued calling her one time after the next throughout his ride in to the office, but she wouldn't respond to a single plea for her attention.

"Damn it, Kelly, where are you?"

Sixteen

Kelly read Natalie's column and knew if the woman were in her face right now, she'd grip Natalie's neck in her hands and not stop twisting until she'd wrung the last breath from her body.

Natalie was an overweight, mean-spirited, busybody who couldn't pass muster as a novelist, so she took her frustration out on people in her newspaper column.

The pictures of Julian leaving the hotel yesterday and the article ate at Kelly until she wanted to scream. So Victoria had gotten what she wanted. Kelly didn't want to consider what might have happened between the couple. The possibilities were infinite and too painful to accept.

Kelly tried to shake it off knowing she wouldn't have to face them anymore. By ending her professional relationship with Julian, she was ending their personal relationship as well. She couldn't deal with him if he believed she'd make up lies just to get her way. And if he wasn't going to be honest.

Aren't you the pot calling the kettle black? Were you honest?

The reflective question posed by her conscience thrust her into the here and now. The elevator doors whooshed open. Office doors clicked closed, voices ebbed and flowed, and the phones bleated muted sounds.

No, she thought. If she had only to speak the truth to herself, she'd admit that she was in love with Julian and had been from somewhere between the first and second hour when she had met him fifteen years ago.

But the rape had changed everything for her.

Kelly didn't realize she'd gotten up, until she focused in on the traffic below her Sixth Avenue office.

A light rain fell on the city, slowing the thready traffic into a sluggish crawl. Colored umbrellas bobbed up and down and men dashed across the street with newspapers covering their heads.

The rain had taken the city by surprise, but the mist that coated her office window mirrored the cloak that had settled on Kelly's shoulders.

A picture of the singer Usher unfolded on the big screen a block away with the title of his multiplatinum recording, *Confessions*, emblazoned across his knees.

The first few words of the hit song ran through her mind, and Kelly folded her arms across her stomach. "I'm Kelly Taylor," she whispered, "and I've loved Julian Blake my entire adult life—until he called me a liar."

If the words had been raindrops, they'd have streaked the window and crashed to the sidewalk below in huge splats. Kelly had never uttered her true feelings aloud before, and she was grateful for the sanctity of her office. Here, no one would dare barge in on her.

She had appointments in an hour, but she took an extra few minutes to reflect on the change in direction her life was taking. She'd expected to be working on the campaign for the next eight weeks, but that had changed. She'd have to explain that revenue loss to her boss, as well as how she was going to make it up.

But George Grant trusted her. She wasn't worried about him.

She was, however, worried about Julian.

She wrestled with the notion that she still wanted to call him. A fifteen-year habit was going to take perseverance to break. She'd have to regroup and figure out how to restructure her time. So much had been dedicated to making sure Julian succeeded.

Before last night she would have imagined them spending late nights doing talk radio shows, their days filled with meetings, inter-views, and making appearances around the city of New York.

She'd imagined fights with other politicians and even with un-happy constituents, but so far those issues were minor compared to having to combat the gossip columnist Natalie Huffman. The woman had the most powerful avenue of access to the public. Ink. And the way she was using it, she was definitely mightier than the sword.

At her desk, Kelly turned on her desktop and buzzed her assis-tant. "Bree, has my briefcase arrived yet?"

"No, but Mr. Blake said he'd deliver it himself."

Kelly's heart flipped and raced and she headed right, then left. She wasn't ready to face Julian. She'd quit and that was that. He'd obviously gotten her e-mailed resignation, and he was probably coming over to have it out with her.

But why?

She grabbed her purse and walked out of her office to her assis-tant's desk. "I'm running to my meeting with New York University. Call my cell when my bag arrives."

"Okay, but Mr. Blake said he needed to talk to you about some unfinished business."

"When did he say that?"

"When I called him five minutes ago to find out where he was."

Kelly examined her watch. It'd take him five minutes to get into the building and up the elevator to her office. Last night was the first time she'd ever walked out on Julian. Today would be the sec-ond, and hopefully the last.

"Just call me when you have my computer in your hands. I'll deal with Julian later."

"What happened?" Bree blurted. "I mean, why are you two angry with each other? You're usually thicker than thieves and now—"

Kelly stared down Bree, whose eyes were wide with concern. She eased back on the remark she'd been about to make about Bree get-ting back to work. "Stop looking like the world is coming to an end," Kelly said calmly. "I don't have time for the campaign anymore. Just call me when the computer gets here and I'll zip by and pick it up. Better yet, you can bring it to me and take a half day off."

"I'm holding you to that no matter what happens next."

"What?" Kelly asked.

"You couldn't wait five minutes to see me? Is that the way it is between us?"

The voice from behind her was one she'd have known anywhere. Kelly closed her eyes and when she opened them, Bree was closing herself in Kelly's office.

She schooled her expression before making eye contact with Julian. "I quit. Thanks for bringing my bag. I've got to run."

Kelly tried to take the case from him, but Julian wouldn't let go, so she did.

"What the hell is going on? You've been the one steady person in my life," Julian said, his dark eyes stormy, his jaw set. "We've never tripped before on each other—"

"I've never been a meddling liar before."

"I was angry. It's not like you've never been angry with me. You've called me a shit head, an idiot, and other things that I didn't take seriously."

"I'm not you, Julian."

"Don't turn into a girl on me, Kelly. You did something that pissed me off, and I let you know about it. How did we end up here, with you quitting, and by e-mail no less?"

How could he have erased everything that had been said? He'd accused her of loving him, as if the possibility was so out of his realm of reasoning, he'd never even considered that she might have those types of feelings for him—or worse, him for her.

But the *coup de grace* was Julian telling her she had no right to be in his personal life.

Kelly gazed at the man she'd never thought she could live a day without. "It never occurred to you that what was said might have broken us irreparably?"

"It can't, Kelly. We're stronger than this."

"Not me. I wasn't aware there was a line in the sand, Julian. I didn't realize there were parts of our lives that were off-limits. I wasn't operating under the same rules, because I wasn't aware there were any. Now that I know, I know I can't play the same game."

"Kelly." His eyes clouded with dark confusion. "Why are you doing this? I never imagined going all the way to the top without you."

"You'll be fine." She eased her bag from his hand and slid it into her office, then closed the door before facing him again. "I'll see you."

Kelly walked past Julian, feeling heavy and hot. She reached the glass doors to the suite and stopped when she finally processed what he'd just whispered. "What did you say?"

"I need you. Don't walk out on me."

The plainly stated words clogged her throat, her resolve suffering a major blow.

"Why shouldn't I?"

"I didn't tell you about Victoria because I was ashamed. All those things you said yesterday about black women fighting for us and loving us despite everything was true for me too. Being with Victoria created a fantasy world where color and hate didn't exist. We laughed and loved and it was beautiful. But as soon as I would leave her apartment, I was black again. I realized I couldn't have it both ways. I couldn't live between two worlds."

"Why didn't you choose her?"

"We were a fantasy. Being black and true to myself was reality. I'm always going to be a freedom fighter. I couldn't give up the good fight for all people for one woman. The night we were supposed to make a decision of where we were going to go with our relationship was the same night you were found."

"You chose to be with—"

"You. For all the right reasons, Kelly. We're best friends and I didn't walk out on you. I need you now." He caressed her fingers. "How about we win this mayoral race together?"

Every instinct in her body said leave Julian alone. That more bad would come from the situation than good, but her heart told another story.

Against her better judgment, Kelly squeezed his hand. "Okay. I'm in till the end."

Julian enveloped her in a hug so tight she thought she'd burst from the love that she held inside for him.

But when he pulled away, love didn't glow from his eyes. Forgiveness and gratitude echoed in the depths.

For a second, his brow crinkled as he gazed at her. "You do something different with your eye makeup?"

Kelly blinked rapidly and hurried for the door. "Yeah, I bought some Bobbi Brown. Look, I'm late for a meeting. Meet for lunch at two to strategize?"

"Sounds good."

Julian stayed behind. She didn't want to, but Kelly looked back and her heart skipped a beat. He was still looking, and his expression said he liked what he saw.

Her Blackberry tickled her side and Kelly unhooked it, sliding into a closing elevator. A chill ran up her arms as she read the note.

We need to get some things straight today. Raja.

Seventeen

Earlier that morning, Raja had raged.

Kelly! That low-down, trifling, conniving, scandalous couldn't-get-her-own-man-if-she-tried, backstabbing, cutthroat, project-spawned tramp! *The Embassy Suites?* If Kelly was gonna go slinking around with a man like Julian, the least she should have done was make him spring for the Ritz Carlton!

And Julian! Could he actually have declined to have dinner with Raja just to sneak in a few hours with a disheveled mess like Kelly?

Flinging her copy of the *New York Weekly* to the floor, Raja crossed her arms over her breasts and lay back in the cooling waters of her morning bath. She closed her eyes and deliberately took deep calming breaths as she mentally recited her self-affirming mantra over and over again.

> *No one but God is more glorious than you.*
> *You have the power to do amazing things.*
> *Whatever you pursue with all your might, you conquer.*
> *You are black and beautiful and female, the envy of the world.*

Damn it, Julian!

His name alone was like a bolt of pain stabbing into her heart and his betrayal filled her soul. Their deceit was a crushing pain in her chest, a thick wad of hurt that clogged her throat. A solid weight of angst that lay heavy in her stomach. Despite her ego-boosting affirmations, angry tears slipped from Raja's eyes and dripped from her chin, disappearing into her bathwater.

She lay there shivering in the scented water, the sanctity of her morning ritual desecrated and violated. The memory of the night she'd lain naked with Julian flooded her mind. The tender way he had held her. The adoration in his kisses. The intimacy of their acts. The whispers of love that had fallen from his lips.

That fucking Kelly.

Raja should have known better than to trust a woman like her. Someone who obviously had so little going on in her own life that she had to get her kicks by scooping up the sloppy seconds of her girlfriends. Kelly was a sneaky little skank with envy running through her veins. She had been dying for Raja to meet Julian. She had practically begged her to give her "friend" a date. She'd even agreed to tag along with them at their first dinner and acted as if she was so thrilled they were vibing and clicking.

And then as soon as it looked like happiness was looming on Raja's horizon, that heffah had made her move. She'd set Raja up to fall for Julian, then thrown herself all over him like the cheap little no-class hussy she was. Yeah, Raja thought. She and Julian had both been set up. Kelly had probably been scheming and planning to trick him into her bed the whole time, and for that she deserved a straight-up Raja Special: an East New York ass-kicking that would teach her some things her mama obviously never had.

Raja unplugged the drain and sat there as the water receded around her. If she had been a lesser, weaker woman she could have sat there naked and wet and wallowing in her misery for the entire day. But weak and less than anyone other than God were no longer apt descriptions of her or of her character.

No. Raja was strong and capable. Women like her were few and far between. Valuable commodities whose worth was beyond question. If Julian had willingly spent the night with Kelly in some cheap little room at the Embassy Suites, then there was no way he could be the upstanding, strong black man that he pretended to be.

His tastes and judgment were flawed and he was beyond redemption. Still, it was hard for Raja to believe she'd been so wrong about him. So far off base about his breeding and character, and especially about his feelings for her.

But Kelly, on the other hand . . . well, Raja had no trouble believing she was scandalous. She was like a snake crawling on its belly. Except she was worse because she appeared anything other than serpentine.

The longer Raja sat in the now-empty tub, the madder she became. She couldn't help envisioning Kelly and Julian with their hands all over each other. Their arms and legs entangled. Kelly enticing her boss to sip her nectar with just as much passion as he'd sipped Raja's.

The images were twisted and unbearable and Raja struggled to push them from her mind. No! she chastised herself as she dried off absentmindedly, and for the first time in a long while she forgot to scrutinize herself from head to toe in the mirror. She was too busy conjuring up the curse-out she was planning to lay on Kelly as soon as she could get dressed and make it downtown to her office.

Raja had far too much class and self-respect to allow any man to think he had hurt her so badly, so getting up in Julian's face and demanding answers was out the question. But she had every right to approach her friend Kelly and confront her with what she knew. If Kelly thought Raja was just going to lie down and act dead while she played games with the man Raja was falling in love with, she was dead wrong. In fact, Raja decided as she picked up the phone and called her boss to request permission to take a personal day off, let them see how flirty Kelly would act when Raja confronted her. After lying up with Raja's man in some midgrade hotel, the least Kelly would have to do was deal with Raja face-to-face and get read up and down for being the shiesty little heffah that she was.

"Can you repeat that? I'm not sure I'm hearing you right," Kelly said, looking up at Raja with tired eyes. She'd been chewing the end of her pen when Raja arrived, and the small smile of greeting she'd been about to offer had quickly vanished when she realized why Raja was there.

"You heard me the first time," Raja said through clenched teeth. "Don't play that innocent shit with me!" She put her hands on her hips. "I'm from the hood, sista, and I know a rat when I smell one. Now what the *hell* is going on between you and Julian?"

Raja watched as Kelly took the pen from her mouth and placed it on her desk. Kelly sighed and frowned, and Raja braced herself for her friend's confession.

"I'm sorry you think so little of me, Raja," Kelly said and had the nerve to look disappointed.

"Don't even try that with me," Raja warned. "It's not about what I think of you, Kelly. It's the fool for a friend that you obviously think you have in me."

"I don't think you're a fool, Raja. But you are mistaken about all of this."

"No!" Raja yelled. "You're the one who's mistaken! Light-skinned chicks like you just can't stand it when a black man prefers a dark-brown sista, can you? It pissed you off to see him all over me instead of you! To see him devouring this dark meat and to know that he prefers his meat this way."

Kelly rose from her chair. "Raja, that's nonsense and you know it! The only person hung up on skin tone around here is you! Nobody cares whether you are dark or light. We're both black women, Raja."

"Yeah, I'm a black woman, but I don't know what the hell you are. You have absolutely nothing on me, Kelly. Not looks, not style, not education, and for sure not class or culture. If you wanted to be one of Julian's little booty-call groupies you could have done that a long time ago. The reason you thought I'd be perfect for him is that I am. You said it yourself that I'm the type of woman Julian needs to take his life and his career to the next level. And then you go and pull"—Raja fumbled in her purse and snatched out a page from *The New York Weekly* and flung it down in front of Kelly—"this kind of stunt on me when he and I were just beginning to vibe?" She shook her head and pushed a few wild strands of hair from her eyes. "I just don't get it, Kelly. Unless you're the kind of freak who gets her kicks from sleeping behind your girlfriends. And that's just crazy, if you ask me. Just crazy."

Kelly held the newspaper in her hand as her lower lip trembled. "You read this?"

Raja rolled her eyes. "All of New York and half of New Jersey has read it. You didn't think crawling into a hotel with a high-profile man like Julian would go unnoticed, did you? And the Embassy Suites?" Raja waved her hand. "I'm not knocking your thing if large families with screaming kids get you off, but it's not my idea of a romantic interlude, honey."

"It wasn't m—"

"What?" Raja mocked. "Say it. It wasn't your idea? You trying to tell me you let Julian pick a hotel for the two of you to shack up in and you agreed on the Embassy Suites? Girl, I don't know how we ever got to be friends, because you are far tackier than I thought."

"Cut it out, Raja!" Kelly tossed the paper back to the desk and narrowed her eyes. "You don't know half of what you're talking about, so just cut it out!"

"Who the hell are you to tell me what to do?"

Kelly pressed her fingers to her temples. "I'm not telling you what to do, Raja. But I am telling you that you have this whole thing wrong. I didn't sleep with Julian."

"Damn!" Raja smirked again. "You mean you let him pull a hit-and-run? Oh yeah. He got caught running out of there right before dinnertime, so I guess y'all didn't get to snuggle and snooze. Hell, falling asleep together is not a mandatory indulgence after getting your groove on anyway, baby. Trust me, I should know."

Kelly lowered herself into her chair and shook her head. "I'm sorry, Raja. Sorry you think so little of me. I introduced you and Julian because I thought you'd make a good match, and I still think so. I have never and would never do anything to interfere with your relationship with him or to violate our friendship. I can't say much about Ms. Huffman's article or speak for Julian at all on this matter, but I can assure you that there's absolutely nothing going on between us."

Raja stared at Kelly for long moments. She'd been a fool not to trust her instincts. To ignore her intuition. Ever since the fundraiser something had been gnawing at her insides, and this just proved that Justine had been dead wrong about Kelly's relationship with Julian being one based purely upon business matters.

Raja mused. It wasn't hard to understand what was in it for Kelly. She'd reap the same rewards for being on Julian's arm as Raja would. The difficulty was in seeing what was in it for Julian. Kelly was definitely not the kind of woman he had claimed to want, and if he *had* wanted Kelly, how could his conscience have allowed him to court and seduce and make such passionate love to one of her close friends? Both of them were shady and scandalous!

"Kelly," Raja said softly. She gathered her purse from the chair where she'd slung it and carefully folded the news article and placed it back inside. "Do you remember back in July of last year when I got a summer flu and you came over to bring me soup and make sure I didn't get dehydrated?"

Kelly nodded. "Yes, Raja. I took good care of you too, didn't I? I was your friend then, and I am still your friend now."

Raja nodded, pursing her lips. "Yes, and do you remember me giving you a key to my apartment and even the spare key to my car?"

"Yep." Kelly patted her skirt pocket. "I keep them both right here on my key ring, just in case you ever need me to be there for you again."

"Uh-huh," Raja said absently, then held out her hand. "I want them back."

Kelly's smile disappeared. "What?"

"Give me my keys. I want them back."

Raja waited quietly as Kelly took out her key ring and maneuvered two keys from the bundle.

"This is not necessary, Raja. What if something happens to you and you need somebody? No matter what Natalie Huffman wrote in that article, in your heart you know you can trust me."

Raja laughed. A high-pitched tinkling sound that would have been infectious under other circumstances. "You should have spent more time hanging out on a few front stoops in the projects, honey," she said. "Every sista in East New York knows a saying that you obviously have never heard."

"And what's that?"

"Scratch a liar, and you'll find a thief!"

Eighteen

"Raja, it's time for you to go. I'm not arguing with you."
"You don't have to. Just admit the truth. You're jockin' Julian like he's a damned rapper, but yo ass ain't slick. I know what's going on and I'm just lettin' you know, Raja Jackson ain't gone give up her man without a fight."

Kelly's heart raced. Raja was dressed in designer threads all the way down to her Louis Vuitton shoes, but the look in her eyes was pure unadulterated hate. In her heart she was a street fighter, a ghetto girl from the hood who no longer greased down her "baby hair" but used correct diction in the boardroom to win her battles.

Except today.

Raja had forgotten who and where she was. The furious look on her face said she was ready to settle a score and she didn't give a damn that she was at Kelly's job doing it.

Kelly stood, key ring in hand. "When you come to your senses, we can have a real conversation. Until then, I don't have anything to say to you."

"I want to know why you're fuckin' a man you set me up with. You're tryin' to take what's mine, and I don't appreciate it."

Ignoring the slip into ghetto-speak, Kelly watched the woman she used to consider a friend. "You've got it all wrong, but fine. Think what you want, but you're getting the hell out of here."

"I'm not leaving until I'm satisfied. I got all day."

"Raja, I'm not one of those white chicks at your job, intimidated and scared of your ass. You want a fight, you'll get one, but I won't end up quivering in the corner. It's going to end up win or lose with your ass being locked up."

"That's all you can do is call somebody," Raja quipped, unaffected. "Why don't you be a woman and give me some answers? Why do you want Julian now that you know he's with me?"

"You're still stuck on stupid. Get out."

"Answer me!"

Kelly glared at her, sure she'd lost her mind. "If he was yours, you wouldn't be here hollering at me."

The words had the same effect as a slap in the face. Raja recoiled, then dropped her hand to her hip and raised her chin in the air. "Oh, he's mine all right." Her confidence had returned with a vengeance. "Anything he has with you is just a nasty diversion. Better now than later. Still, I want to take you apart limb by limb."

Kelly resisted popping Raja. She was on a sky-high ego trip, one that could be deflated with a good ass-kicking, but she wasn't about to jeopardize everything she'd ever worked for to fulfill a momentary impulse. She'd grown up in the streets, but the streets had never been in her. She wasn't going to let a thug mentality rule her now.

"You're confused," Kelly told Raja. "You seem to have forgotten that you're on my turf, in my office, acting a fool over a misunderstanding."

"I'm not confused about a damned thing. I know what I've seen with my own two eyes. You've been trying to play me for a fool for too long. Why isn't there a man in Kelly's life? I've often wondered. Is she gay, or is she just a man-hater? Neither, I realized. I recognized the type of woman you are from way back. Had an aunt like you."

"What the hell are you talking about?"

"Your ability to get and hold a man is so weak, you can't be with a brotha unless he belongs to someone else. Then there's no pressure on you to have to try to keep him."

"Raja, you need to step, and you need to do it before one of us regrets what happens next."

Raja sighed dramatically. "My aunt died, bitter, defeated, and alone. I'm sure you recognize the parallels."

From the corner of her desk, Kelly picked up a crystal vase and before she could talk herself out of it, hurled it against the wall. Glass exploded, spraying tiny shards like crystal sparkers. Feet thundered and stopped outside her door. "Ms. Taylor, you all right?"

Security had come. Incidents of craziness happened every day in PR offices across the country when people realized that their one stupid act would affect their livelihood and possibly their freedom.

More feet thundered and her door handle was pushed down. Cecil stepped into the doorway, tall, black, and ferocious-looking. "Ms. Taylor?"

"It's under control. I'll only be a minute more."

Cecil hesitated, never having seen the unflappable Kelly Taylor flustered. He closed the door behind him, making it known he wasn't going to be far away.

Before Kelly's eyes, Raja tucked her feral attitude back into its closet and fastened the door closed behind her smooth Bobbi Brown makeup. She smiled at Kelly, but joy never reached her eyes. Eyes that were now skimming the open file on Kelly's desk.

Kelly cringed at her mistake of leaving the business of two New York star athletes open for prying eyes, but hoped Raja didn't see too much.

Tucking her finger beneath the folder, she flipped the top down and positioned Raja's house and car keys directly in front of her. Raja lifted the keys, the significance sinking into Kelly now that the cool metal was nestled in Raja's palm.

Their ties were breaking, the years of friendship being unwound in a matter of moments. Every relationship, no matter the person, ended this way with Kelly and she was emotionally exhausted. She wanted Raja gone. If they were going to be enemies, she'd rather know now.

She opened the door to her office and waited. Raja strolled around the desk, ignoring her. "Kelly, I don't live in the land of regret. That's how I got where I am today. But you . . . you can't let the past go. That's why you're chasing a man who could never want you. I'm giving Julian everything he needs and wants. It's my bed he warms, so have your little fantasy. I've had the real deal time and time and time again." Raja sighed aloud, smiling big.

Her words disturbed Kelly, but she wouldn't dignify Raja's comments with a response.

Raja strolled out. Kelly let the door slam behind her. "What a fucking day. First Julian and now his girl."

Kelly's assistant stuck her head inside the room. "Is it safe or should I go to an early break that will last an hour?"

"Call maintenance first, please, and then come on in."

"You got it, boss."

Kelly walked to the window and looked out. The traffic on the street below flowed with a jerking rhythm that was controlled by four streetlights and two cops. Overhead a plane screamed past, and Kelly grew jealous. She had no idea where the passengers would end up, but it had to be a helluva lot better than being here.

Suddenly, she hungered to be away from New York and Julian, Raja, Victoria, Natalie—all of them—leaving the overpowering drain of their bullshit behind. Her eyes watered and she massaged her temple with her fingers. How had her life spun so quickly out of control?

Her office door opened and closed. "Kelly, you have a meeting in an hour with Mr. Rasheed and Mr. Silverstone."

"Who?" Kelly asked absently.

"John Rasheed, second-round draft pick for the Jets, who can't seem to decide if he's in the pimp business or football. Mr. Silverstone is the attorney that represents Tommy Whiteis, the Anglo player for the Mets. He can't seem to keep his mouth shut while he's flapping his Confederate flag and pickup around Manhattan."

Kelly cringed, remembering. She'd take a case of a married gay governor any day to avoid having to deal with stupid white-boy racist shit. "Pass that off to Paul."

"He gave it to you. The client requested you personally. Remember?" Bree coaxed. "Silverstone wants New York to know that despite his client's actions, he isn't a racist, so he hired a black PR firm. Good strategy," she commented into the growing silence.

"I want you to get rid of them. Triple my rates."

"Already done."

Kelly rolled her eyes. "Triple them again and if they still won't go away, push the meeting back until ten—"

"Thirty," Bree said softly. "Already done. You're now going to be making twelve hundred fifty dollars an hour."

Kelly tuned out the traffic, airplanes and the noise of controversy in her head. "I suppose you gave yourself a nice raise too," she said, eyeing her savvy assistant.

"I'm thinking of moving off the third floor in my brownstone to the vacant unit on the second floor."

For the first time that day, Kelly cracked a smile. "I guess if you gone tip, tip your damned self well."

"Amen to that." Bree didn't crack a smile as the level of understanding passed between them.

Distantly Kelly wondered how long it'd be before Bree would leave, taking all that she learned from Kelly with her.

She decided not to reflect on the future. She needed to get through this election with Julian and then she'd sit down and seriously look at the course of her own life. Preferably while sipping something delicious in Costa Rica.

"Would you like to sit in on the meeting with Mr. Rasheed?" Kelly offered.

Bree practically salivated. "I think I'm going to faint."

Kelly grabbed her briefcase. "Remember, he's a wannabe pimp, and the other one thinks a good time is getting a cap busted in his ass for waving the wrong flag."

"But you're going to make a killing today."

"Ain't America great?"

Kelly left the second meeting with Silverstone and his idiot client Tommy Whiteis having made nearly five thousand dollars. Not only had she inflated her fees, she'd managed to give them both a piece of her mind for trying to use her. Her stomach did a slow push and roll at having to work with the racist pig, but as Bree put it, money was green and it spent the same.

Kelly eyed her watch. Lunch had come and gone and so had her meeting with Julian. She flipped open her phone and dialed as she slid her car into the parking garage and drove on automatic pilot to her assigned space.

"You don't mind standing me up, do you?" Julian answered the phone with a cool air of nonchalance.

Kelly sighed into the mouthpiece. "I've been arguing with people all day. My feet hurt, my head aches, and my back feels like—" Kelly stopped herself and took a deep breath, then started coughing.

"Feel better now that you've inhaled a double lungful of Manhattan exhaust?" Julian said softly, chuckling.

"No," Kelly said, whining to the only man who had ever seen her vulnerable. "Where are you?"

"Where you think?"

"Hopefully somewhere buying some food."

"I bought lunch."

"You ate without me?" She pulled into her space and parked the car, grabbing her bags and purse in one hand, the door handle with the other.

Instinct made her look over her shoulder as she exited the car, her keys between her fingers. Kelly scanned the parking lot as she walked quickly to the elevator. "I can't believe you didn't bring me anything. I can't believe you ate without me."

"Kell's Bells, it's six o'clock. Hell yeah, I ate without you. What happened today?"

Frustration made her words tumble out. "Arguing, all daggone day long. Raja, then the pimp, then the racist. Sometimes money isn't everything."

"Tell me about the pimp, that sounds the funniest."

"J, when the cops busted him, he had on a five-finger diamond ring that said *imapimp* and his pro jersey." They laughed at his stupidity. "It's almost too bad he can play ball. The talent will be wasted when he's doing five years in the state."

"What about the racist?"

Kelly pushed the button for her floor and waited for the door to close. She didn't relax until she was safely sealed in the elevator. "He's a farm boy who thinks he can espouse his opinion by driving his F-150 up here with the Confederate flag waving. Then he's mad when his car is vandalized and fans boo him. He and his lawyer are ridiculous. But the craziest part of the day was Raja."

"I thought you were kidding about having an argument with her. What happened, or should I ask?"

Kelly got off at her floor and a thrill danced up her stomach to her chest. Julian was standing outside her door.

He waved the bag of Italian food, then took her keys and opened the door to her apartment, letting them in.

Kelly slid off her shoes and into her heeled slippers, leaving everything but the food on the foyer table. She followed Julian into the kitchen.

"Raja thought she'd better come to my office and let me know you're off-limits. I've obviously overstepped my boundaries by staying your friend while you're fucking her."

"Hey," he said, taking umbrage with her terminology.

"In any case, she decided she wanted to fight me and let me know how she felt."

"You're lying," Julian uttered in disbelief. "You mean argue."

"No," Kelly said assuredly. "I mean 'put your fists up and I'm kicking your ass' fighting."

He laughed but his eyes were serious. "Tell me you're exaggerating."

Kelly removed the plates from his hand and set them on the table. She moved around him to get the serving silverware. Julian tugged on her suit jacket until it was draped carelessly over the kitchen chair. Kelly knew he was reading her with his eyes so she stopped moving.

"You're not lying," he finally breathed in disbelief.

Kelly pulled her blouse from the no-waistband skirt. "I don't lie to you. She wanted to fight me. Things got a little out of hand."

He glanced over every inch of skin available to see. "She didn't hit you?"

Kelly snickered and served the food. "Let's not trip. I got upset and threw the flower vase against the wall."

Julian wiped his mouth. "Who the hell does she think she is? She doesn't own me." He stalked over to his suit jacket, pulling out his cell phone. "I'm setting her straight right now."

Kelly licked Alfredo sauce from her thumb before reaching over and putting her hand over the numbers. "Quit trippin'. She left after that. It's over."

"No, it's not. Raja doesn't own a damned thing over here. And she was in your office, too?" His faced twisted in disgust. "I work with your firm. I'll bet security showed up—" When Kelly didn't answer, he threw up his hands. "I'm not having somebody that's associated with me going off on you at your job. That's bull—"

"Mr. Mayor-to-be, stop cursing and sit down. You don't need to call her. Come on and eat. I fixed your plate."

"She embarrassed you in front of your coworkers. And she embarrassed me. She owes you an apology."

Julian paced the floor while Kelly sat down and waited. She dug in Julian's plate for a seasoned piece of sausage and he took the fork and ate the meat.

"Eat, then we'll talk about how to deal with Raja," Kelly said, no longer the angry one. She was starving, while Julian picked at his food. He kept looking at her, concern mirrored in his eyes.

When they were finished, the table cleaned, the containers stored in the refrigerator, she poured two glasses of red wine and sat down in the living room. "What are you going to say to Raja in my defense, Julian?"

"I'll tell her the truth. We're not messing around."

"I think it's better to let her believe we've got something going on."

"Come again?" Julian sat down beside Kelly, his head down, looking at her sideways.

"Raja," Kelly said, imitating Julian's voice, "I'm not sleeping with Kelly, but my ex–white lover happens to be my baby's mama, the child I've never seen. Oh, and by the way, her husband is my opponent, Alex Nixon."

He leaned his head back against the couch, silence enveloping them. "I can't have her thinking that you're deceiving her. You two are friends."

"Leave it alone, Julian. It's for the best."

"Best?" He wiped his face, picking up the remote to her entertainment system and working the buttons until John Legend poured into the room. "What's best? I don't know anymore," he said around the soulful music.

Kelly watched Julian wax poetic, hating to admit that she loved being a witness to his slide back to his roots. He stood there, wine in hand, and in one swoop pulled Kelly to her feet.

"Hey," she protested, as he rocked his hips to the music, draining his glass. "I don't feel like dancing."

"Come on and shake your ass, girl. This is good stuff."

Kelly laughed as he imitated his father, a man she'd met a handful of times, who always seemed to have a song on his lips, a suave dip to his step.

Mr. Blake had been *fine* in his heyday, and as Kelly watched Julian Blake Jr. she saw where he got his good looks. Julian's eyes were closed, his arms raised, his body swaying.

At this moment he was free from burdens, demands, and deception. Julian was what he'd always claimed to be. Just one man. Here he was safe.

He reached for her and Kelly went into his arms, dipping and turning as they fell into an easy rhythm.

"We're supposed to be strategizing for the debate," she reminded him as he sang in a surprisingly smooth tenor.

"Shh," he said, "I'm trying to concentrate. This brotha can sing."

"I hope he lives in New York, because he may be your only vote if we don't get some work done."

"All work, Kell's Bells. Come on, girl. Let's just chill a minute."

"Ten minutes is all you're getting," Kelly said, dancing around the coffee table to the center of the floor. Julian joined her.

They danced together and apart. Laughing and talking, they took a ride down memory lane, remembering the dance moves, the people, the times, and the house parties that their friend Disco used to give. Off beat and on, they bumped, slid, and rocked through time until the CD changed to the crooner Kem.

Kem was the moment of reckoning. Too romantic, too personal. They stopped moving as if in silent agreement that they had to remember who they were and what they'd been discussing a mere hour ago.

The spell was broken and reality settled on their relaxed faces. Kelly worked the remote until the music faded.

Julian clapped his hands and stuck out his chest, smiling. He looked like a college boy again. "Damn, Kelly, I wish you'd quit playing around and let me get some work done."

She went to the kitchen, smiling at him over her shoulder. "I'm getting some food. I've worked up an appetite again. You want some?"

He patted his stomach. "I did work up an appetite." Julian pulled three-by-five cards from his briefcase before coming into the kitchen.

"Those your interview questions?" she asked him, heating up their leftovers.

"Yeah. Look," he said, plate in hand, fork in the other. "I'm going to have a conversation with Raja and let her know what she did wasn't cool."

"And I think you should leave well enough alone until the right time—after the election."

"I know I have a lot more to deal with than just Raja, but I don't appreciate her showing out on your job. She's got to understand that we work together and we're friends. We go way back and nothing and nobody is going to change that."

Kelly's chest constricted as she stirred pasta onto her fork. "She isn't trying to hear that, I promise you. You need to save the me-and-Kelly-are-just-friends speech for a time far from now. Preferably never."

"Then what would you suggest I do?"

"Make sure your answers to the debate questions are tight. There are ten opponents. You have to sound better than all of them. You have to be ready for whatever is thrown your way. Personal drama can't have any part of this election or you'll lose.

Let's start with the first question. You've never held more than a council seat in government. What makes you qualified to negotiate contract disputes between laborers and management?"

Julian started talking about his history, his successes, and what he'd learned along the way. He sounded confident and self-assured, but never arrogant.

They worked through each one, Kelly reminding him of details to mention and hot buttons to stay away from.

Eventually they migrated back to the living room where she opened the drapes to her picture window of the distant Manhattan skyline.

Time had flown by, but neither was tired.

"Your schedule is hectic this week. I've confirmed everything with all of your assistants, so you're in the clear to hit seven to ten places over the next two weeks. Some days there are ten events."

"You're really trying to keep me away from Victoria."

Kelly drew back, looking at him. "I'm trying to help you get elected to the highest office in this city. I think that deserves your time and attention. Do you feel differently?"

"No," he said, lacing his hands behind his back and giving it a good crack. "I didn't intend for it to sound that way."

"Focus, Julian. Stay in the zone and you can't go wrong."

"You never asked what happened. Don't you want to know?"

Kelly couldn't answer honestly. "No. Not while you have only a few weeks left. How bad do you want this?"

The answer came slowly, but as he thought, Kelly could see the depth of his commitment. "Worse than anything I've wanted in my whole life."

His cell phone rang, breaking their peace. The outside world wanted in and Kelly lowered the music again, letting Kem croon only to her.

"Hey, Raja. Yeah, let me call you right back."

Julian's sheepish look told her he had feelings for Raja.

Putting her feelings back in her chest, Kelly waved him on and nodded.

Julian closed his phone, warily looking at Kelly. He wasn't the type to make excuses, but she felt one coming on.

"Call me late afternoon tomorrow. You can tell me how the appearances went and maybe we'll need to fine-tune some things." He pulled on his jacket and headed for the door, Kelly trailing.

"Kelly, don't worry about Raja. I'll take care of it."

"I'm not worried about her, Julian. Let's get through these next two weeks and after the election, you can do whatever you damned well please."

"I don't know about that," Julian said before unlocking the door. "But I feel you. Later, girl."

"Bye," she said and was startled when he turned around suddenly and hugged her.

Kelly would have settled for a quick touch-and-go, but Julian held on. "I love you."

"What?" she said, too shocked to say more.

"You always got my back. I love that about you. See you tomorrow."

Julian released her and was gone in an instant.

Kelly locked the door and slowly walked into the kitchen.

She'd longed to hear those words from someone for all the right reasons, but it hadn't happened yet.

She cleaned the kitchen and turned off the lights, determined to go to bed early and forget the worst parts of the day.

After bathing, she doused herself in creamy lotion, pulled on her nightie, and climbed into bed.

For Julian's sake, she hoped Natalie's spies were out in force tonight and would catch him leaving Raja's apartment tomorrow morning.

Sleeping with Raja was the best thing.

Kelly slid to the center of her king-size bed and drifted to sleep before her brain could think any more.

Nineteen

Tired of the lies and deception that didn't exist in his life before seeking the mayor's job, Julian was having more second thoughts than usual about bowing out of the race altogether. If it hadn't been for the constant prodding from minorities and important business leaders, he would have caved in a month ago. Julian was beginning to understand how the price of passion and success could overlap and cause more backseat drama than he ever expected. An old flame, even a white one, was manageable had Victoria simply been a no-name one-nighter, but she was much more than that. The fact that she resurfaced with a husband on the campaign trail and Julian's daughter multiplied his anxiety exponentially. Now this Natalie Huffman had gotten it in her thick head that Julian had a lot more to do with Victoria than he'd ever admit, so she was dogging him too. Raja and Kelly had fallen out over some ridiculous misunderstanding, a newspaper photograph picturing him exiting a hotel lobby, and their own insecurities regarding his affection for the other.

What a fine mess, Julian thought, as he motored through the dissipating Manhattan traffic. *I need a long, hot shower and a close shave to scrape off some of the mud they've been hurling at a brotha trying to make a difference. If I was really doing dirt, the kinda dirt that some of my opponents have made a fortune getting away with, they'd crucify me for*

breakfast and be dumping flowers over my cold dead remains by lunch-
time. I've got to find a way to slow this runaway train before it jumps the
track and gets somebody killed, including me.

Julian continued on thinking about his career, his illustrious past, his problematic present, and pondered over an extremely uncertain future. Just when it seemed the darkest of night had fallen, his cell phone buzzed from the car console. Julian pressed the telephone icon on the steering wheel to activate the speaker feature. "This is Julian," he said, neglecting to look at the caller readout information.

"Ooh, you sound worn," Raja's smooth voice purred. "Where you been? I thought you were going to call right back."

"Here and there," Julian answered casually, trying to avoid having to lie. Unfortunately, Raja wasn't willing to let it go so easily.

"I hear you but I don't follow. Where exactly was *here and there?*" she said, more definitively.

"Nowhere really. I had some meetings with legal colleagues that backed into one another and wouldn't you know it, both of them ran long? I'm going to force myself to be more assertive when it's time to move on, despite how undiplomatic it may come across. Whoever said that success was a journey, not a destination, must have run for mayor before me, 'cause he was dead-on like I'm dead on my feet now." Julian hoped his lengthy dissertation put so much on Raja's mind that she couldn't spot the cow chips in the midst of the muck he'd shoveled. When she continued the same line of questioning, Julian wasn't sure what conclusion to draw.

"Legal colleagues?" Raja repeated suspiciously. "Why is it that I have the distinct feeling whenever you're not ready to tell me where you've been, I'll get this 'with some legal colleagues' brush-off? Hmmm, look at you, already politicking me."

Julian chuckled. "You did say politicking?"

"Unless you'd rather be doing something else to me right now," Raja quipped. She let the ending of her proposition dangle in the air so that Julian wouldn't have any problems snatching it.

"Dayyyum, that sounds inviting."

"Consider yourself invited. Since you won't come right out and tell me where you've been, I'll settle this one time for where you are now." Raja was lying across her bed on an oversized bath towel, air-drying after a steam-filled bath.

"Actually, I'm close to home. Why, is there something you want me to know? Something you want to ask me?" Of course Julian knew that she wanted his company and more importantly what he had provided the last three times they were alone together, window-rattling, bare-assed sex that rendered Raja breathless and begging for a chance to get it back.

Raja held the phone against her ear, trapped with her shoulder.

She was blushing and Julian sensed it. When she wanted to get nice and naughty in a heated escapade, she batted her eyes, bit her bottom lip ever so slightly, and twisted strands of hair around her index finger.

"If I have to ask, it's obvious that you don't want it as badly as I thought you would," she whined seductively. "Now, is there something you want to ask me?"

Pulling his luxury car over on the shoulder of a well-lit avenue, Julian flashed a curious furrowed brow. "Question, are you batting your eyes right now?"

"Uhhh-huh," she moaned.

"Question, are you biting on your bottom lip?"

"I was when I called you but now I'm sucking on it." Raja giggled softly.

"Ohhh, you're killing me. One more question. Are you twirling hair around your index finger?"

"Nope, they're all busy doing something else at the moment. Too many questions, I guess." Raja painted the kind of visual that men can't resist, a woman who had nothing to do with her hands.

Julian whipped the car around and burned rubber in the opposite direction. "I'll be there in a few minutes, don't stop. I want to watch," he told her in no uncertain terms. "Then I'll give them a break and take over where they left off."

"I ran your bath. It's hot, very hot," Raja cooed like an alley cat in heat. "Don't let it get too cold." She heard the phone click but wasn't certain he'd made up his mind. "Hello? Julian?" When he didn't answer, she had hers. Julian was definitely on his way over to do a lot more than watch.

Minutes later, Julian whipped his car into Raja's underground parking garage. Suddenly, he blew out a deep, labored sigh. Visions of his evening with Kelly played vividly in his mind. It reminded him of the fun they'd had when she initially moved to the city and crashed at his place for two months until the entry-level publicity position she'd interviewed for came through. In good and bad times, Kelly always held up her end of the fun. The more Julian thought about it he realized how she'd always been there for him as well, even now, going out on a limb to take the weight over the hotel incident. Kelly had put herself in the middle of him and Raja in order to protect both of them. Only a true friend would have gone to such lengths to do that. Julian sat there contemplating how to come clean with Raja and tell her what kind of friend she had in Kelly.

Julian popped the trunk from the inside, threw in his briefcase, and then charged up two flights of stairs.

Fostering the best intentions, Julian had his mind made up to set the record straight. When Raja opened the door, wearing baby-doll high-heel pumps, a sheer nightie, and nothing else underneath, Julian's good intentions disappeared and undoubtedly ended up where most of them do, on the road to hell. His leering gaze scanned her body head to toe and up again. As soon as his mouth fell open, Raja stuck her tongue in it, allowed it to dance, and then she held up her naughty fingers to his mouth.

"Ahh-ahh. Hush, baby," she demanded adamantly. "You've said enough for one night. Whatever you had on your mind, we'll discuss it tomorrow." Julian had never been so happy to shut the hell up while being led inside by his front belt loops. Raja stamped an indelible exclamation mark on the situation when she kicked the door closed with her heel of her shoe.

When they reached Raja's bedroom, well lit by scented candles of ginger-peach, she took her time undressing Julian. He considered lending his assistance, but why bother when she was having such a good time doing it? The atmosphere called for creative juices to flow uninhibited and without regard for virtue. Raja had reached into her bag of tricks and come out with a show-stopper. "Don't be afraid," she told him, while pulling the blindfold over his eyes. "I promise to take special care of you. It's not going to hurt, much," she added to arouse his curiosity. "First we need to get all of the city dust off you so I can get down to business."

Raja led Julian to the bathroom by the hand. He was smiling below the blindfold and standing at attention below that. After being bathed and pampered, Julian was toweled off and pulled into the dining area where a small cart rested alongside Raja's dinner table. Still blinded by a black cloth strap, Julian began sniffing as a familiar aroma tickled his nose. "I smell chocolate," he whispered. However, he couldn't recognize the other scents commingled within the sweet fragrance that Julian swore made him hungry for ice cream.

"Shhh! Quiet," Raja fired back at him. She placed her hands against his chest and pushed until he began backing toward the table. As Julian's muscular thighs brushed against the rim of the table, he stiffened as if bracing himself for a fall. "No, baby, you're safe but I need you to lie down," she instructed. "Here's the deal. You get dinner and then I'll get dessert." Not that Raja was looking for Julian's consent; she just wanted him to be aware of things to come. Having her way with him was a special treat, but feeding his desires with the core of her essence, that was worth its weight in gold.

After Raja slipped a satin pillow underneath Julian's head she ran her fingertips along his skin while circling her prey. "Whatever you do, do not remove the blindfold," Raja ordered. "I want you to commit this occasion to memory so whenever . . . you close your eyes, tonight will be there waiting on you."

Julian nodded slowly that he planned to comply, and then he licked his lips and swallowed hard.

Anticipation was what Raja had in mind most of all. Julian was about to burst, he wanted her so badly. "Come here," he begged. "Ahhh, come on."

"Okay. Enjoy," she answered while climbing atop Julian and straddling his face. "Uh-uhhh, slower," Raja moaned. "Slower, baby, much slower." Julian's tongue danced between her thighs just as she requested. "Oohhh, that's it. I like that, Julian. A little faster now," she whined, whipping her head back and forth. "Faster, Julian. Faster. Right there, right there, right there. Now suck it, baby. Oohhh, it's so good. Don't stop sucking it, oh yeah, just like that! Ohhh, shit, I'm there, Julian. I'm all the way therrrrre!"

Once Raja regained her faculties, she slid off Julian to gather her ingredients. From the cart, she picked up a warm bottle of chocolate syrup. As Raja hoisted it above Julian's chest, she cooed, "This is going to be tasty, very, very tasty." She poured a generous helping of it on all the places she wanted to lick, and another measure on the place she wanted to lick the most. Julian squirmed as the liquid topping streamed closer to his prized passion, the family jewels. "Be still," Raja hissed. "I have to make this sundae just . . . the way . . . I like it, with lots of nuts."

Julian chuckled then, thinking the syrup wasn't such a bad idea after all, but as soon as the cool whipped cream landed on his skin, he wasn't so sure. There he was, squirming again.

"Uh-uh, we already talked about that. Don't move. All you need now is a cherry on top."

Julian enjoyed every wet stroke of Raja's tongue as she satisfied her sweet tooth, although his favorite part occurred when she put the cherry exactly where he needed it, spread out over the nuts.

Twenty

"**D**amn," Raja sighed. She took a sip of her cold coffee and pushed a strand of hair away from her face. She'd been sitting alone in her office making a halfhearted attempt at working down the mound of paperwork on her desk, but even after dredging up the last bit of her energy reserves, she was getting nowhere.

"And how could I?" she asked herself aloud. Between the less-than-earth-shattering night she'd spent in Julian's arms, and the neck-popping, eye-rolling, call-a-sistah-out encounter she'd recently had with Kelly, there was simply no way she could concentrate on anything else for more than three straight seconds.

"Justine is dead wrong this time," Raja muttered. Pushing away from her desk, she stood and walked over to the small window and promptly shut the blinds, darkening the room. Sex with Julian last night had been physically pleasing, but emotionally flat and mechanical, nothing like their usual intimate, soul-stirring lovemaking. Raja had done her best to engage Julian's emotions while he moaned and grunted on top of her, but she'd gotten the distinct impression that Julian was simply making love to a hot female body, and that the act itself held no passionate connection to her as a person.

She'd called Justine to discuss her fears, and her friend had insisted that Raja was paranoid. "C'mon, Justine," Raja had pleaded. "Stop trying to make it seem like I'm overreacting or creating something out of nothing. First I read about him coming out of some hot-sheet hotel, and then he climbs on top of me and screws me like I'm some nameless, faceless, booty-call. Something is up, girl. I just know it."

"Well," Justine said in a rational tone, "I know y'all talked things out before getting deep in the sheets, right? Didn't you at least ask him what he was doing coming out of that hotel?"

Raja pouted. "No," she admitted. "There was no time for a conversation, and besides I was too afraid to talk. I drug him into my apartment by his belt loops and practically jumped him. I ran his bath, rubbed him down with oils. . . . I did all the sweet things for him that men usually do for me. I guess I wanted to get with him physically to try and relive that emotional connection we shared the last time we made love. But maybe I imagined that whole thing."

"Wow," Justine said softly. "You're supposed to know better than that, Miss Raja. If you don't own a man's heart vertically, you can't possibly earn it horizontally."

"I know. It's just that prior to all this drama with the hotel and the fiasco with that backstabbing Kelly, I was absolutely positive that there were long-term vibes stirring between us. That he felt for me the same way I feel for him. At least that's what he said."

"And you still don't know that he doesn't mean that, Raja," Justine said. "I think you're jumping to conclusions. About him and about Kelly. I know I've said that before, but you just can't seem to hear it."

Raja had sighed again. "I would love to be wrong about Julian, but I'm almost positive that Kelly wants him for herself. I've zeroed in on enough men to know when another woman has zeroed in on mine, and no matter what you say, Justine, Kelly wants Julian. I'm willing to put my last dime on it. I just have to find out if Julian is crazy enough or desperate enough to want her too."

"Better keep your little dimes in your purse, Raja," Justine warned. "No need to go broke over something that seems pretty baseless to me. If Kelly had even the tiniest spark of feelings for

Julian, there's no way she would have hooked the two of you up. She would have kept that prize all to herself. That's how we do, girl."

Raja had hung up feeling worse than before she called Justine. She was unaccustomed to being so conflicted over a relationship, and as angry as she was with Kelly, deep inside she hoped her instincts were off and that her girlfriend wasn't trying to edge her out of Julian's life on the sly.

But still . . .

Denying one's intuition didn't make that intuition wrong, Raja knew. Besides, there was no refuting Julian's lack of connection to her in bed, and if Kelly wasn't gunning for his heart, could there be someone else out there trying to beat her time?

"Uh-uh," Raja said aloud, shaking her head to purge the distasteful thought. "Julian might be a fine, rising star, but brother better not be trying to play no aging mack-daddy roll with me. Have me yanking out some sista's weave and wrapping it around his neck! Hmph . . . don't make me go East New York on you, Mr. Julian Blake!"

Raja feigned interest in the paperwork on her desk for a few more minutes, then flung the whole stack aside and picked up her purse. An early lunch was in order, so it seemed, and even though she didn't feel hungry the walls were closing in on her and getting out of the office was suddenly paramount.

After visiting the restroom where she washed her hands and reapplied her makeup, Raja took the stairwell down to the main lobby. There was no way she wanted to stand in front of the elevator banks and risk running into someone who wanted either to talk shop or get in her business.

"Have a good lunch, Miss Jackson."

Raja was just about to push through the revolving doors when she turned around and saw the aging black security guard waving at her. "Oh, thanks, Mr. Brooks," she said with a small wave. The guard was old enough to be Raja's father and then some, but he refused to address her by her first name.

"Joseph," said the smiling gentleman, initiating their private joke.

"Raja," Raja replied in turn, conjuring up just a little sunshine to add to her brief smile.

Outside, Raja strutted down the Midtown streets with confidence and finesse. With her designer wear, appropriate jewelry, and perfect hair, no one would ever guess how much inner turmoil and emotional distress was brewing inside her.

Several professional men eyed Raja's assets, nodding their interest and trying to make eye contact to see if she'd flirt reciprocally. She ignored them. The last thing she wanted to do right now was meet some new man, chip away at all the bullshit and drama in his life, and then find out that after all of her hard work he was somebody's nobody, just another wolf on the prowl.

The scent of pizza was in the air and even though she hadn't been hungry, Raja's mouth began to water as she stepped into a local shop.

"I'd like a vegetarian slice and a bottle of Evian, please."

Raja gazed around the pizzeria as she waited for her order. The booths and tables were filled with an early lunch crowd. Men discussing business, groups of women laughing and no doubt discussing men. Friends. Lovers. People relating to other people. It hit Raja suddenly that aside from her close friendship with Justine, she hadn't really forged any meaningful relationships that could sustain her through rough times like these. While she loved Justine, her girl wasn't what you would call sophisticated, and they certainly didn't travel in the same circles. Raja would love to be sitting four to a booth, eating her slice while bouncing her thoughts about Julian and Kelly off three worldly, trusted friends.

Instead, she took a seat alone at one of the few available tables toward the back of the eatery. Folding her slice in half, Raja bit into the V tip and chewed slowly as she took a bit of self-inventory regarding her personal friendships. Most of her childhood girlfriends either were smoked out on crack or had ten baby daddies, or worse, were locked up in jail. Those who were doing well in their lives couldn't seem to shake off their project personas, and reconnecting with them was as distasteful as it was unthinkable.

The women at her job were no better. True, many of them had

pedigrees and came from families with old money, but Raja wouldn't dream of revealing the slightest bit of herself to some white chick who thought all black women were fat and inferior and all black NBA players were hung like horses. The whole lot of them were a bunch of trifling airheads. Especially that blond-haired Phinius, who of all things had gotten a promotion that very morning. Raja wasn't above using what she had to get what she wanted, but white women like Phinius played the corporate game on a gutter level. If she hadn't been so consumed with her quandary over Julian and Kelly, Raja would have torn up the carpet at First American Bank that morning when the watercooler news about Phinius's promotion reached her ears. Phinius wasn't nearly as educated as Raja, and had next to no experience working with the detailed international documents that were the bane of the industry, yet she'd managed to snag a position equal to Raja's in half the time it had taken Raja to earn hers. And she was making more money too, which burned Raja up to no end.

But the money didn't fry her nerves half as much as did the fact that Phinius had recently set her sights on Darren, a bespeckled brother who had a wife and three children, and who was one of the only black men at their branch. Nibbling on her pizza crust, Raja redirected her anger and permitted herself to fume over Phinius and her scandalous intentions. Darren was short and scrawny, not much to look at in the least. But it wasn't looks that Phinius was after, Raja knew. It was the thrill of illegally copping something that belonged to a black woman, the satisfaction of taking a brother out of a happy black home and luring him away with the appeal of that forbidden white fruit.

Raja was no stranger to that scenario. In fact, it was that very thing that had set her early life on a path of ruin, and launched her and her mother smack into a tenement in East New York. She took a sip of her water and used her napkin to pat the beads of sweat she felt rising on her nose. *Calm down, girlfriend,* Raja cautioned herself. Sister to sister, she was almost compelled to call Darren's wife and hip her to the game Phinnie, the black man slayer, was trying to run on her husband, but it really wasn't her place. In fact, it was

such a call from a well-meaning sister that had sent her mother fly-
ing off the handle, forcing a confrontation with her father that
ended with him choosing his dowdy white tramp over the two
beautiful black queens in his life. For want of a white woman that
fool had totally rejected the black queen he had married, as well as
the one he had fathered.

To say Raja's mother had become bitter after his betrayal would
be an understatement. She'd constantly cautioned Raja about getting too close to any woman or sacrificing too much for any man.
She'd also drilled it into her head that white women only wanted
one thing from black women.

They wanted to be them.

As such, the only person in the city that Raja had really connected with was Kelly, and turning her attention back to the situation at hand, Raja found it hard to believe she could have been so
wrong about her ex-friend, and perhaps the man she was growing
to love as well.

Raja was surprised to look down and find she'd not only finished
her pizza, but had devoured every bit of the high-carbohydrate
crust as well. "Oh well," she murmured, then drank the rest of her
water and discarded her trash in the can by the door.

Back outside, Raja walked back to work in a fog, her mind totally
immersed in the loneliness and ugliness that had suddenly become
her life. She was swept up in the crowd and wrapped in her thoughts
when she stumbled over her feet and found herself being steadied
by a pair of strong male arms.

"Sorry—" the man said, steadying her with his hands.

Raja clutched her purse and got ready to go Brooklyn on him.
This was an old trick. Bump into a woman on the street and slide
off with her wallet.

"Yeah," she said sharply, making sure the zipper on her Fendi
bag was still closed. She was nobody's damn victim. "I bet you are.
Hustle somebody else, asshole."

"Damn, sister. I said I'm sor—Raja? Is that you?"

For the first time Raja looked into the face of her accoster, and
the person she saw froze the nasty words on her tongue.

"C-Calvin? Calvin Jennings?"

His handsome face broke apart in a huge grin and Raja's first thought was of his beautifully clean teeth and awesome smile.

"Raja Jackson!" he exclaimed, hugging her to him and holding her close. "Raja, Raja, Raja, *Raja*!" Calvin planted a big kiss on Raja's forehead, his exuberance that of an overgrown puppy. "Girl, how've you been? Beautiful as ever! A sight for sore eyes!"

Raja smiled brightly and allowed him to hold her in his arms right there on the busy street, her gloom and emotional turmoil totally forgotten.

"Calvin Jennings," was all she could say as she blushed down to her Victoria's Secrets. He had been her first love, her truest love, and memories of the trust and innocence of their relationship as well as their incredible sexual attraction came flooding back to her.

"Damn, girl," Calvin said, his grin ever widening as he stared into her eyes.

Success was all over him, Raja noted with pride and satisfaction. From his custom-made suit to the two-thousand-dollar shoes on his feet. Calvin had done something with his life, just like he always said he would. He'd made something of himself and Raja felt her heart swelling as they stood there grinning at each other like two love-struck kids.

"How've you been?" Calvin asked. "How's Justine? What are you doing in Midtown?"

Raja giggled. "I've been fine, Cal. Better now that I've run into you, though. Jus is fine. I work a few blocks away, at First American Bank. What about you? I thought you were out in California. What are you doing bumping into young women in the heart of New York?"

Calvin laughed and took her hand. "It's not every day that I get to bump into a woman as beautiful as you. I'm here on business, but I have a few hours before I need to be at a meeting. Can I buy you lunch? You know, spend a little time with you so we can catch up on each other's happenings?"

Raja smiled and felt a happiness that seemed to run through her blood and creep down into her bones. She'd cut out early for lunch, and had just eaten a slice of pizza, but so what? Let Phinius handle whatever issues arose in her absence. Give her an excuse to earn her new salary. Besides, she'd gladly push some food from one side of her plate to another if it meant sitting across from Calvin Jennings, the man who'd not only made her a woman, but who'd lived to keep her happy and make her feel secure.

"Of course," she said, taking the hand he'd extended out to her. "I'd love to catch up with you. You know. Chat for a little bit."

As they walked down the busy Manhattan streets hand in hand, a thousand questions flooded Raja's mind. Was Calvin married? Did he have any children? Was he in New York to stay? She was suddenly so happy she felt giddy. One question she didn't have to ask though was whether or not their chemistry was still working. As Calvin held her hand, running his thumb joyfully over her fingers, Raja had forgotten all about the woes of her present and was gleefully looking forward to reliving the one crowning highlight of her past.

Twenty-one

The computer keys moved easily under Kelly's fingers as she gathered ammunition on Alex Nixon's voting record. Her research would pay off in a big way for Julian during the debate.

Alex was against many issues that were important to the black community. She shook her head at his record of voting regarding the MLK holiday. He'd voted no twice. No three times to Affirmative Action, and no against state aid to help the underprivileged. He'd even argued against children learning African-American and Hispanic history in elementary schools. His inability to hear his constituents wouldn't bode well with the communities he needed to sway.

Kelly dragged and dropped his record into her grid, then gave her fingers a break for a minute.

Julian would annihilate Alex. Julian was savvy, had name recognition, and he'd been a part of the fabric of New York before and after 9/11. He'd done good work, serious work, and people wouldn't soon forget that.

But she couldn't help but face another reality.

Alex was a golden boy. Good-looking with the perfect life in Atlanta, the perfect political career, and the perfect family. Although his record for issues regarding the middle and lower classes was questionable at best, he'd authored bills for stem cell research, stronger EPA controls, and homeland security.

Despite the short period of time Alex had spent in New York, he'd become the candidate to beat.

Kelly moved her electronic organizer over and made a note to ask Julian if they could publish some of his photographs with several of his friends that had survived the Trade Center bombing. The group of firemen and police had started an after-school program for young victims of September 11, and Julian volunteered his time and talent with the kids once a week.

Julian was protective and had given strict orders that he and the children not be photographed. He didn't want them exploited. They'd already lost a parent.

Their privacy wasn't for sale.

Kelly perused the voting records for the past five years and saw Alex's name pop up, this time against any type of health care for illegal aliens. She popped in the DVD of his speech in defense of his voting record taken by an AP reporter last year.

"Americans should each take care of themselves," Alex said, to a handsome Italian reporter.

What is his name? Kelly struggled, then scribbled *Santos Tucci*. She underlined his name to reference later.

"Why should the government have to support freeloaders with welfare?" Alex continued. "Most of them don't want job training, but will have more babies because their checks will increase. I say no more. End the welfare system. I support privatization of managed health care, and public aid only in the most extreme cases. My great-grandfather came to this country with three dollars and eighty cents in his pocket. He taught my grandfather, who taught my father, who taught me the meaning of the words *hard work*. I'm a proponent for hard work, and I will continue the legacy by teaching my daughter those same ethics."

"What about the people who don't have babies, yet can't care for themselves?" Kelly noted Santos's face grew angrier as he asked the question.

A twinge of pleasure tickled her when an annoyed Alex jerked his head back after being lightly tapped on the mouth by the microphone.

"Score one, Italian guy," she cheered.

"Mr. Nixon, your great-grandfather was an immigrant," Santos continued, although Alex had ignored his first question. "Should he have been denied health care?"

"My great-grandfather scraped and labored for every dime he earned."

"So he's a better immigrant than the people coming to America today?"

Alex ignored the other reporters and focused on Tucci. "You're trying to put words in my mouth. I didn't say that."

"Three dollars and eighty cents," Santos said clearly.

Alex was annoyed, no question. His face had reddened, his mouth set in a firm line. No other reporter spoke, leaving Alex hanging by the noose of his words.

"That's right. That's all he had when he arrived in America."

"That's not much more than some of the working poor earn an hour after taxes. With rent in New York starting at fifteen hundred a month, what part of that three dollars and eighty cents should go to health care, Mr. Nixon?"

Alex blanched, and for the first time since Kelly'd made the acquaintance of Alex and Victoria, she saw Alex flustered.

"Listen here, Mr. Tucci, all that my great-grandfather ever got he earned. He worked until his hands curled with arthritis, his body bowed from eighteen-hour days for sixty-seven years. Say what you will, but I share his ethics. I will work my fingers to the bone and I will take care of my family. Every adult should feel the same."

Some of the reporters cheered, having been won over by the passionate speech.

Tucci's expression seemed to say he was in agreement with Alex, but Kelly detected the glint of a predator in his deep brown eyes.

"Do you consider giving council members, yourself included, a three hundred percent raise 'hard work'?"

Several of the reporters scribbled furiously, while others kept their film rolling.

Alex looked like a boxer, his mouth turned down, forehead glowing with the beginnings of sweat. "I won't justify that with a response. That information is unfounded."

"So you're saying your hard work is more important than those who don't get to vote on their increases?"

"I'm done with you. Is there another question?"

"How much do you make?" another reporter asked.

"Do you have government medical benefits?"

"Are you and your family covered for life?"

Questions assailed the councilman, until he raised his hands. "Thank you. Have a nice day."

Alex smiled as if he had just been electrocuted. Too wide. Too bright. Fake.

The DVD ended and Kelly sat back. She recalled reading in *USA Today* that they'd only been granted a 35 percent raise.

Poor Alex, she thought, feeling a lot more sympathy for the man who didn't know the woman he was married to or her past involvement with his archrival.

Kelly got up and stretched, taking her glass of wine with her as she gazed out over the piece of New York's skyline that she could see. So much was happening, but Julian could win this race. He just had to keep things together for another two months and the seat would be his.

They were juggling a lot of balls, she knew, hitting the remote. Grating hip-hop charged the air in the room and she bopped to her one secret indulgence.

Truly she was too old for the music, but every now and then she had to keep it real and go *there*. Back to the hood, back to the streets when hip-hop lyrics were her mantra. Back to the days when being poor and black was an honor. When gettin' that paper from college meant hope, when dreams were all they had.

Hip-hop took her to the days when she and Julian and the rest of the homeboys from New York and Atlanta claimed D.C. as their home away from home.

How often had they driven to Micky Ds eight deep in Disco's ratty Lebaron, and begged the manager for some free food?

Disco had been the pleading beggar, but Julian had been all about finesse. He still was now.

Kelly smiled at the memory. They'd often driven away from those fast food restaurants with food to spare.

They'd been some hungry Negroes.

Where was Disco? And Root, Baller, and Malcolm? Where had those brothers gone? They'd been her friends. The brothers she'd never had.

Kelly fingered her wineglass, the memories making her nostalgic.

She picked up her phone and tapped the keys on her computer, searching online for Disco's number. When she found it she dialed.

"Yo?"

"You run a car dealership with that mouth? I wouldn't buy a car from yo tired ass."

"Kelly! Girl, it's been a minute!" Disco roared, his effervescent laughter engulfing her. "Where you at? You in Houston?"

"Hell no. I'm in New York where I'm supposed to be."

"I see," he said with a slick smile in his voice. "Still chasin' that butterfly coalition, reach out and touch somebody, circle of love bullshit with Julian?"

Kelly laughed good and hard. Leave it to Disco to trivialize their efforts. "No, I got my own thang goin' on, thank you very much."

"Oh, you do? What you up to?"

"I'm in public relations for a firm in the city. I do my thing so that you like the athletes you see on TV every Sunday when you lay your ass up on your wife's couch."

"Shit." He laughed. "I bought it, I can lay my fat ass on it!"

They cracked up. "Really," he said, "how are you?"

"I'm good," she replied, basking in the genuine warmth of her friend's voice. "I got to thinking about the old days and goin' to eat for free at the fast food restaurants, and you popped into my mind. The red Lebaron," she sighed.

"I go back there too," he said of his memories. "You married yet, Ms. Taylor?"

"Nah. That isn't for me."

Disco mimicked her, then chuckled. "You still waiting for that knucklehead to wake up?"

"Hell no, Disco. I'm just being me. Tryin' to make it in this world on my own. You understand?"

"More than you know."

"What you talkin' 'bout?" she asked her old friend, forgetting decorum and diction. They were just two friends keepin' it real.

"Ciara took the boys and left."

"No! Why? When?"

"She found something better," he said, sounding sad for a minute. "No, she found something different. I took her to France for our tenth anniversary and one day I was chillin' in the hot tub and she went shopping. In more ways than one."

"She's in France?" Kelly was stunned.

"Yeah. But hey, what can I tell you? I know I'm a good catch. The boys will be back soon and we're going to go on from there."

"Damn, Disco, I'm so sorry," Kelly said sincerely. "Why don't you come and hang out with me and Julian after the election?"

"Don't play now. I might just do that. Hey, Kelly? I was checkin' him out on the Internet and saw another somewhat familiar face. The wife of one of the candidates looks like a blast from the past. Seriously."

Kelly's joy seeped away under the pinprick of his sharp memory. No matter how they tried to ignore Victoria, if Darrell Disco Blain could put together memories of the past, so could someone else.

The phone clicked and Kelly looked at the caller ID. *Private.* Hmm.

"Disco, hold on a minute." She clicked over. "Kelly Taylor."

"Ms. Taylor, this is Natalie Huffman with so much good news to share I'm about to burst."

"I'm on another call."

"Oh, fiddlesticks. I wanted to tell you I've been promoted."

"Good for you, Natalie. Congratulations. Good-bye."

"Don't you want to know to what?"

No! Kelly clamped her lips together. "Just a minute." She clicked back over. "Disco, I've got to go, duty calls."

"Kelly, it was good hearing from you. I may come up there in a couple months, so don't act like you don't know a brotha."

"Never," she promised. "Love to you," she said and clicked back over. "Okay, Natalie. I'll bite. What's your new job?"

"I thought you'd never ask," she said like a cat, playing with a helpless bird before the big kill. "Investigative reporter. And my first assignment is an exposé on Alex Nixon, his beautiful wife and Julian, and their secrets. Care to share?" She laughed.

Kelly did something she'd never done in her career. She hung up the phone.

Natalie's laughter rang in her ears as her heartbeat thundered against her rib cage.

Julian.

He had to know what was going on.

And they had to find a way to stop Natalie or she'd ruin their dreams.

She was startled when her phone rang again.

Julian?

Her breath quickened.

Natalie was calling back.

For the second time in her career, Kelly did the opposite of everything she'd ever preached to new public relations personnel.

She refused to answer her phone. Before she spoke to anyone else, she needed a plan.

Twenty-two

Julian sat in the law library reflecting on the night he'd spent with Raja and his early morning dash from her apartment. Raja was stretching for her three-mile run as he fumbled around the bedroom looking for his wallet.

"You could call in to the office and tell them that you're all tied up," she offered, her hands flat on the floor with her behind in the air. "I'm nearly finished warming up. Another horizontal workout with you sounds like a great idea to me."

Julian smirked, fixing his eyes on the roundness of her sculpted attitude. Raja's body looked just as tempting in a half leotard. His mouth fell open again. However, this time words actually came out of it. "Hmmm, you don't know how much I'd like to put another stamp of approval of that ass, but I really need to get mine into the office. I can't believe I'm doing this but I've got to pass. I'll make it up though. Call you later." Once he located the wallet underneath a stack of pillows on the bed, he planted a gratuitous smack on Raja's lips and bolted down to his car before he had the mind to serve up Raja the way she had done to him the night before.

Leaving her home was always the same for Julian, filled with mixed emotions. Satisfaction of the sinful nature swirled around his conflicted feelings that perhaps Raja wasn't the right one for him. Although, that human-sundae-on-the-dinner-table stunt she pulled gave him second thoughts of feeling right at home while covered in whipped cream and a beautiful bronze goddess with a bona fide kinky streak. Raja was fine and crazy-sexy-cool, Julian couldn't refute it, but there was something missing. It wouldn't be long before he discovered exactly what that was. Tougher decisions were sure to follow once that discovery became crystal clear.

Julian stared at a mound of important documents spread over one of the small conference tables in the firm's legal library. He thumbed through a case file, searching for a brief to review. When a certain written court decision wasn't inside it, Julian dug through his briefcase to get at his cell phone. He lifted flaps and checked the briefcase throughout. After going over it again, he'd concluded it wasn't there but had a pretty good idea where he had left the small flip phone. "The last time I had it," he thought aloud, "I was headed up to Raja's place." Julian picked up the office phone, selected an open line, and dialed Raja's work number. Several rings later, a voice message chimed in.

"You've reached the office of Raja Jackson. Unfortunately I'm away from my desk but I will return your call if you leave a brief message and a number. Thanks. Have a good day."

"Raja, this is Julian. I may have left my cell at your place this morning. Please get back with me as soon as possible. I need to swing by and get it today. You know the number. Oh, wait. That's right. I don't have my cell phone. Tell you what, call me at my office, I'll be there after eleven. Thanks, sweetheart. Bye."

Julian gathered the case file and accompanying document, then shuttled them into his briefcase. He was stuck with the missing court decision to do further research for his case. The county courts would have to go back and find that brief so he could continue making preparations to represent his client. He called the legal aide, who had been handling the paperwork for this case, informed him what he needed, and then instructed him how to expedite getting it immediately. "And don't take no for an answer, Jerry. Make it happen today. Thanks," Julian added after dictating his demands.

Now that the wheels of progress were in motion, Julian had the time to plan out the remainder of his day and the time to think. Usually, during a stagnant break in his busy day, Julian palmed his cell phone and hit 1 on his speed dial to check in with Kelly. *Kelly*, he thought, *I wonder what she got into after I left last night. Maybe she's got a private boy-toy stashed away somewhere to help her get by. Hmm, if she does have a tune-up man on call for lonely nights and lazy afternoons, why hasn't she told me about him?* Suddenly something strange washed over Julian. He didn't recognize it at first, but soon enough it hit him like a ton of bricks. Julian was jealous, jealous at the mere thought of Kelly being with another man, despite having just shared a backbreaking freak marathon with Raja.

Before Julian knew what was happening to him, he'd sprinted up three flights of stairs when the elevator took too long to arrive on the eleventh floor. Huffing and out of breath, he flew past his administrative assistant waving hello. Behind closed doors, he called Kelly's office. Impatiently, he paced back and forth behind his desk. Kelly had been a good friend, a great friend for a long time, and he was at odds about giving a damn about her private social life, but there he was, pacing and jealous. "Hey, Kelly," he panted, as she picked up the phone.

"Yes, Julian?" Kelly's voice was uneven while she was trying to get a lock on Julian's. She noted his quick pitch and exasperated tone and waited to see what lay behind it.

"Uh-uh, hold on, I was just exercising." Julian clutched the telephone in both hands and took a deep breath. "Okay, I'm back."

"What's wrong?" Kelly asked suspiciously. "And why are you working out in your office?"

"I . . . I was just wondering how your day was going," he lied. "And if you got enough sleep last night. I mean, my campaign manager has to be on the ball."

"Sure, I got what I needed last night. Thanks for asking." There was a long stretch of silence as Kelly replayed their discussion in her head and still couldn't make sense of it. "Julian, is there something else you wanted to ask me?"

He wanted so desperately to come out and ask if she had a late-night visitor after he left, but it was inappropriate and he couldn't see changing the structure of their friendship. Julian was caught in the middle of loving Kelly like a dear friend and developing all of these new feelings he couldn't explain. The most prominent barrier that stopped him from sharing what he was going through was the possibility of rejection. He couldn't see making a fool of himself and causing her to start acting weird around him after going off for overstepping unwritten boundaries. If Kelly did want him for herself, she wouldn't have hooked him up with Raja, Julian reasoned, so he decided to let it go and pretend it never happened. "No, Kells," he answered finally. "I just called to say thank you for doing what you do for me and that I'm grateful."

"Okaaay," she said, with her furrowed brow. "I'm going to get back to work, tough client who's got his mind set on being the next mayor so—"

"I get it," Julian said awkwardly. "Have a good day, Kelly." He hung up the phone, collapsed in his chair and stared at the ceiling. "What are you doing, Julian?" he heard himself say. "What are you doing?" Unfortunately, he had no idea what he was doing or what he was going to do about it. In a short time, Raja had made herself appear irreplaceable. Kelly's stock was rising every time Julian conjured up another vision with Kelly and some other dude doing the dessert thing he enjoyed so much. And then there was Victoria. She was holding all the cards in the game she played with Julian. He'd promised himself a long time ago that one woman would be the only mother to his children, but that didn't work out according to plan either. His daughter would be an extended part of the immediate family he'd more than likely create with Raja. *More than likely?* Julian winced when he admitted to himself that he wasn't absolutely sure about his and Raja's future although she was the woman of the hour with outstanding potential.

As the office phone rang repeatedly, Julian exhaled. "I'm getting too old for this shit. Hello, this is Julian." Immediately upon hearing the voice on the other end, he sat up straight in his chair. "CJ? Boy, I haven't heard from you in a month of Sundays. I can't believe it, Calvin Jennings, as I live and breathe." Julian's high school buddy always made him feel young again and longing for the kind of male bonding that was considered ridiculous once the school days ended. "So, CJ, how the hell are you, man?"

"I'm in town for a few days, Jay. We're in the play-off hunt and it looks like your New York Stankies want a taste of this West Coast whoop ass."

Julian beamed. It had been years since someone called him Jay. "That's right, it is baseball season. I'm sorry to say that I don't keep up with your stats like I used to, but I'm still your biggest fan. What's it been, fourteen years in the majors? Don't you think that two league MVPs with the Dodgers are enough?"

"Not as long as I'm batting three-oh-one and leading the West in stolen bases," CJ answered, with as much testosterone as he had spewed in school. "You remember how I was always quick to 'hit and git.'"

Julian laughed heartily. "Yeah, I remember that quick in and out of yours got you in some big trouble when the principal's daughter made your personal wall of fame. I thought for sure your dick-and-ditch days were behind you after that."

"Not hardly, I just tipped my hand that time," Calvin admitted. "I've lost a step since the old days, in a few ways at that, but I haven't lost my ambition."

"Is that her name? We used to call her Palm-Ella," Julian jested, implying that Calvin was spending time stroking his own ego instead of having one of his groupies handle that for him.

"Ahhh, that same Julian. You still got jokes. What I'm going to put on those pin-striped punks this weekend won't be funny," Calvin fired back. "Hey, that reminds me. I flew in early to check on some off-season business prospects. You have a minute to hang out with an old buddy or are you too busy politicking to be seen with the likes of me?"

"Never too busy for you, man." Julian flipped through his day planner. "How's a four o'clock work for you? I'm in the city so name the place. . . . Uh-huh, I've been there," he informed his old friend. "They have great steaks and even better atmosphere. All right, see you then."

Julian agreed to meet Calvin at the Widow's Window, a happening restaurant where the young and inspired law crowd huddled for happy-hour elixirs and a chance to forget about their troubles of the day. When Julian arrived, he looked over the busy eatery, swarming with bright legal minds and those looking to get together with one of them. There in the back, a hoard of autograph seekers lavished Calvin with free drinks and accolades from his past accomplishments. "Yeah, CJ, my dad thinks you suck," announced a young barrister who'd had too many whiskey sours. "But that's only because he loses money every time he bets against the Dodgers." The crowd erupted with laughter after the great Calvin Jennings raised his beer to losing money when betting against his team. When he spotted Julian standing on the fringes of his fame, he excused himself from the slew of idol worshippers to hang with a true-blue friend.

"Julian Blake, you old dog." Calvin saluted with a stiff handshake following by a brotherly embrace. "Man, you look great. It must be something in the water, because I know you're not putting anything in your mouth but beer and big titties."

"Calvin CJ Jenkins," Julian sighed as if he'd seen an apparition from his youth. "I had to grow up sometime and start taking care of me. We can't all be pro athletes and big ballers like you, getting millions to help you keep a body like that. Some of us have to hit the gym and get fit the new millennium way, pay a personal trainer to do it for us." Julian was in amazing shape, but it was hard not to envy Calvin's chiseled frame, cut from granite.

"Hey, let's snag a table over there and catch up," Calvin offered, gesturing toward the far side of the restaurant. "By the way, whatever happened to that skinny little underclassman that used to run behind you? Uh, what was her name? You know, the cute one, Kelly Taylor. Have you kept in contact with her?"

"Actually, I spoke with her today," Julian answered, wearing a brand-new grin. "Kelly's all grown up too, filled out nicely, and running my campaign like a well-oiled machine. I'll tell her that you asked about her. She'll like that."

"Please do, Kelly was always a real go-getter. It's important to keep people you trust around you. Lawd knows I've had to learn that the hard way. Between housekeepers stealing my personal stuff and selling it on eBay and ex-girlfriends selling their stories to the rag mags, I'm leery about saying two words to people off the record or letting my guard down with folks on my payroll." Calvin downed one of the mixed drinks sent over from two adoring blondes across the bar. He nodded thanks, avoided a conversation with the women, and then continued on with a discussion he did care about. "It's times like these I wish I had a special somebody to go home to, crawl into bed with, and know that she was watching my back instead of going through my pants as soon as I fell asleep."

"I feel you, CJ," Julian agreed wholeheartedly. "I was just saying this afternoon how I felt too old for the foolishness. It's definitely time to settle up and settle down. If I hadn't done it by now, probably didn't need to."

"Whuut? Not Julian Blake, 'the man it takes to make the ladies quake,' " Calvin chanted.

"How many times do I have to tell you I'm past all that, CJ? Well, almost anyway," Julian reiterated. "I'm trying to be respectable now. I've got a woman who's making that a lot easier to do than I imagined. Got me thinking about the house in the burbs, kiddies and all that." When that brand-new smile made a second appearance, Calvin called him on it.

"Is that why you're grinning like an alley cat who humped the rat? It's that Kelly girl, ain't it? She the one got you all lit up like Times Square? I guess she is all grown up at that."

"Nah, you've got the wrong idea. I'm kicking it with a superfine superwoman with some real good . . ." Julian bragged until he glanced over at CJ getting all excited, so he squashed the compliments. "Well, let's just say that she's top of the line and has a sweet tooth for chocolate sundaes. Maybe you'll have time to meet Raja before you leave town."

Suddenly, Calvin's easygoing expression changed. "Raja, huh?" he said, mulling over another thought in the back on his mind. "She sounds exotic. Her name, I mean. There can't be too many sistas with that name. This Raja, she must be special if you're thinking about her and two-point-five kids. Is, uh . . . she the one?"

"She's definitely one of a kind," Julian stated fondly.

Calvin stared into the distance, barely connected to his conversation with Julian at all. "Hmmm, I'm sure she is," he murmured over a second complimentary stiff drink. "I'm sure she is."

Twenty-three

Lunch with Calvin had been the bomb. She was still in a daze. His sexy eyes, honest smile, and the memories they shared all served to infuse Raja with renewed energy and a spirit of hope. The despondency she'd been wallowing in over Kelly and Julian was totally gone. In its place were the warm feelings that Calvin had ignited in her so many years ago, feelings that had been tucked away in her heart, and had now resurfaced with a vengeance.

They'd spent two and a half glorious hours together at a nearby Italian restaurant, and it was well after the lunch crowd had dissipated before they noticed the passage of time.

"Wow!" Calvin had exclaimed, glancing at his watch. "Raja." He said her name with a boyish laugh. "You always could make me forget the rest of the world. Here I've been monopolizing your time as if you don't have a job to get back to and I don't have a meeting to attend."

Raja had simply smiled. Job? What job? She hadn't given that bank one single thought from the moment she'd laid eyes on the wonderful hunk of man sitting before her. She hadn't thought about Julian either, and wasn't trying to think about him now.

"Yeah," she said softly, gathering her purse as Calvin signaled for the waiter and handed him a platinum charge card. "I guess it's time to get back to the grind. It was nice talking to you, Calvin."

"But hold up," Calvin said quickly. "Can we get together later on tonight? I mean—if you don't have plans, I'd like to see you again."

Raja shook her head. "Sorry. I have a previous engagement," she lied. "But I'm open for tomorrow. Would that work for you?"

"Absolutely," Calvin replied. "I can pick you up at your office, or I can swing by your place. Are you still in New York?"

Raja suppressed a shudder. "Um, no. No. I live in Montclair now. In New Jersey."

Calvin nodded. "I hear that's a nice town. I tell you what. Let me jot down your address and I'll pick you up at seven. Cool?"

Raja giggled. Calvin and his "cools." Just like when they were kids.

"Cool, Calvin," she said, then blushed inwardly when he took her hand and pressed her fingers to his lips.

"It's good to see you, Raja. Even better to talk to you. Everything about you is as perfect as I remember. I'm glad you've done so well for yourself, and I hope whoever you have in your life is making you happy. You deserve the best."

Raja could only sigh. And then sigh again as they rose and Calvin pulled her into his embrace. She permitted herself the luxury of those strong, safe arms. The bliss of his scent and the sureness of his touch.

"Yeah," she said when their arms finally fell away. "I hope somebody is making you happy too, Calvin. The best always deserves the best. And you, brother, are the best."

Raja had allowed Calvin to escort her back to the bank, and for the first time ever the Midtown blocks were far too short. They'd kissed on the cheek before parting, with the promise of dinner and perhaps a movie in a little more than twenty-four hours.

Raja wasn't sure if she could wait that long. Her heart resounded with something that had lain dormant for so many years that she'd convinced herself it was dead. And her body. Lord have mercy. Just the sensation of Calvin running his fingers all over her hand as they walked along the streets had done a job on her flesh. Her nipples were erect beneath her suit jacket, and there was a heat missile lurking in the bottom of her belly, just dying to explode.

"Hey," the security guard called out as Raja pushed through the revolving doors that led into the bank's foyer. "Long lunch, huh? I was starting to get worried about you."

She gave Mr. Brooks a smile that was a million times stronger than the one she'd flashed him before she departed. "Yep! Long lunch. Great lunch. Thanks for worrying, but actually . . ." Raja reached into her purse and retrieved her cell phone. "I'm about to take that 'extended lunch' thing to a whole new level."

She pressed a number on speed dial, then stood grinning at Mr. Brooks and gazing through the bank's glass doors as her boss's secretary answered her desk phone.

"Sheila?" Raja spoke into her cell cheerily. "This is Raja. Do me a favor, sweetie, why don't you? Let Bob know that I'm not feeling well and I won't be back for the rest of the day. Oh, really? I sound great?" Raja laughed out loud. "Well, I try to make it a habit to not only look but sound better than I feel. Tell Bob he can pass my workload on to Phinius for the day. I'm sure she's highly qualified to handle things without a glitch. You guys have a swell afternoon, okay?" *Click!*

With a wink at Mr. Brooks, who was belly-laughing at her antics, Raja pressed another number on speed dial and waited until the phone was answered.

"Justine!" she nearly screamed into the receiver. "Girl, you are *never* gonna guess who I just had lunch with! Honey, stick a bottle of Apple Malt Duck in the freezer. I'm leaving work early and I'm on my way to East New York."

As the subway raced toward Brooklyn, Raja swayed in her seat, too high on Calvin's vapors to be annoyed by the hefty woman who had not only squeezed her forty-five-inch hips into the six inches of seat space between Raja and another woman, but whose head lolled against Raja's shoulder as she snoozed as if she were in her own bedroom.

She replayed every syllable of her conversation with Calvin over and over in her mind, a warm glow heating her insides as she remembered the intensely erotic look in his eyes as he gazed at her. By the time the train arrived at the New Lots Avenue Station she could barely wait to talk to Justine. She'd played the what-if game over and over in her mind for an hour straight, and each time she was forced to conclude that maybe she'd been wrong to let Calvin go. Wrong about who he was as a black man and where his true desires lay.

"Open up!" Raja pounded on Justine's door, playing around the way they used to when they were kids. "This is the po-lice, damn it! We know you're hiding in there!"

Justine came to the door laughing and untying her apron. Flour dusted her nose, her arms, and the front of her pink shirt. "Well, look at you!" she exclaimed. "All glowing and things. Get your butt in here, girl, and tell me who put that gorgeous smile on your face. It was Julian, right? See? I told you he was legit. Did he take you out to lunch and propose to you? Or did ya'll do the nasty in the back of a limo and call it an afternoon delight?"

Raja shook her head, inhaling the rich aroma wafting in from Justine's kitchen. "Uh-uh, honey. You're way wrong. I smell sweet potatoes. You baking pies?"

"Yep," Justine said. "And I have a couple of extra ones on the cooling rack, so you be sure to take one home with you. Now go get comfortable on the couch while I break out the Duck and some glasses. By the look on your face I know this is gonna be one hell of a story."

By the time Justine returned with the drinks, Raja had kicked off her shoes, retrieved her house slippers, and settled down in her favorite spot on Justine's sofa.

"So I was walking down the street minding my business, right?" Justine nodded. "Uh-huh."

"And out of nowhere, I tripped over my own feet and some guy grabbed me. You know I thought he was going for my purse, right?"

Justine laughed. "Yeah, Miss Paranoid. The man was probably just trying to stop you from cracking your teeth on the concrete."

"Whatever!" Raja giggled. "I almost cursed him out, but when I looked up into his face and saw who it was I almost fell on that concrete for real."

"Who?" Justine breathed. "Raja, who was it?"

Raja closed her eyes, clenched her fists in the air, and squealed at the top of her lungs, "*Calvin Jennings!*"

Justine's mouth flew open. "Oh, Raja. Oh . . . Raja. Calvin? You ran into Cool Cal?"

Raja nodded, beaming. "Yes, I did. And he is still as cool as they come. Fine, sweet, funny. The whole nine. You know the deal."

"Damn," Justine said, disbelief and joy on her face. "I bet seeing him made your day. Hell, your year. What's he doing in New York?"

"His attorneys are negotiating a new contract for him. His father took sick and he wants to be closer to him. If things go well, he'll be moving to New York before next season."

Justine took a sip of her malt. "Speaking of his father, Raja, did you guys talk about what went down between you?"

Raja shrugged. "A little bit. You know, I don't usually admit this, but I might have been wrong about Calvin, you know."

"Please!" Justine waved her hand. "Of course you were wrong about him! I tried to tell you that twelve years ago. You had the finest man in the neighborhood, Mr. Most Likely to Succeed, and you kicked him to the curb like he was a scrub. That man loved you, Raja. He really, really loved you."

Raja nodded slowly, her eyes sad. "Yeah, I know. I loved him too. With all of my heart. I've never met a man who made me feel as good and as special as Calvin did, and of course like you, he knows my entire past. But after that drama with his father messing with that white woman . . . and the way Calvin defended that old man even though his poor mother was brokenhearted to find out that her husband had been creeping on her so hard that he had a half-white baby . . ." She shuddered and shook her head. "All that just hit too close to home for me, Jus. I just couldn't get with Calvin defending his father, who was too old to be creeping anywhere anyway. Plus, my mind started messing with me, and I ended up constantly wondering if Calvin had the same appetite for white meat that his father had. It was too much for me to bear. I had to let him go."

"But did you have to cuss him out and cut him completely off too?"

"Yeah, Jus. I did. Because any man I give my heart to has to also have my complete trust. If I have to second-guess where his attractions lie, then that means he's not worthy of me."

"That's true," Justine agreed, "but Calvin never gave you the slightest reason to think he was anything except totally in love with you. You took the sins of his father and placed them on his head. The sins of *your* father too. And just look at how things turned out. You're still alone, single, and looking for Mr. Right. Maybe you already had him."

"Maybe," Raja mused. "But still . . . I have to feel a hundred percent sure about a man if we're claiming to be serious about each other. That's why I'm so uneasy about this Julian-Kelly situation. Something tells me Julian is not being straight with me about his feelings, and if that's the case, he's a big-ass fraud and his pillow talk is full of lies. I can't get with that."

"Uh-huh," Justine replied. "But what about Calvin? Is he married? Does he have any kids?"

Raja brightened. "Girl, no. Not married, and not in a serious relationship either. You know I asked all that. And absolutely no kids. He claimed he hasn't fathered any children in all these years because the only person he's ever wanted to mother his offspring has been me! Girl, can you believe that?"

Justine laughed. "Hell no. I can't even see you sacrificing those proud thirty-four Ds to breast-feed a baby. But whatever. Where's Calvin staying? Are you gonna see him again?"

"He's at the Hilton Hotel. Living large, honey. And yep. We're going out tomorrow night. He's picking me up at my place. He wanted to get with me tonight, but I pretended I already had a date and said no."

"Raja, you need to stop. Why you fronting with that man already? For all you know, running into him is a sign from above."

Raja sighed. "I know, Justine. But I needed time to think before seeing him again. Time to bounce all this off you, and to put it into perspective. No lie. My heart didn't recognize a single one of those twelve years since I saw him last. For me, it was like yesterday, and just his smile brought back all the love and the goodness of our relationship. Damn. Just think. If it wasn't for his nasty-behind father, we could have been married with a couple of kids by now."

"His father didn't break ya'll up, Raja. It was your lack of trust that did it. And if you don't mind me calling it like I see it, I think you've been chasing his phantom for the last twelve years. Manipulating men, controlling relationships, all in an effort to protect that place in your heart that you only thought Calvin had wounded."

Raja sighed again, then nodded. "Yeah, I'm guilty as charged. Confused to the max, too. But Calvin swore to me over lunch that his feelings about me haven't changed. He says he's never so much as dated a white woman, and swears that just like he told me years ago, he's not attracted to them that way."

"Well, hell! Didn't I tell you that a decade ago? See, you're just too hardheaded, Raja. You could have saved yourself a lot of time and worrying if you would have listened to what me and Calvin were both trying to get through your thick skull."

"Well, you were probably right, Dr. Justine. So what now? You gonna start charging me by the hour to sit on your couch and shrink my head?"

Justine grinned and took another sip of her drink. "Not hardly, girlfriend. My love is free."

The first thing Raja did after arriving home was check her voice mail.

"Hey, Raja, this is Calvin. It was wonderful seeing you today, lady. Just talking with you made me feel good, and I can't wait to see you again tomorrow. Be cool, lady. Bye."

If she grinned any wider she knew she'd split her face.

Feeling ecstatic, Raja pranced into her bedroom and sat on the edge of her bed. The suit she'd worn to work that morning was wrinkled from lying around in it on Justine's sofa, but Raja didn't care. It would get dry-cleaned that weekend and would look next to new in no time. She was reaching down to unstrap her black designer shoes when she saw it.

A cell phone.

Julian's cell phone.

On the floor, partially hidden by her chenille spread.

Retrieving the phone, Raja stared at it for a moment, then set it on her nightstand. She should probably call him to say she'd found it, but after the afternoon she'd just spent with Calvin, she wasn't quite ready to speak to Julian. She'd just give it back to him whenever she saw him next.

After kicking off both shoes, Raja removed her jacket and pulled her shirt over her head. Standing in her bra and skirt, she eyed the cell phone again, and without a second thought she picked it up and pressed 123 to retrieve the three messages that were indicated on the screen.

The first two messages were mundane. Bids, contracts, city council meetings, and so on and so forth. But the last message was quite a bit more personal, and certainly more interesting.

Raja listened intently as Kelly's panicked voice flooded her ears.

"J . . . listen! We have a problem. Natalie Huffman is on to you and Victoria. We need to plan some damage control. Call me!"

Raja's eyebrow went up as she replayed the message again.

Victoria? According to Kelly, Natalie Huffman was on to Julian and somebody named Victoria. Who the hell could that be?

Frowning, Raja racked her brain trying to recall a sista in Julian's world by the name of Victoria. She came up blank. Her first thought was to call Julian and relay Kelly's message, and then demand an explanation. But the longer she thought things through, the less inclined Raja was to show her hand.

Nah, she told herself. *Chill, sister. This ain't the time to break. Don't let him peep your hold card.* Instead, she saved the message as new and put the phone away.

Twenty-four

Fresh from the shower, Raja was slathering her brown flesh with Jafra's Royal Almond Oil and mulling over Kelly's cryptic message to Julian, when the phone rang. "That's probably him now," she muttered under her breath and frowned. "No doubt he's desperate to get his hands on his precious little cell phone."

But with one glance at the caller ID, the frown fell off her face.

"Hello," she said, regaining her cool and adjusting her tone until it was deliberately low and sexy.

"Calvin Jennings here," boomed a deep masculine voice. "I'd like to speak to the gorgeous little brown-skinned beauty who blessed me with her presence over lunch this afternoon."

A surge of heat shot through her body and Raja blushed so hard the oil on her skin tingled warmly. "Well, that would be me," she said smoothly, a small tinkle of laughter slipping from her lips. "How are you, Calvin?"

"Not good," he replied. "I came into town on business, but I can't seem to concentrate. I can't think straight, and my chest has started to ache."

Raja frowned. "My, my. That doesn't sound good at all. Maybe you're coming down with a cold, huh? You'd better hope it's not a summer flu."

Calvin laughed on the other end. "No, baby. I don't have the flu and I hardly ever catch a cold. My problem is far simpler than that."

"Oh, really?" Raja toyed in return. "Well, what might your problem be?"

"I've missed you, Raja. And I can't get you out of my mind. My head is swimming with thoughts of you, and while the little bit of time we spent over lunch was wonderful, it just wasn't enough. Can I see you tonight?"

For once, Raja couldn't think of a thing to say. Calvin had always been so forthright about his feelings for her. He'd always given her the deepest compliments without a bit of reservation, and she'd loved him for that openness. For not being the kind of man who was guarded about his feelings or who tried to make his woman guess about who was more in love with whom.

But after years of dating and playing the field, and especially in light of her current relationship with Julian, who was less than expressive about his feelings unless they were in the bedroom, she didn't know how to respond to Calvin's unabashed adoration.

"I had a great time with you today as well," Raja said gently, "but I told you I had a previous engagement tonight, and we agreed to meet tomorrow, remember?"

"Yes, I remember. But that doesn't mean I'm satisfied. Look, I know I can't just breeze into your life and expect you to drop your friends or neglect your relationships on my behalf. I just thought I'd take a chance and see if your plans might have changed, or if you'd finished up your evening early and wouldn't mind coming back out to have a few drinks with an old friend."

Raja smiled into the phone, reveling in his earnest plea.

Well, she thought quickly. There was no way she would admit that her "previous engagement" consisted in gushing about him over sweet potato pie with Justine. "Actually, I am free for the rest of the night. I met with someone earlier and took care of some business, so drinks sound wonderful. Where should we meet?"

Less than five minutes after she'd hung up from Calvin's call, Raja's telephone rang again. She'd gone into the bathroom to reapply her makeup, and her heart fell at the jingling sound of the phone. Maybe Calvin had changed his mind. She was surprised at the level of disappointment that filled her with that thought. She hoped he wasn't calling back to cancel on her. Raja rushed into her bedroom and over to the phone, then stopped dead in her tracks.

Julian's home number glared at her from the caller ID.

She stood there fuming and staring at the phone as it rang, thoughts of the mysterious Victoria in Kelly's earlier message plaguing her. To hell with Julian, she thought, letting the telephone ring. She knew why he was calling, and it sure as hell wasn't to declare his love for her. No, Julian wanted his cell phone back, and that was the only reason he had bothered to dial her number.

The phone stopped ringing. "Raja." She listened to his voice as his call rolled over to her voice mail. "Hello, darling. You must have turned in early after that episode we had last night, huh? It was wonderful for me too. Making love to you is always beautiful, and I guess you turned me out so badly that I forgot my cell phone at your place. It's like a lifeline to me, of course, so I'd like to stop by and pick it up tonight. I really hope you get up to get a drink of water or something and check your messages, because I need that phone back ASAP. Thanks, love. Good-bye."

Raja sneered at the telephone, disgusted. "Oh, so you need your phone back, huh? Well, fuck you, Julian. And fuck you, Kelly. And you too, Victoria. Whoever the hell you are. All of y'all can kiss my cute black ass tonight because Miss Raja is going *out!*"

An hour later Raja was being driven to her destination by a local car service. Since she'd just showered before Calvin's call, it was simple work to complete her body pampering and slip into a tight pair of Donna Karan jeans and a white cotton shirt that fit snuggly around her jutting breasts.

"Calm down," she told herself. She was so excited about seeing Calvin that her heart was thudding and she couldn't get to him fast enough. They'd agreed to meet in the lounge at Calvin's Midtown hotel, and while traffic wasn't very heavy, the trip was taking longer than she could bear.

In the dimness of the backseat, Raja checked her perfect nails, rubbed her lips together to ensure the evenness of her gloss, and tossed her hair until it settled around her shoulders. Everything was perfect except that nagging little thought in the back of her mind, the one she kept trying to sweep into her subconsciousness, the thought of Julian that just wouldn't leave her alone.

Fuck him, she thought. Her intuition had been telling her Julian wasn't being honest with her for weeks, and after hearing Kelly's message she smelled a rat stinking to high heaven.

Calvin was waiting in the lounge when she stepped into the hotel, and at the sight of his bright smile and broad shoulders Raja beamed. That man could sure 'nuff hang an outfit. He was dressed in a pair of casual brown slacks and a white polo shirt, and his thick, well-toned physique made him seem like the most powerful man in the room.

"Wow," he said, opening his arms and gathering her in his embrace. Raja felt small and protected huddled against his rock-hard chest. "Raja, baby, you always could wear a pair of jeans. You look great, sweetheart. C'mon." He took her hand. "I reserved a booth. What would you like to drink?"

Raja smiled. "Ginger ale would be fine."

Calvin grinned. "You still don't touch alcohol, huh? Great. I admire you for taking such good care of yourself, Raja. I really do."

"Thank you," Raja replied, eyeing his physique. "I can tell that you still take really good care of yourself, too."

Calvin led her over to an intimate booth and waited until she was sitting comfortably before taking a seat across from her. He signaled to the waiter and ordered a ginger ale for her and a large glass of orange juice for himself.

"So," Calvin said. "We caught up some earlier, but I want to know more. Like, how you spend your free time, what are some of your hobbies, you know. It's been a lot of years, Raja. Let's fill in a few of the blanks."

She laughed. "Sure, I'd love to. Tell me about some of the cities you've visited. The places you've been. In your line of work you've probably seen half of the world."

"Oh, man." Calvin grinned, showing deep dimples. "You're

really good. I ask you to tell me something about you, and you redirect my question back at me. But okay. I'll tell you my life story because I'm really interested in hearing yours."

Fifteen minutes later when Calvin finished recounting his college days and giving her an insider's glance into the world of professional baseball, Raja continued to stare at his sensuous lips.

"And now," he concluded, "Mama is dead and Pops is sick, so I'm thinking about coming back to New York to be closer to him."

Raja nodded slowly.

"I wanted to tell you," Calvin continued, "that no matter what you thought about my father and what he did, he always liked you. I know you hated him when he stepped out on my mother with Allison, and for a long time I blamed him for making me lose you. But honestly, Raja. No matter what his choices were, they were his to make, and I just couldn't stop loving my daddy just because he made a mistake. Hey, we all make them."

Raja thought about Julian and shuddered inside.

"You're right," she said. "I was very immature back then. I took what your father was going through and made it a template for the pain my mother and I had experienced in our lives. I just couldn't help it. White women have been the bane of my existence, Calvin, and I couldn't seem to stop thinking that since you defended your father so strongly and refused to condemn him, maybe you were hiding a secret desire for white women as well."

Calvin shook his head. "Never, baby. Never. I have too much pride in my sisters and too much love for my black self to ever go that route. I don't knock those who do, but believe me, I've never had a single desire to get with a white girl. I'm just not built that way, Raja. Brown skin turns me on. Drives me crazy, in fact. And nobody except a sister can speak my language and understand my flow. It's all about black women in my life. Black mothers, sisters, aunties, and future daughters, and that's not just a promise, it's a fact."

Raja just stared at the wonder sitting before her, kicking herself for being blind to his heart all those years ago and wasting so much precious time apart from him. "So," she asked softly, "who's the lucky sista in your life right now? And how could she let a man like you travel to this big bad city all alone?"

Calvin shook his head slowly. "As I said earlier, I was in a relationship not too long ago, but it's over now. She was a lovely young lady, but there was something missing. Something that before coming back to New York, I thought I'd never find again."

Raja lowered her gaze, unable to meet the intensity in his.

"And how about you, Raja? Who's the lucky brother whose time I'm trying to beat tonight? Who's taking care of you in this dog-eat-dog world? Whose shoulder are you leaning on? Whose arms are keeping you safe from harm?"

Raja was speechless. It had been so long since a man cared so much about her life, about her world, that she'd forgotten what it felt like. Julian was always busy with some political thing or the other, and when he wasn't running around the city or holding "meetings" with Kelly or conferences with the press, he was distracted by the rigors of his position and found it hard to relax. Forget about taking care of her or providing a shoulder for her to lean on. That just wasn't happening in their relationship.

She trusted Calvin, and knew he'd give her his best advice regarding her situation with Julian, and she was right on the verge of blurting out his name when a tiny voice told her to be still. Why ruin a great evening by injecting negativity into the groove?

"Um," she stammered. "My relationship is not that deep, actually. It's not really important enough to discuss." She took a sip of her ginger ale and smiled. "Nice band here tonight. Do you still love jazz?"

Calvin held her gaze for a second longer. He didn't look ready to let the conversation go, but Raja knew he respected her, and she was glad when he finally nodded.

"Yes. I still love jazz. Would you like to dance?"

Their dance turned into a romance as an hour later Raja found herself naked in the bedroom of Calvin's hotel suite, soft music flowing through the semidarkened room. She moaned on the soft sheets as Calvin's muscled body loomed above hers.

"Oh, baby." He kissed her neck and breathed in her scent. "I've waited so damn long to taste you again." His tongue swirled along her collarbone before sliding south to the peaks of her eager breasts.

Raja drew him toward her, nearly crying out loud as his lips found her nipple and sweet remembrance filled them both. She took his manhood in both hands as they explored one another, becoming reacquainted with each other's bodies and whispering their long-banked love.

The years that had separated them disappeared, and once again Calvin was making love to her with the utmost tenderness and passion. He was a giving lover, and pleasing Raja was also his pleasure. As they tangled themselves in the sheets it was all Raja could do to stop the tears of joy from falling from her eyes. She moaned and whimpered and sighed in ecstasy as every wonderful emotion long buried in her heart came rushing to the surface.

And the moment Calvin entered her, all of her pretenses fell away. Once again she was seventeen and in love with the most wonderful man in the world. She was soft and new, trusting and vulnerable, raw with longing and totally without defense.

"Give it to me, baby," Calvin urged as they climaxed together, his first and her third. Her body convulsed and the tears slipped free as his name fell from her lips. "I still love you, Raja," Calvin whispered into her ear. "And I want to be with you forever."

The night was still as Raja left the comfort of the hotel room and stepped out into the night. She'd slipped from Calvin's room minutes after he'd fallen asleep, and after stopping by the concierge's desk to order car service, she stood outside the hotel waiting and confused. Physically, she was more satisfied than she'd ever been in her life, but her heart was filled with more confusion than she knew what to do with.

Julian. Raja felt terrible for reducing him to an afterthought. Forty-eight hours earlier she'd been eager to marry him and help him climb the political ladder to success. And now she was slinking out of a high-priced hotel after getting lost in the emotions of someone from her past.

She'd never do it again. She just couldn't. As complete as she'd felt in Calvin's arms, there was no way she should be doing to Julian the very thing she had accused him of doing to her. Yeah, she had enough class to be coming out of the Hilton and he'd been spotted slinking out of the Embassy Suites, but still. His wrong didn't make her right.

As she folded herself into the backseat of the hired car, Raja closed her eyes and sighed. She'd have to find the strength to tell Calvin she'd made a mistake. A way to make him understand that she was involved with a special man and that their night together could never be repeated.

As the car raced toward home, Raja sighed again.

Julian. Calvin. Julian. Calvin. Calvin. Calvin.

Calvin.

Twenty-five

The moon was making a slow getaway beneath the heavy clouds as Julian neared his home after laboring with union chiefs and leaders from the "We Teach to Reach" educators association. He never knew teachers could be so demanding. Perhaps if they were as determined in getting their students to score higher on standardized tests as they were securing a pay raise for themselves, Julian reasoned, there would really be "no child left behind." He left the arduous meeting with only one regret. Not saying what he wanted to regarding a referendum that would have tied the teachers' salary increases to the rate of increase achieved by the students was eating at him on the inside like a cancer. If he was elected, that referendum was going to receive the highest priority, whether teachers ranted about it all the way to the Supreme Court. It was about time that someone be held accountable for the children, Julian thought with a deep sigh. It was about time.

As the traffic dissipated, Julian swerved over two lanes to take a right on Ninety-second Avenue. He was surprised to find Kelly standing directly in front of his building, with her arms crossed over her chest and her high heels impatiently patting against the concrete. She was still wearing her business suit, hair pinned up in the back, and an exasperating expression on her face. "What the . . ." Julian mouthed while sliding down the driver's-side window. "Hey,

Kelly," he shouted from the car, idling near the curb. "Let me pull into the garage. Meet me at the door." Kelly nodded as if she couldn't find the words to articulate her agreement. Julian eyed her suspiciously while whipping into the narrow entrance of the underground parking structure.

Kelly was so worked up that it struck Julian with an uneasy feeling. The look plastered on Kelly's face had him wondering what could have been so jacked up that she couldn't discuss it with him over the phone. That's when he realized that she'd probably been calling his cell phone but couldn't reach him so she was forced to show up unannounced instead.

"Sweetheart, come on in and sit down," Julian offered when Kelly leaped through the door huffing.

"No, I'll stand!" she objected adamantly. "I couldn't sit down if I wanted to. Too much drama to take it sitting down," Kelly added in a short and snappy manner.

Julian blinked his eyes, trying to keep up, but his mind didn't readily grasp what she was talking about, so he just stood there silently until Kelly's wide-eyed expression begged him to say something, anything. "I have a fishy suspicion that I'm supposed to know what you're talking about and why you were out front a minute ago stomping a hole in the sidewalk, but I don't."

"Damn it, Julian, this isn't the time to stop checking you voice mails," Kelly spat, mad at the world in general but aiming her anger at Julian. He gulped before he spoke.

"Yeah, I, uh, misplaced my cell last night. It's probably here some place." Julian turned his head to disguise the embarrassment of leaving it at Raja's while imagining a second round of "build your own sundae" as she waved her behind in his face. When all of the guilt had passed, he faced Kelly, then loosened his silk necktie. Kelly motioned toward the wet bar, suggesting that she needed a stiff drink before she could get to the bottom of what had her about to have a conniption in Julian's living room. He caught on and poured her a tall glass of rum and Coke to soothe her mind. "Now then, what's all this about anyway?"

"Hell, I don't know where to begin," she answered, sipping from the cool concoction. "Listen, you're not going to like this but the jig is up. Natalie Huffman is on to you and Victoria. Don't ask me how she did it but she knows everything and that bitch is threatening to run the story on the front page." Kelly caught her breath as Julian began to lose his. She wanted to feel sorry for him, but there was no time for that. Something had to be done, and fast. "What in the hell are we going to do about it before the wheels come off this freakin' campaign and expose you like some ghetto deadbeat baby daddy from the projects?"

Stunned, Julian lowered his head, to think. "When . . . how did all of this happen?" was all he could muster to say.

Kelly started pacing the floor and wringing her hands. "I dunno, but she knows everything and I do mean everything. When I finally called her back, she agreed to hold off for twenty-four hours, but don't go thinking it was a random act of kindness that initiated it. That trifling cow wants to save it for Friday's early addition so the entire city will be salivating over her dirty byline by lunchtime."

There was nothing Julian could say to that. Kelly was right, but then she always was. He threw his head back and stroked his chin. "Okay, okay," he sighed. "This is the worst-case scenario, but we should have seen it coming. I need to defuse that story before it plows one helluva mile-wide trench in my life." He lowered his head and stared deeply into Kelly's eyes. "We'll come up with something," he said, the wind taken out of his sails.

"Damn straight we will!" Kelly agreed. "You're going to come clean and make this right before it goes so wrong that we can't survive it. If this shit hits the fan, it'll cause such a stink that they'll be holding their noses in Poughkeepsie."

Although Julian didn't care for the way Kelly browbeat him, he knew she was correct. He sighed again and sat down on the sofa. "I'll talk to Victoria. It's the only way. I don't have any idea how she'll take it, but I'm not going to jeopardize my daughter." Julian hung his head in his hands. His world was splitting in half and he could see it happening. It wouldn't have been fair to allow Brittany's world to dissolve in the process. The child he hadn't met was in danger of being hurt over learning about the father she didn't even know existed. Doing the right thing long before now had crossed his mind, but there was no way he planned on rattling old bones before the election. Julian had hoped that a sensible resolution would have presented itself until it was certain that his past and future were about to collide in grand fashion. With resolve shrouding his face, he shrugged. "If it has to blow up, I'd better be the one lighting the fuse. At least that way, I can warn my child and shelter her from the blast somehow," he concluded finally. "Brittany didn't sign up for this and I won't let her get jammed up in the middle. I can't let it go down like that. There has to be a way to keep the lid on this until—"

"Until what, Julian?" Kelly asked bitterly as if she had as much in the kitty as he did to lose. She shifted her weight and stood back on her heels. "You might not want to hear this but I'm going to lay it on you anyway. As your campaign manager and as your friend, I'm advising you to put your foot down and stomp a mud hole in Victoria's ass if you have to. If you don't handle this, but quick, Natalie Huffman is going to be the end of your political career. You know as well as I do that New Yorkers love only one thing more than their celebrities and that's their celebrities' dirt. You'll help that nosy reporter sink your ship if you don't head her off at the pass with both guns blazing."

Kelly was so angry because she cared about Julian in ways he couldn't have imagined. Her love was boiling over and for the first time since admitting to herself that she was head over heels for him, Kelly didn't give a damn about letting it show. Only thing was, Julian didn't recognize it. He assumed that her duty-bound responsibilities were guiding her steps.

The surprised look in Julian's troubled face said what he was thinking. "You mean, an ambush?"

"Damn that, I'm talkin' a good old-fashioned Gotham City–style jack move," Kelly insisted wholeheartedly. "Steal that goat Natalie's thunder. Check it out. If someone has the goods on you, it'll work out in your favor if you spill the beans and put your slant on it before they do. That's right, spin control in its purest form. Think about it. Two people, two perspectives. Which one is the public more apt to believe?"

"The first one they hear," Julian answered correctly. "A bald-faced lie is almost believable when it precedes a watered-down truth. Kelly, you're a genius." He hopped up from the sofa and paced circles around Kelly with the renewed vigor of a man preparing to do battle. "I have an idea. Can you stay for a while?" he asked with pleading eyes, praying that she didn't have another man to run off to when he really needed her.

"Uh, sure, I can stick around," she replied, unsure but interested in what Julian had cooked up in that complicated head of his.

When Kelly agreed that she was willing to hang for a while, Julian slapped his hands together. "I was wondering, since you're here, would you mind working on a plan of action? I mean, if you're up to it." Kelly nodded agreeably, hiding a smile behind her concerned expression. "Great. That's why I love you," he told her, slowing his stride to embrace her. "You've always been there for me, Kelly, unwavering and at my back. We need to map it out from beginning to end, if this spin-control idea is going to work." Julian was glad that she decided to stay. The thought of having her close to him, for an extended period, appealed to him unlike ever before.

As he stood close enough to smell Kelly's expensive French perfume, which he had sent her from Paris on her last birthday, Julian's heart rate quickened. He licked his lips and unleashed a cordial grin while noticing how her eyebrows were perfectly arched and her breast cleavage conjured up the same visions he'd had the other day, of Kelly's toned body glistening with sweat during a sordid sexual tryst with some dude she'd kept hidden. However, these new visions had him playing the role of sexual stud and her sweat was caused by the blissful hours of unbridled passion he'd put on her. Julian liked the new visions a lot better. So much in fact that he wanted to "go there" when he never would have conceived putting it out there on the table in the past.

"Before we get down to business, I wanted to tell you how grateful I am to you for everything that you've done. I know I've said it before but it warrants saying it face-to-face. You've put up with my bullshit, dealing with all of the political foolishness, and you're still as cool as a West Indian island breeze," he complimented her with the utmost sincerity. As Julian coddled Kelly, surprised at how much he wanted to undress her and serve up years of suppressed and deferred yearnings, he collected himself and backed off. Kelly had closed her eyes, waiting on what she had longed for as well, but Julian pulled a fast one. Instead of kissing her, he shook the devilish thoughts from his head, backed away, and chucked her on the arm playfully like a big brother proud of his kid sister. "My girl," he gushed. "Where would I be without a friend like you? Now let's get down to business."

Suddenly, Julian retreated to the bar to pour himself a much-needed drink. He had come so close to making a huge mistake, he reasoned. Women came and went but good friends were a rarity. Kelly was one friend he wanted to keep, despite how seriously he felt about making love to her. Speaking of women coming and going, the burning question of Raja's sudden change of character danced around in Julian's mind before he'd taken a sip of the aged cognac swirling around in his crystal goblet. Why hadn't Raja returned his calls? he contemplated, knowing her well enough to see that it was out of character. That wasn't like her, he thought, but what really bothered him wasn't so much that something may have happened but that she hadn't called him back. Why, Raja, why?

Twenty-six

Light reflected off the Schwartz crystal clock on the corner of her desk and Kelly smiled at the expensive indulgence. At the store today, she'd reasoned that she deserved something special for working with those asshole athletes who thought just because they could handle a ball they ruled the world.

She adjusted it again, the timepiece her most expensive bauble yet. There was more of this to come if she and Julian really teamed up. They could both retire extremely wealthy people. Separately or together.

The thought dragged her slowly back through time to last night. Julian loved her. That much she knew. But behind his invasive questions about her private life had been personal, real emotion. It was as if he'd wanted to locate the intimate spaces and fill the darkness.

When emotion had shaken his voice, her mouth hit the floor, but her heart, damn it, had done one slow somersault after another.

Julian was screwing with her head, getting all nostalgic and silly. He loved her, but he didn't really *love* her, did he?

The indecision left her wondering.

How could he? Julian was dating the craziest, most beautiful woman in New York, and that was Raja Jackson. Yeah, her attitude sucked and she had a vicious jealous streak, but she was still model beautiful. Men adored her, and with good reason. Raja was smart, sexy, educated, and ambitious. She'd made the most of her assets and now they were working with the power of a microchip. She didn't have the scars of life embedded in her soul. With the right man, Raja could conquer the world.

Knowing all this didn't stop Kelly from wondering what a personal life with her best friend would be like . . . if she indulged the fantasy that had been nudging at her all day . . .

Julian walked into Kelly's office, midday, his eyes as alluring as the first day she'd met him. He inclined his head, the gesture bringing her to her feet. Meet me halfway, *his eyes said, asking her to join him not just on a for-the-moment journey, but something more substantial. Something permanent.*

"Where's my kiss?" he asked.

Though she'd kissed Julian hundreds of times, that didn't stop Kelly from wondering what this kiss would mean. Friendship or finally something more.

Somehow she knew . . . His eyes told her just before their lips met . . . this time meant the beginning of forever . . .

A resounding screech and thud of cars crashing into one another on the street below thrust Kelly out of her daydream and back into the figures on her desk.

Who was she kidding? Daydreaming was for teenage girls. Julian wasn't going to get into office by himself.

Kelly grasped her pen and trained her thoughts to the finer details of the fund-raiser. The time was growing near when they wouldn't be able to accept donations anymore, and she wanted to maximize the days they had left.

Dialing the Terrace on the Green, she asked for Aspen, the event coordinator. Getting his voice mail, Kelly ran down her final list. "I want magnolias on each table, gentle lighting, one wireless microphone, a Sommelier like you promised, and the jazz group Pieces of a Dream. And—"

Her phone beeped and Kelly glanced at the caller ID. Julian.

Her heart fluttered. What the hell was going on? How many times had that brotha called and her body didn't react at all?

"Aspen, I'll have to get back to you." She clicked over, feeling a little breathless. "Hey, what's up?"

"You talk to Raja?"

"She's not taking my calls, why?"

"I misplaced my cell phone and I can't get in touch with her."

A light rain burned the heat off Kelly's fantasy, leaving it hazy. The stinging slap of reality left her aching from the pain and Kelly embraced it. This emotion she understood.

"I haven't talked to her."

She lost her voice for a moment, unanswered questions racing up her tongue, but never leaving. *Did you sleep with her? Was she good? Is that what you want?*

"Julian?"

"Yeah, baby?"

How could he twist her heart and not hear it screaming? They weren't intimate like that.

"Why not just cancel the damned thing, get another one, and keep on going? We've got too much ground to cover the next couple days to be worrying about something so insignificant. In fact, you need to call the company right now. You don't know who's got it and using it to potentially make you look bad."

"Damn, that's why I love you so much. You're thinking before I can fully comprehend what day and time it is."

Knowing he was unaware that he'd just stomped on her heart-strings, Kelly had to hold her breath from equal levels of yearning and piercing pain.

"Why aren't you running for mayor?" he asked, his spirit lighter than she'd heard in days. Raja must have really broken him off a piece.

"I curse too fucking much," Kelly said, a bark of laughter shooting from her mouth. *Too harsh*, she silently chastised herself. Her phone clicked again and she eased it from her ear, then back. "Hey, I've got to go. I've got Tavis Smiley's producers on the line. What you up to later?"

"Kell's Bells, you're funny as hell. I'm not doing anything. Call me. Damn! No phone. I'll call you."

"Please get another one right now. Bye."

Kelly clicked over. "Kelly Taylor."

"Ms. Taylor this is Warren from the Tavis Smiley show, and I've got two dates for you. August fifteenth and September eighth. Which do you prefer?"

"Neither. It has to be this month. The primary is in September, barely two months away, so he has to do his appearance before the upcoming debate. Otherwise we'll be talking a whole different interview."

"Unfortunately we don't have anything available."

"Come on now. This is important news. How much exclusive time are you giving the councilman?"

"Six minutes."

That was a lot, but Kelly wanted Julian on for the entire show. He had a lot to talk about and he needed that time, but she wouldn't push on that. "How about this, for the entire twenty minutes I can get Tavis an exclusive with Barry Sanders—but that's if you get Julian in by next Thursday?"

Warren sounded like he was hyperventilating. "How are you going to get billionaire recluse Barry Sanders to come on our show? When he retired from Wall Street, everyone heaved a sigh of relief."

"Barry's a friend. Did you know he's creating his own stock exchange called Blackstreet? It's a stock exchange for blacks to learn how to invest their money in businesses that support our communities. His plan includes teaching people how to own their own businesses and how to create their own financial empires."

"I've never heard of such a thing. Kelly," Warren said, his voice conspiratorial, "I'll kiss your toes if you get him on our show."

Kelly laughed. "And Julian?"

"Oh, he could have next Thursday, Friday, any day he wants, if we get the exclusive with Mr. Sanders."

"I'd like Wednesday."

"Done. Just send me a signed agreement with Sanders for an interview with Tavis. I'll get back to you to firm up the Wednesday evening with the councilman. Talk to you in twenty-four."

Kelly shook her fist in victory and placed another call. "Barry, it's time to go public with Blackstreet. I just booked you on Tavis. You're going to do this, Barry. Remember our agreement? I spin your affinity for secretaries and you owe me one colossal favor. It's payback, baby, and this won't hurt you one bit. Thank you, dear. I'll call you later with details."

Kelly hung up feeling confident, her thoughts gravitating to Natalie. After their recent conversation Natalie hadn't contacted her again. What was that witch brewing?

Julian needed to be straight with the public about his daughter instead of this secret shit. Damage control was never as effective after the fact. And beating Natalie out of a byline was extremely attractive.

Kelly replayed her run-in with Victoria, surprised that the ivory-skinned woman hadn't made her second crucial move.

Had Julian kept this from Kelly?

He had good reason if he did. She'd botched his last confidential communiqué. Why should he feel comfortable sharing his secrets? She had to make this up to him. She picked up the ringing phone and pressed it to her ear.

"Hello." The person coughed, then settled back down, his voice painted with tobacco juice. "This is Ronald Harper. Kelly Taylor, please."

Kelly ran in circles, holding the phone away from her ear. She stopped smiling long enough to blow a quiet stream of air through her pursed lips.

"This is Kelly, Mr. Harper. What an unexpected surprise. How can I help you?"

"I've been following Julian's career and I like what he's done for our community. I want to make a sizable donation to his campaign."

Kelly's Blackberry buzzed and she read an e-mail from Bree. *Go to the* Times *Web site. Exceptional news for Julian.*

"How sizable?" she asked, as she logged on to the *Times* site and was shocked to see they'd raked in three top endorsements from the teachers' union, the waste disposal union, and from the local teamsters.

"The maximum limit allowed."

She sat forward. "Why?"

Harper coughed and cleared his throat. "Blake saved my ass this past year without knowing he was helping me. I have properties all over the world, but here in New York my investments are a bit top-heavy. When the waste company went on strike, I couldn't continue to build. The new laws regarding commercial trash removal about crippled me. I couldn't bring in a private company. Blake negotiated the end of the strike and that saved me millions and kept my crew on schedule. Donating to his campaign is the least I can do."

"All right, Mr. Harper. We certainly appreciate your generosity. Would you be interested in having drinks with me tomorrow evening?"

"Now that's an offer I can hardly refuse. However," and his voice dipped toward intimacy, "I heard that you and Blake were more than business associates."

Kelly squirmed in her chair. "Where'd you hear that?"

"It's the word on the street."

"Don't believe everything you read in Natalie's column, Mr. Harper."

"Trust me," he said, his voice edgy. "I have no interest in Natalie Huffman, now or ever again."

"Again. That sounds interesting."

"It's a well-kept secret, but I've had intimate dealings with Natalie and that mistake won't happen again."

Intrigued, Kelly glanced at the computer screen with the endorsements, but couldn't help but concentrate exclusively on the conversation. "Again? Look, Mr. Harper, we don't do business with people who do business with Natalie Huffman."

"Then I'm your man. A lifetime ago, I was married to Natalie Huffman. Leaving her was the best thing that ever happened to my life and that of our children."

Kelly was stunned, her mind working. Perhaps Harper was the key to shutting Natalie down. "Mr. Harper, you are definitely an interesting man. Let's meet tonight at Café Blondie, seven o'clock."

"See you then."

Twenty-seven

"So the bottom line is," Raja said quickly, interrupting Phinius's long-winded monologue and directing her gaze at each member of the international banking department as they sat around an oval table in a large conference room, "we need to pursue our high-end accounts more aggressively, and once they've firmly committed to a relationship with us, we have to trample the competition by providing our clients with medium-cost, top-notch banking services." She raised an eyebrow in a gesture of finality. "Agreed?"

Murmurs of concurrence and nodding heads abounded, but Raja hardly noticed as she rose from the table and slipped her Palm Pilot into her designer purse. Meeting adjourned! She wasn't about to spend an hour in a fifteen-minute meeting. Not today. Raja grabbed the small stack of reports that Phinius had prepared, then exited the room before the rest of the staff were even on their feet.

Her stiletto-pump shoes clicked rhythmically across the floor as Raja made a dash toward her office, her hips swaying beneath her sexy, but appropriate Greystone skirt. Calvin had called. Well, she admitted, blushing inside, he'd done more than called. He'd called and asked if he could stop by her office when he was done with his morning meeting, and ever since she'd hung up the phone her body had been running warm with excitement.

She stopped in the ladies' room and splashed cold water on her wrists. There was no way in hell she wanted to be in that damn meeting when Calvin arrived. He couldn't give her a definitive time other than between twelve and one, but she planned on being available whenever he got there.

Raja checked her hair and makeup, but really, she was perfect, as usual, and didn't even need to reapply her lipstick. She'd just dried her hands and stepped out of the restroom when she heard her name being called.

"Raja!"

Calvin!

Her heart leaped as a grin split her face. She forced herself to turn around slowly, when every ounce of her wanted to spin around like a five-year-old and jump into Calvin's strong, honest arms.

But it wasn't Calvin's perfect teeth and broad smile that greeted her.

"J-J-Julian?" Raja stammered, shocked to the core. "What are you doing here?"

Even in her disbelief Raja noted Julian's well-groomed appearance and suave air. She could see why Kelly would be attracted to him. Any woman would. Julian's outer package was clearly all that, but something inside told Raja his insides were filled with lies.

"Good to see you, baby," Julian said, closing the distance between them with three long strides. "As always, you look great."

Raja studied him. Damn. Did he want his cell phone that bad? He'd never just "dropped by" her office before, and Raja knew from years of experience that whenever a man showed up unannounced on a woman, somewhere shit was stinking.

She smiled and led him into her office and closed the door. "You look great too, Julian. And likewise, it's good to see you." She put her hand on his arm. "But is everything okay with your campaign? Are you feeling well? What brings you into the bank today?"

They were standing close enough for Raja to read his thoughts, but she was caught by surprise when his hands encircled her small waist and his nose sank into her flesh, nuzzling that spot he loved at the base of her neck.

"Yummm," Julian murmured. "I just needed to touch you, baby.

To feel you. You smell delicious. How about I treat my special lady to a nice, intimate lunch?"

Raja pulled away, her mind racing with thoughts of Calvin.

"Oh!" She glanced at the clock. It was close to twelve. "Lunch? Oh, Julian. As wonderful as that sounds, I just couldn't." She gestured toward the stack of papers she'd just set on her desk. "I'm bogged down with accounts today, sweetheart."

She couldn't believe the look of disappointment that fell across Julian's face.

"Aw, baby," he said, his voice deep and sexy. "Can't you spare an hour to spend with your man?" He took her face in his hands and slowly massaged the back of her neck with his fingers. "I know I've been busy lately, but I don't want you to feel neglected. I have a few free hours right now and I'm choosing to spend them with you."

Raja forced herself to smile up at him with shining eyes, but all the while her heart was pounding as she considered what would happen if Calvin was to show up while Julian was molesting her in her office.

"How sweet!" she exclaimed as if delighted. "It's great to know I have such a place in your heart, Julian. It really is."

"You have the number-one place in my heart, Raja," he said seriously. "We both agreed that we want this relationship to move to the ultimate level, remember?"

Raja remembered. She just wasn't sure if Julian was being honest when he'd declared his feelings for her and talked about their future together. How could he be a straight-up righteous brother if he was trying to play her and Kelly at the same time? And no matter what Justine said, there was something going on between the two of them. If it wasn't yet a physical thing, it was damn sure an emotional thing. Raja suppressed a small shudder as she maintained her smile. Julian was a damn liar, and so was Kelly. They were both trying to play her.

"I remember everything you've ever said to me, Julian," she answered, slipping out of his embrace coyly. "I remember all the promises you've made, and how you say you feel about me as your woman too."

Julian spoke earnestly. "So have lunch with me, Raja. I'm hungry. No, starving. Let's sit down to a meal together and talk more about our relationship. More about our future. Let's try and sort things out and understand our feelings more fully, okay?"

Hell no, Raja thought. She planned to be right where she was when Calvin arrived, and not even Julian's sugary words could sway her. The funny thing was, she couldn't understand why Julian had deceived her. If he wanted a slouch like Kelly, he could have had her a long time ago. Neither of them needed to bring her into their sordid little game. It just wasn't right.

"You know how much I'd love that, don't you, baby? But I just can't get away today. Maybe you can come back tomorrow?"

Julian frowned. "This is so unlike you, Raja. I thought by surprising you with an offer of lunch it would make you happy. Please you. Excite you. But you seem a little distant, baby. Distant from me. Why?"

Raja shook her head prettily and sighed. "Not distant, Julian. Just distracted. You wouldn't believe all of the nonsense that I have to deal with at this branch. It's getting so bad that I'm thinking about requesting a transfer."

"That bad?" Julian asked, and Raja saw real concern in his eyes.

She sighed again. "Like you wouldn't believe. Remember that white girl, Phinius, I told you about?"

Julian nodded.

"Well, just like a typical white tramp, she's at it again. This time she's got her claws in Darren the brother who works here in the accounting department. I swear." Raja crossed her arms under her breasts and fumed. "She's a black man slayer. I don't understand how these weak brothers keep falling for that type of crap. They feel so inferior to white men that they're in awe of them. They seem to think that by getting with a white woman they can come up to the white man's status, when it's really the white man who needs to come up to theirs."

"Maybe she really likes this guy," Julian offered.

"Not even," Raja seethed. "For one, he's married. For two, she already has a black boyfriend—who she stole from a sister who works at our sister branch. And for three, she has absolutely no respect for black women, let alone for the black men we give birth to and raise into manhood. The only black men that white women like her are fit for are those dumb-ass NBA players who dish out all their money just to be seen with them. Then they act all confused when she 'accidentally' gets knocked up and they end up with a half-white baby and a disgusting amount of child support to pay each month." She glanced at Julian and shook her head. "Trust me, Julian. Black men like you are rare. I'm glad you're so attracted to black women. It says a lot about your character, and about how much you love your culture, your ethnicity, and yourself."

A look of pain crossed Julian's face, and Raja was on it.

"Oh, I'm sorry for going on and on when you've already said you were starving! Please—" Raja ushered Julian toward the door. "You've got to get yourself something to eat, Julian. There's absolutely no way I can join you, but I don't like seeing you hungry, so go grab a bite to eat."

"Then can I see you later?" Julian insisted.

Raja agreed. "Sure. Later would be fine."

"Your place? Eightish?"

"Eightish is fine. But hold up a minute." Raja reached back and retrieved her handbag from her desk. She extracted Julian's cell phone and smirked. "I don't think you want to wait that long for this. I'm sure you've *really* missed it."

"Right!" Julian took it quickly. "I can't believe I forgot to ask for it!"

"Yeah," Raja said, her voice crisp and dry. "I can't believe you forgot to take it home with you in the first place."

Julian pulled her into his embrace. "Thank you, baby. I appreciate you holding it for me." He lowered his open mouth to hers and sought out her tongue, kissing her deeply as he circled the tip of his tongue deliciously along her lips. His hands slid from her waist down to the roundness of her hips and back up again, the tips of his thumbs brushing her nipples as his mouth pressed hotly against hers.

It was Raja who broke contact first.

"Okay." Julian grinned. "I apologize for that. I know this is your place of business, so I'll respect that fact. But I can't wait to see you tonight, baby. Eight o'clock, right?"

What the hell? Raja screamed inside. That kiss was hot, but Julian had to go! For all she knew Calvin could be walking through the bank's doors at this very minute, and there was no way she could risk the two of them bumping into each other.

"Yes," she said, regaining her composure long enough to reach up and dab away a smear of black rose lipstick from Julian's bottom lip. "Eight o'clock."

Julian was barely out of her office when Raja collapsed into her chair, her legs and arms akimbo. *Calm your ass down*, she told herself, taking deep breaths. This was no time for an anxiety attack, and for the first time ever, Raja conceded that she was getting old. Slowing down. Her game wasn't nearly as tight as it once was. How tight could it be if Julian had slipped up on her blind side and nearly frazzled her with his enamored kiss? Maybe it was time to settle down and get married and have a bunch of babies, because juggling Julian and Calvin was beginning to feel too much like standing in the center of a congested highway and praying the trucks wouldn't crash and hit.

Her phone rang, scaring her upright. It had to be Calvin calling from the front desk, and if so, he'd just missed Julian.

"First American Bank. Raja Jackson speaking, how may I help you?"

"Well, hello to you, Miss Jackson!" came the chipper voice. Definitely not male, definitely not black, and definitely not Calvin.

"Hello," Raja replied. "How can I help you?"

"Well, I think the question is more like how can we help each other!" The caller laughed. "This is Natalie Huffman, columnist for *The New York Weekly*. I'm writing an article about the upcoming mayoral campaign, and profiling a few people who are important in the lives of our candidates. It seems as if you've become a necessity in the life of Julian Blake of late, and I'd like to interview you to give the public a glimpse into the softer, more personal side of the man who has the greatest chance of moving into Gracie Mansion."

Raja could barely think. "Um . . . wh-when? When would you like to interview me?"

"Today," Natalie said firmly. "It's a last-minute story idea that was pitched, and unfortunately my deadline is tomorrow morning at nine. Can we meet for drinks tonight? Say, around six? I only have a few questions and I promise it won't take long."

Raja thought quickly. She got off work at 5:30 and she had agreed to meet Julian at her place in Montclair at 8:00 p.m. That didn't leave much time for her commute home or for her to change clothing before Julian arrived, but hey. She'd worked more with less before.

"Fine. I'd love to. And yes, I can do six."

Natalie laughed. "Great. Let's meet at Iridian's Restaurant and Jazz Club. Do you know where that is?"

Raja smirked. She was a native to this city and knew it like the curve of her own hip. "I'll find my way," she said.

"I'll be sitting at the bar," Natalie said. "And wearing a bright red shirt and white slacks."

Raja said good-bye and hung up. Natalie Huffman wanted to interview her! So much was happening at one time! She thought about her trifling ex-friend Kelly, and how much it would hurt her to see Raja's name linked with Julian's in the press.

Yeah, she'd give Natalie an interview, all right. And put an end to that "unnamed beauty" nonsense about her on Julian's arm. Natalie Huffman might not know it, but she was about to give the world a treat. All of New York would have the privilege of knowing the name of the woman whom Julian professed to love. And Natalie had better spell it right too. The name was Raja Monet Jackson, and after *The New York Weekly* got a hold of it, not even Kelly would be able to forget it.

Twenty-eight

Raja's vacant expression kept flashing in his mind as he climbed into his car. While checking the messages he'd missed, he reflected on the subtle way she'd backed out of his embrace. By the time the last voice mail ended, Julian concluded two things: that he hadn't missed anything important while estranged from his cell phone and that trouble was brewing inside the woman he'd just begun falling in love with. As he pulled into traffic, he glanced at his diamond-studded Rolex and sighed. "Like I don't have enough things to worry about."

The short drive up Fifth Avenue would allow him to think of what awaited him at his next stop. Before Julian knew it, a valet attendant was standing outside his car beckoning for him to unlock the door.

"Sir, are you checking in?" the uniformed kid asked once Julian snapped back into the present.

"Uh, no," he replied. "I'm here to visit a guest. Keep it near the front for me."

"Yes, sir," the attendant gushed when he noticed the ten-dollar tip resting in his palm.

Julian peered up at the broad Embassy Suites sign. He shook his head as it occurred to him that it looked much larger than it did when it had loomed ominously behind his photo in the newspaper.

He couldn't shake the unnerving feeling that he was making the same mistake twice. There was no way around it. Victoria was holding all the cards and if he wanted to see them, he'd have to play the hand that misfortune dealt. Like it or not, he was in up to his neck against a stacked deck and praying for aces.

As he rapped at Victoria's suite, the knot in the pit of his stomach began to twist and turn. Thoughts of Raja, wrinkled sheets, and their future together had long since been put on the shelf. He'd need all of his faculties if he stood a chance to battle the tiger on the other side of that door. The last time he had entered her den, he scarcely escaped without wearing her claw prints up and down his back. With bated breath, Julian promised himself that he'd be more ferocious the next time he traveled into the wild. When she opened the door, scantily clad in a pale blue silk robe, matching the color of her steely eyes, and nothing else, he realized immediately that he'd better have his A game or expect the same result as before. Shamelessly, Victoria let her eyes wander over his Italian navy blue three-button suit like a lioness that hadn't eaten in weeks. She was leering at Julian, and it was obvious that she had made reservations to have him for dinner. "Mmmm, tasty," she moaned sensually. "Come on in," said the spider to the fly.

Like a bronze statue, Julian stood in the hallway contemplating. Sure, it was a trap, but he had to fight his way through it if he wanted to end up on top, instead of on the bottom with his pants around his ankles.

"Really, you couldn't expect me to be stupid enough to come in there and the only thing standing between you and me is a yard of imported silk," he said, biding his time. The way Victoria was undressing him with her eyes answered that question in grand fashion. Not only did she think he was stupid enough, she had the wherewithall to prove it.

"Look, Julian. Either you can come in and get what you came here for or we can debate the future of your illegitimate child through the doorway." Victoria glanced down at her loosely fitting robe with a firm set of implants popping out. "Obviously, I have nothing to hide."

Julian weighed his options briefly, then took a deep breath.

"What if Alex was to bust in and see you like that . . . in front of me?" he asked wearily.

"That would take some doing. See, he's in Atlanta, about six states away," Victoria replied, annoyed and horny. "Not that you care but I'm getting a complex standing here all fresh and showered up. You know I never could stand rejection. Perhaps you'd better make up your mind before I forget the whole thing." Victoria stepped aside, allowing room for Julian to enter before he came to his senses and bolted in the other direction.

After Julian acquiesced, he lowered his head, slid both hands into his pants pockets, and slinked inside the luxurious suite. He'd put up a good front but both of them knew it was a foregone conclusion that Victoria always got what she wanted. Once Julian had stepped inside her lair with the door slammed behind him, it was clear that he had glided way past stupid as it was earlier suggested. There was no doubt about it, he was a damned fool.

"You sure that Alex isn't planning to drop in to check on that honorable wifey of his?" Julian asked, peering from side to side as if he expected someone to spring out of the closet.

"I told you, he's far . . . far away. He's bringing Brittany up to the Big Apple so she can see what all the fuss is about. Alex wants the family together for the debates. You know, the whole putting on a good show for the press sorta thing. Although, he'd better get here quick because I'm curious to see if all the fuss I'm hearing about you is warranted. Neither of us is getting any younger but I'm still good for three rounds." Victoria unfastened her sheer robe and approached her prey. Julian sneered, after taking a gratuitous look at her last birthday present, and then took a calculated step backward. "Uh-uh, don't be scared," Victoria cooed, southern girl style. "I won't bite, maybe nibble here and there, but I won't leave a mark."

"Hold on, this is low, Victoria. Even for you," he snarled. "I consider Brittany a part of my family too and I plan to protect her with my life if need be."

"Save that for the reporters, Julian," she spat back, her hands resting on her narrow hips. "If you were that concerned about Brittany, you would have stepped up and made it clear to her in the very beginning. It's a little late for grandstanding now, don't you think?"

Venom gathered in the back of Julian's throat. He was mad enough to spit nails. "This is nothing but a game to you! I love that girl. I always have. Sure, I made the mistake of letting yo silly-ass daddy keep me from her. I regret that but I'll have to live with it. That might not make a damned bit of difference to you and I'm determined to become a big part of her life if she'll let me, but I will not let you use her to get at me or drag her through the mud so your trusting husband can back-door his way into the mayor's office."

"You've got your nerve!" she shouted, standing firm on her legs and drawing her robe around her. "If you were half the man you're pretending to be, we wouldn't be in the mess we're in. You were scared shitless when that silly-ass daddy of mine punked you into hitting the road with your dick in your hand." Victoria huffed and turned away in disgust, leaving Julian to look the silly ass now. "I can't believe I thought we had a chance." She chuckled, wiping her tears. "I guess I'll never learn."

Julian was torn. He didn't know what she was talking about as her confession seemed to fall from the sky. Thoughts of embracing her passed quickly through his mind, but he battled against them. She had been a friend, after all. "Victoria, what are you saying?" he asked eventually.

Turning to face Julian, Victoria sniffled. "You mean you can't tell that I'm still in love with you? God, Julian. I've been throwing myself at you since I got here. I guess my aim isn't as straight as it used to be."

"I . . . I didn't know," Julian answered, with surprise shrouding his face. When nothing else came to mind he decided to play it honest and right down the center. "I can't say that I feel the same way about you and besides *you're married*."

Victoria chuckled again, this time like a drunken housewife at her wits' end. "Oh, that? I'm leaving Alex. The divorce should be final about forty-eight hours after the election."

Needless to say, Julian was even more shocked than before. "I'm speechless," he sighed. "Victoria, you and me . . . that was a long time ago. We were young and—"

"Yeah, tell me about it." She laughed sarcastically. "And I was white, you left that part out." Suddenly, the drunken housewife sobered up. Victoria dug her nails in and wouldn't let go. Julian should have seen it coming and ducked. "Funny, how time doesn't come close to healing old wounds. Come to think of it, you haven't changed at all. You look the part, all grown up, but you're still the same old coward who hopped the first thing smoking when your back was up against the wall fifteen years ago." Victoria's eyes floated to land on Julian's in a devious manner. She unleashed a devilish grin and bit down hard. "As a matter of fact, you weren't man enough to deserve this pussy in the first place."

Julian was chuckling then but the joke was on him for getting involved with Victoria on her terms. "I should have figured as much. You can't get your way so you resort to being the crass bitch your silly-ass daddy raised, huh? I'm outta here!" He headed toward the door with long, measured strides and Victoria coming up fast behind him.

"Hit the road then, you coward!" she hissed. "Get the hell out! Run, punk! Run like you always do when things get a little hot." Julian wrested the door open and flew through it. "You're weak, Julian. Weak!" she yelled down the long hallway. "If you can't be man enough to handle this, I will. I'll tell it allll!"

Julian heard Victoria's rants loud and clear but he refused to look back and address them. As he neared the elevator, other hotel guests were stepping on. When he saw their faces gawking back at him, he knew they had heard every word as well. Too embarrassed to ride down, he hit the stairs all the way to the lobby floor. His blood was boiling. "To hell with it," Julian barked, much to the chagrin of the hotel manager seeing to a group of Japanese businessmen. He was willing to face the music Victoria had decided to groove to. It was high time to dump the dirty laundry and sort through the funk. There was only one thing left to do, call Kelly and prepare a press release before Victoria, or Natalie Huffman, for that matter, beat him to it.

Twenty-nine

The words on Julian's "coming out" statement ran through Kelly's mind, garbled and confused. She'd been rewriting it for hours until she just couldn't think straight. Never one to give up, Kelly numbered the last lines and started reading the statement from the beginning.

I feel it necessary to announce that a private matter from my past has fallen into the wrong hands and will become a public issue. Before this matter is presented to the world in the wrong manner, and to protect all parties involved, I feel it prudent to speak up about it and explain the circumstances. Sixteen years ago I was an undergraduate. Sometime later, I was informed that a brief union produced a child. I was stunned but my child's mother and I decided that it was best for her to raise the child with her then new husband as their own. Throughout the years I have faithfully sent child support and hope that one day when my daughter is ready, she and I will develop a beautiful relationship.

I am making this matter public because in today's world private matters are no longer private and innocent people can become hurt by the insensitivity of others.

I can handle the scrutiny of the public, but my daughter should not have to answer questions about the actions of her parents from

years ago. I ask everyone to leave her alone, and if you have questions
about my life, campaign, or where I stand on issues regarding New
York that are not answered on my Web site, call me at my office.
For everyone involved, thank you for your respect and attention.

Kelly reread the letter and felt as if something critical was missing. Unable to put her finger on it, she felt herself drifting to sleep and forced herself to sit upright.

Her chin itched, the beginning of stress bumps dotting the smooth surface.

Life had gotten too complicated and she had reached the burnout stage. But this announcement superseded everything Julian had done politically to this point, and if it wasn't handled correctly, it would end his career.

Kelly thought of all the scandals that had befallen powerful men like Bill Clinton, Marion Davis, and Kobe Bryant. From sex to drugs and more sex, these men and many more had stumbled, but not been brought to their knees by their actions.

Julian would overcome this personal and political hiccup, and if it was handled properly, he could still win.

Bree walked in. "It's late, almost nine. You about ready to go?"

"No," Kelly sighed. "I have to edit this press release again and notify the media of Julian's press conference."

Bree walked back to her desk and returned with her calendar. "What press conference?"

Kelly closed her computer and stood. "Let's talk about it over dinner."

"Your treat," Bree said with a straight face.

"Oh, hell no. You just got a bonus. If anything you're paying for me."

Her assistant shrugged. "All right, but you only get one appetizer. I know your greedy type. I can't afford to feed you and myself all the time."

Kelly laughed as they locked their office and headed down the elevator, Bree's droll humor a welcome change. "For someone who didn't know anything about public relations and campaigns before coming to work here, you sure are comfortable talking junk."

Bree exited the elevator, her four-inch heels only making her as tall as Kelly's shoulder. "I'm a quick study. Why is Julian in trouble?"

Kelly gave a noncommittal shrug. "Iridian okay with you?"

"Sure," Bree said, following Kelly to her car. "Afterward, I can get the subway and go home."

They drove in silence the four blocks to the restaurant and Kelly turned her keys over to the valet.

Inside, the nightlife was chilled, the after-work crowd thinned to those who didn't have anyone to go home to and those who just didn't want to go home. Kelly and Bree were seated by a glass-covered wall, Kelly's favorite spot. Listening ears would be kept to a minimum. She sat facing the crowd as Bree settled in across from her.

She ordered her drink and food at the same time and Bree followed suit. The waitress delivered the drinks and drifted away, leaving the two alone.

"He's not gay, is he?" Bree asked.

She chuckled. "Thankfully not. But he's got a child and Natalie Huffman is on to him."

"So what?" Bree asked. "Who doesn't have kids? Known or unknown?"

"This is a little different. His daughter is fifteen years old and—" Kelly took a drink of water. "She's Victoria and Alex Nixon's daughter."

Bree blinked rapidly. "Well, he's a politician. He doesn't believe in doing things small, does he?"

Despite Bree's cool response, Kelly felt as if a load had been lifted from her shoulders. She hadn't realized how stressful keeping Julian's secret had become. "No, but this could destroy his immediate political dreams for the obvious reasons."

"Because Victoria's white?"

"Yes, and because Julian's constituents are predominantly Black and Hispanic."

"I would think the bigger political bomb is that the men are adversaries *and* related. That's the trip of this whole scenario. How do we spin that?" Bree asked.

If only Bree knew, Kelly thought.

Their food was delivered while Kelly contemplated how much to tell her assistant. Kelly didn't want to dog her best friend and she didn't want to stand in judgment. Most of all, she didn't want Bree judging Julian harshly. The public would formulate their opinions soon enough.

For several days Kelly had been wondering the best way for Julian to make this announcement. The ideal situation would be to get the entire family together and make the statement as one. But the likelihood of that happening was slim to none. Especially since her talk with Victoria had ended with the woman announcing her intention to leave Alex and make one big happy family with Julian and her daughter.

No way would the men be sharing a podium. If anything, Alex would think Julian had continued his affair with Victoria over the years.

"Maybe duo press conferences," Bree suggested, twirling fettuccini around her fork.

"No," Kelly disagreed, knowing too much inside information. "It would be better if things were kept separate. That's cleaner."

"I'm thinking we shouldn't even have a press conference. I'd release statements to the media and do one controlled interview about everything. Why not on Tavis?"

"That's a very good idea. I'll run it by Julian. We don't have much time. I know Natalie wants to run her article Friday. I think we should hit the media Wednesday."

"That just leaves tomorrow to pull everything together. Is Julian booked on National Public Radio?"

"Yes, but for Friday," Kelly replied, her food forgotten. "He's on Tavis Wednesday. Have the press statement after the radio interview. I want to save the biggest bang for Tavis's show. That will guarantee great ratings and us great exposure."

"Always thinking ahead. You'd better eat. We're going to need our strength," Bree predicted.

After saying good-bye to her assistant, Kelly pulled her car to the exit of the restaurant facing the Lincoln Center. Now that rush hour had passed, fewer pedestrians filled the sidewalks, and those who were still out moved at a more leisurely pace. New York was experiencing a mild summer night and restaurant owners were overjoyed. Kelly pulled onto the street, but noticed an accident up ahead. Several cars had been involved and New York's finest had blocked the way, leaving drivers no alternative but to turn around and head back the other way.

Distracted from her earlier thoughts, Kelly put her car in reverse and turned around. Putting the gearshift into drive, she looked up and her heart beat double time.

Outside the Iridian were Natalie and Raja!

Mouth agape, Kelly stared at them as they walked together talking, ignoring the attempts of an eager doorman to earn a tip by flagging them a taxi.

She slowed and cars behind her blared, but the women ignored the traffic noise, engrossed in their conversation.

This isn't good, not at all, Kelly thought following at a snail's pace.

Julian had to make his announcement within the next twenty-four hours. Or he'd lose everything.

Thirty

Cradling the receiver between her shoulder and her ear, Raja kicked off her shoes and took a sip of lemon water, then sighed into the telephone. "Justine, I'm serious as a heart attack. Hell, I wish I was lying. Natalie and I just had drinks at Iridian's, and I nearly flipped backward off my bar stool when girlfriend dropped that little bug in my ear."

"Raja, stop!" Justine squealed. "I just can't believe it! I never would've suspected Julian of having a secret daughter."

Raja smirked. Her head had been reeling so badly from the news that she'd barely made it back to her apartment in one piece. "According to Natalie Huffman he has a secret daughter and a secret white woman fetish, too. I tell you"—she put her friend on speakerphone and set the receiver in its cradle—"if what she says is true, he hid that mess real good. A white lover? I never would have known. Every time we made love he'd constantly rave about my beautiful brown skin, swearing up and down that he loved my rich, earthen tone."

Justine's voice flooded the room. "But remember, that Natalie chick is messy, Raja. Digging up a scandal is how she makes her living. How do you know she's telling the truth?"

Raja shrugged, then sat down at her vanity table. She began straightening her toiletries even though they were already perfectly organized and aligned. "She can't be, Justine. She just can't be telling the truth. For one thing, Julian is far too smart to allow someone to get that kind of dirt on him, and secondly, if something like that were true, he would be the first to announce it. The brother is politically savvy. He's running for office. There's no way he'd let someone get the jump on him and hold a brick like that over his head. He just wouldn't."

"But," Justine interjected, "didn't Natalie say she had pictures of him coming out of the Embassy Suites, and isn't that where the white girl is staying?"

Raja fell quiet. She hadn't wanted to validate that connection, preferring to hold on to her initial belief that it was Kelly whom Julian had gone there to see, but hearing Justine speak it out loud made the truth irrefutable. "Yeah," she said finally. "Victoria is staying at the Embassy Suites, and she was staying there the night Julian was seen leaving. Natalie showed me a copy of her room registration and her current receipt. She also showed me a photo, Justine, and even though that child has blond hair and blue eyes, she also has bronzed skin and full lips, and that nose came straight off Julian's face, Justine. Right along with that pouty bottom lip and the dimple in her chin."

"Damn," Justine breathed. "So she looks like him, huh?"

"Like he spit her out. I played it off when Natalie whipped out a news file and showed me her picture, but deep inside I could tell right away that I was looking at Julian's child."

Justine made a sympathetic noise deep in her throat, and Raja sighed in return.

"I'm sorry things went down this way, Raja. I know how much you liked Julian and I wish he would have been honest with you."

Raja shrugged, knowing her friend couldn't see her. "I've been telling you all along that Julian hasn't been honest about things, Justine. I thought it was only Kelly he was digging, though." Raja pulled off her jeans and walked around the room in her panties and blouse.

"Maybe Julian was just afraid to share this with me, or maybe he was hoping his skeletons would stay locked in the closet and his political career would be safe. Or maybe, just maybe he didn't even know about his daughter. Remember, Justine, I was practically ready to marry this guy, and regardless of how I feel about this latest news, I don't see Julian as the type of man who would just abandon his child. Remember the kind of father I had? I'd never be attracted to a man who could do that."

"True," Justine countered, "but remembering the kind of father you had, you'd never be attracted to a man who was into white women either."

Raja shuddered. "Not knowingly, girlfriend. Not knowingly."

"Well," Justine said brightly, "let's look at the positives here for a moment. At least now you know your friendship with Kelly was good to go. Since it was Victoria that Julian was more than likely seeing at the Embassy Suites, you were probably wrong about Kelly wanting to get next to him. See, your girl didn't deceive you after all."

"Uh-uh, Justine," Raja said quickly. She stood and put her hands on her hips. "That's a load of bull. Regardless of what kid Julian has with whom, I know for a fact that Kelly has feelings for him, and I suspect he has feelings for her as well. I just think it was foul and low-down for Kelly to use me like that. She's known Julian for a long time. The two of them could have gotten together without involving me. I mean, damn. What if I was really head over heels in love with Julian? Girl, I could have gotten hurt!"

"So the thought of the two of them being together doesn't hurt you?" Justine sounded doubtful.

Raja sat on her bed, then lay back and stared at the ceiling. "Hell yeah, it hurts. Kelly betrayed me, and Julian tried to play me. They used me when they should have just left me out of their little cat-and-mouse love game."

Raja was on her feet again. "Jus, I gotta go. I need to get down to the nitty-gritty on this and find out what's really what."

"Where are you going, Raja Monet?"

"To get my straw straight from the horse's mouth. I'm going down to the Embassy Suites to talk to Victoria. I'll start there, and if I find out that Julian hid his relationship with her and knew about that little love child of his, then I'll know for sure that he's capable of lying to me about his feelings for Kelly."

"Don't bust up in there like you back on the block, Miss Jackson. I know you. You're probably snatching out your earrings and slapping Vaseline on your face right now. If you absolutely have to know, then maybe you should just call and talk to Victoria on the phone."

"Nope," Raja said, sliding her firm body back into her designer jeans. "We're gonna do this face-to-face, and somebody better be straight up with me or I'm coming up out of my Brooklyn bag."

It had taken every ounce of control she possessed to drive under the speed limit, but now that she was parked outside the Embassy Suites, Raja's feelings bounced all over the place. Taking the key out of the ignition, she frowned and shook her head. She couldn't decide if she was more hurt, more angry, or more humiliated. Just the thought that she may have been sleeping behind a white woman for all of these months blew her mind, no matter how long ago Julian had had this relationship. And if Natalie was right, then perhaps it wasn't so long ago at all.

Raja gazed at the twelve-story building and forced herself to breathe easily. Part of her wanted to rush into the hotel and confront Victoria for the truth, yet another part of her wasn't certain if the truth even mattered at this point. Whatever Raja might have had with Julian was surely over. If he wasn't seeing Victoria, he was certainly emotionally involved with Kelly, and either way she just couldn't tolerate that kind of dishonesty in her life. She could just imagine turning into her mother, always doubting and suspecting her man, never sure about his true intentions or his real inclinations. No. Never.

But you've lied too, a small voice nagged from inside. Yes, Raja admitted to herself. She'd been less than honest with Julian about her East New York upbringing and about her educational background, and true, she'd slept with Calvin and discovered hidden feelings she'd thought were long buried, but unlike Kelly, she hadn't consorted to betray a friend, and to her, that not only violated the girl-friend rules, it was low-down and dirty.

"Fuck it," Raja spat, then slid her key into the ignition and turned on her engine. Why go in there and harass a white woman over a black man's lack of good character? Kelly, Victoria, whoever. None of them were worth the energy or the aggravation.

"Just fuck it!" Raja screeched into the air, peeling out of the parking lot. She aimed her car toward where she knew a true friend, a brother of honor and truth, would be waiting. Yeah, Julian Blake could have whoever it was he wanted, and whoever happened to want him—as far as Raja was concerned, he was up for grabs.

Thirty-one

It was nearly 10:00 p.m. Julian worked feverishly in his office with the door closed. Tension was riding high from every imaginable position. Another call from the Teachers' Union proved unsettling as they propositioned several additional points of promise in an agreement to back him as their candidate of record. Julian considered what their association meant to him and then reluctantly agreed to meet each of their concerns if elected. Two of his biggest contributors asked for personal guarantees that he had his hands around the rumors circulating that his private life was getting out of control. Julian swallowed his pride and answered both queries with an affirmative "Yes, of course I do." Not to mention the Victoria mess and the impending press conference. His head was pounding.

When Julian's cell phone rang, he felt the muscles in his shoulders contract because he wasn't in the mood to deal with another fire blazing on the other end. Glancing at the caller readout, he almost managed a smile as Kelly's name flashed in blue illuminating letters. "Hey, Kell, I'm—"

"I'll give it to you straight, no chaser, and we'll take it from there," she said, cutting him off. "This deserves your undivided attention."

"How bad is it?"

"Very."

Julian squeezed his eyes shut and massaged his right temple. "Okay . . . give it to me."

"This evening, I had an after-work powwow with Bree."

"Yeah, so . . ." he baited eagerly.

"So, I saw Natalie Huffman all chummy with . . . Raja coming out of Iridian's Restaurant." She blew out a breath. "Now, it could have been nothing," she quickly added, "but it sure did look like a helluva lot of something. The bottom line is, Natalie Huffman and Raja Jackson don't mix. It can't be anything but trouble. I'm sure Natalie was trying to get as much inside information on you from Raja as possible. And . . . she may have spilled her guts about Victoria, just to see if Raja could substantiate anything."

He slammed his fist down on the table. The nightmares just kept coming.

"I would have told you sooner but I've been placing calls to see if anything concrete had hit the newswire. It hasn't, so whatever Natalie is planning to do must be rolling off the presses in the next run."

"I need to talk to Raja first. I have to try to explain things to her before she reads it in the papers. Maybe, just maybe Huffman didn't . . . Shit!"

"Calm down, get to Raja and try to work it out. I'll do what I can on my end." She paused. "I'm sorry, Julian."

"Yeah, Kell, me too." He hung up the phone.

As soon as he had taken a minute to collect himself, he punched in Raja's number at home and got her answering machine. After several attempts to get Raja to answer her cell proved futile, Julian grabbed his jacket and briefcase and dashed out of the office.

Julian called Raja's cell intermittently, on the way to her apartment. He was thinking of all the ways to undo whatever Natalie may have told her concerning Victoria. Prepared to do whatever it took to salvage the relationship with Raja, the woman he wanted to make a life with, Julian was champing at the bit to make it right. He wanted desperately to tell Raja about Brittany before she became national news.

Julian's heart was already racing when he pulled up in front of

Raja's building. The scene that caught his eyes as he parked the car caused it to thump like a steel drum. On the other side of the street, Raja was hugging his old friend Calvin around the neck with her lips locked to his like glue. Julian jumped from the opened car door and sprinted across the avenue. Venom coursed through his veins as he approached his woman in the arms of another man.

"What kinda shit is this, CJ!" he barked. "Huh? Is this what's it's come to? Ain't enough women on the West Coast? You got to come way up here and sniff around mine?"

Raja backed away wide-eyed, her hand covering her mouth. Then she tried to step in between him and Calvin to calm the waters. "Julian, please," she begged. "Don't make this worse than it is."

"What!" Julian answered, with so much animosity that it made Raja shiver. "You don't have a damned thing to say to me. After I heard about your little meeting with Natalie Huffman, I drove all the way over here thinking how I owed you an explanation. I was a fool to think you were ever worth my time." He took a threatening step toward her, then stopped, looked from one guilty face to the other. "You two make a fine pair," he said, sneering, and stepped to Calvin. "A fake-ass gold digger and backstabbin' no-game chump," Julian raged.

Raja didn't know what to do. She'd never seen this side of him and was afraid that he was capable of kicking it up a notch. She glanced up, noticing that many of her neighbors had begun peering out of their windows to take in the scene escalating on the sidewalk.

"CJ!" she yelled. "Talk to him. I don't need this happening outside my apartment."

"Raja's right, Julian," Calvin said, as calm as he could. He extended his hand to usher Julian inside the building so that the drama could be contained, but his gestures fell on deaf ears. "Let's go on up and hash things out like adults. Raja and me, we've been seeing each other. She didn't know that we were friends and I didn't know that y'all had a thing until you told me the other day."

"I see," Julian said, shifting his eyes back and forth between Calvin and Raja. "But you didn't let finding out keep you from tapping it, huh? Nah, that's one thing about you, CJ, you never could pass up an easy lay."

Several people from the audience, which had gathered to watch the fireworks, laughed at Raja after Julian had insulted her. She crossed her arms and sneered back at him, although she was wise enough not to address Julian directly.

"CJ, are you gonna stand there and let him talk about me like that?"

"He'd better mind his place before I loosen some of those store-bought teeth down his throat," Julian threatened. "CJ, you can't be crazy enough to get yo ass whooped over a conniving trick like Raja. I know that thing she does with her tongue is real nice but—"

Suddenly Calvin lunged at Julian with both hands outstretched. The crowd cheered as the men wrestled like bitter enemies. Calvin twisted Julian's arm and slammed him against a parked car along the curbside. The car alarm sounded, adding to the mayhem that embarrassed Raja to no apparent end. Julian spun away and then handed a solid jab on Calvin's chin. Like a house of cards, Calvin tumbled to the hardtop on his behind. Julian came at him again and Calvin dodged his furious blows, literally from the seat of his pants. Raja screamed frantically in the background, amidst chants from a riotous crowd.

The sidewalk brawl ended when sirens sounded and the police arrived and separated both men, disheveled, dirty, and bleeding from scraped knuckles and skin abrasions. The first cops to appear on the scene had to call for backup when the spectators turned disobedient. They refused to back up and allow the officers a chance to sort things out.

Julian couldn't tell whether Calvin had gotten a good shot at him or if one of the cops had sneaked in a punch or two during the separation, but he was bleeding from his nose nonetheless. As Julian huffed, he used his tattered shirttail to wipe the trail of blood away, and that's when he realized that an unmarked car idled in the street. The back window was lowered and someone had been taking photographs of the entire incident. Julian spat on the sidewalk again in disgust, although this time he tasted his own blood.

Calvin was arguing with one of the officers when a sergeant arrived to help straighten out the situation. He was ready to throw the hooligans in jail for public disorderliness until he recognized that one of the hooligans was Councilman Julian Blake. Since Calvin refused to press charges for assault, the crowd was dispersed and Julian let off with a warning.

Seething over getting involved with Raja and letting himself get worked up enough to fight Calvin because of her, Julian left the skirmish minus a long-term friend and a great deal of his self-respect. He hadn't felt so foolish in years, but the way Calvin's head snapped back when he was socked on the chin, and Raja's stupid expression when he let her have it in front of her neighbors, almost made it worthwhile.

Thirty-two

The chilled bottle of Pinot Grigio mellowed Kelly, momentarily allowing her to slip into the restful place between awake and asleep. This abyss should have guided her into the land of dreams, but instead she drifted, the babble in her head drowning out the sounds of New York City's ever-bustling streets.

Pressing her body into the center of the mattress, she strove to find a comfortable spot, then stopped. Forcing herself to rest negated the point of drinking the entire bottle of wine, something she hadn't done in years. Alcohol had never been her crutch for facing reality, but today, it seemed, she needed to bolster her diminished bravery. Sleeping alone in the center of the bed wouldn't fix what ailed her.

Out of habit she rolled to her right side, the full-length body pillow accepting the leg and arm she threw over it, but her mind and body warred. Ghostly memories of ten thousand yesterdays had stolen her peace.

It was time to deal with herself about the rape.

Kelly shifted to the right side of the mattress and looked into the mirror at the woman she was now.

She saw her face, smooth and bronze and strong. Her eyes, dark and wise and cautious. Her mouth, full and capable and oh so ready to offer what her body begged for.

Whispered words slipped from her lips.

I forgive you.

The lightning bolt crease struck between Kelly's brows, causing her nostrils to flare and her eyes to weep as guilt bound like old newspapers broke the bindings.

Accepting forgiveness for the anguish of lost innocence took time, and Kelly finally recalled little bits of the horror.

After the tears, the eighteen-year-old eyes of the child/woman looked back at her with vulnerability and yearning.

It's not your fault.

Kelly pushed to her knees and her hands rose, capturing her face. Chills raced over her body like a waterfall, the gesture endearing.

She quickly pulled off her nightgown and visualized the once garish bruises and touched each one in recognition of how they started and what they'd become.

They were hers, woven into the fabric of her life, yet not the whole of her being.

Looking into the mirror, Kelly saw both sides of herself, the older and younger, each seeking that last vestige of closure.

Their lips moved as one.

I love you.

Cool air washed Kelly's naked skin, as peace filled all her empty spaces.

Lying down on her left side, Kelly knew that she was now ready to share the center of her bed.

The Blackberry on her nightstand bleated, her house phone ringing too. Kelly sat up, reaching for the instruments, knowing before she was fully awake there was only one person who'd interrupt her sleep.

"What's up?" she answered.

"I'm in the hallway and my key is in your door. I'm coming in."

In all the years Julian had had a key to her home, he'd never used it.

"On my way," Kelly said.

Her feet hit the floor and she saw her bare image in the mirror.

Kelly didn't look away from the scars, yet they didn't hold her captive either.

She pulled on her satin negligee and had one arm in her robe sleeve as Julian walked through the front door.

"Kelly?"

Belting the waist, she walked toward him as his presence filled her space, large and masculine and affected. Frustrated anger billowed from him in waves.

This is bad, she thought and stepped out of his way and let him have the floor.

His navy blue Kenneth Cole suit showed signs of a scuffle, the tie stripped from the blue-and-white pin-striped shirt. But his face bore the brunt of his encounter, his cheek red and slightly swollen.

Kelly saw his red fists. Julian wasn't a street fighter.

"What the hell happened to you?" she asked.

Kelly considered giving him a drink, but didn't want to get off the couch where she'd drawn up her legs so he could walk.

"I saw Raja and Cal. Kissing. Cal and I got into it. Two idiots tussling over a woman. Raja was crazy. Screaming and carrying on. Hell, it was insane."

"Whoa. Cal, your friend, and Raja? She accused me of being with you and all this time she was stepping out. Damn." Kelly regarded Julian's remorseful expression. "I didn't know you cared so much to get into a fight over her—or anyone."

"I don't," he said, tightly. "My ego reacted like a typical jealous male. *That's my woman*," he mimicked. "The bitch of it is, I don't want Raja."

"Say what?"

Julian yanked off his suit jacket, tossed it onto the leather easy chair, and sank down on the couch beside her.

Kelly wanted to stroke his neck as he worked through his thoughts, but kept her hands to herself. Seeing him this way for anyone beside herself made her heart ache. She wanted Julian free and clear from the encumbrance of any other woman.

He shrugged his shoulders. "This sounds silly, but my feelings were hurt, like I'd been played. I'd confided in Cal about some personal things, including Raja, and then he turns up with her. I was being stupid." He looked sheepish. "We were photographed scuffling. The police showed up, and had it not been for the fact that they recognized me, I could have ended up in jail for the night."

Julian scrubbed his face with his hands. "Damn, that was stupid. This whole campaign is a ridiculous mess, one scandal after another, and I'm at the center of all of it. I swear, if I were a constituent and saw me, I'd think 'he's got too much drama to be running for mayor.' But I can't give up. Something inside me won't let go. This is crazy, huh?"

Kelly smiled, pointing to papers she'd been working on before going to bed. "Yeah, but we can fix it. If we have to stay up all night working on interviews for the morning news, we'll do just that."

"I don't love Raja. I never did."

Without hesitating she replied, "I know."

"How?" Pulling her feet into his lap, he moved his hand slowly up and down her leg.

The caress left her speechless until she collected her thoughts. "Y-you were always with me. If you were in love, she'd have been more of a priority."

Kelly stood up, the belt unwinding, her robe slipping open.

Julian fingered the white satin, creasing it into a fan between his fingers. "Your logic is impeccable as always and correct. I wanted to be where I was." The silence between them lengthened and before she did anything stupid, Kelly tried to maneuver around his feet.

Julian stretched out his legs, keeping her captive until she looked at him. "You won't give up on me, will you?"

Her heart raced. "No. Never."

Julian folded the belt end over end, looking into her eyes. "Why?"

"Because you're my best friend."

"And?" As he reached past her and set the length of folded satin on the table, his cheek brushed her breasts.

Julian's large hands captured her lower back, his face pressing into her abdomen.

Kelly's throat tightened, her eyes filled with tears as her shaking hands reached for his face. She made him look at her. "I love you. For a long time, I've loved you."

"I know," he said. "I love you too."

Although she'd waited her entire adult life to hear those words, Kelly wasn't prepared for the joy followed by passion that engulfed her.

"What now?" she whispered, touching him for the first time as an adult in love.

Julian didn't speak as he brought her down to straddle his lap. His mouth grazed her chin and Kelly leaned into him, seeking what she'd never given herself permission to have before.

Her hands slid up his shoulders to his neck and jaw, where Julian captured them. Slowly he kissed her fingers, then tilted her mouth toward his. The first touch of his lips against hers was soft and safe. He didn't seem to want to startle or push her too fast.

Kelly appreciated his thoughtfulness as the newness of their love abounded. Letting him know it was okay, she leaned in a little more.

Their chests met.

Julian snaked his hand behind her head and brought her closer. His mouth covered hers and the kiss deepened, conveying a passion she'd never known.

Urgency filled her and she couldn't help wanting him. She'd been in love with him since five minutes after they'd met.

Tonight they would consummate their love and she didn't care if it took all night, Julian would know she was the woman for him.

He slipped the satin robe from her shoulders and it slid to the floor. She tried to stay in the moment as he pulled down the thin straps of her negligee, but in one fleeting second insecurity snuck in. Tears slipped down her cheeks.

"You are the sexiest, most beautiful woman I've ever known."

Kelly stood up and let the negligee slide down her hips and pool on the floor with the robe. She stood before Julian bare—in body and soul. "This is me. All of me. Can you handle it?"

Sitting there in his expensive shirt and slacks, Julian didn't hesitate as he kissed the front of her thighs, her navel, and her breasts until she gasped with pleasure.

His hands and mouth made lifelong promises. Within minutes, Kelly lay with Julian in the center of her bed naked, his mouth sending her to new heights. "Make love to me."

"With pleasure."

Hours later, Kelly lay with Julian curled around her, feeling so sexy she didn't believe she'd ever need clothes again. "You think we can still be friends in the morning?"

He laughed, his hands cupping her breasts. To her surprise her nipple blossomed against his palm. "Oh yeah," he crooned. "We'll be better than friends."

She breathed unevenly. "Better than," she murmured. "How's that possible?"

"Just go along for the ride. It's going to be big."

He pulled her up and sat her on him until she felt as if she'd burst. With his mouth he claimed her neck, lips, and breast, then stroked her clit. A climax slammed into her and he gave her time to recover before moving inside her.

He smiled, sexy and confident. "The big ride is us. We're forever, baby."

Kelly swam in the pools of love in his eyes and prayed this feeling would last forever.

Thirty-three

The morning after making love to Kelly, Julian kissed her good-bye and headed off for home knowing that he'd have to walk the last mile alone.

During the drive home, Julian tried to remember why he wanted to be a politician. Fighting the cynical side of himself, he smiled when the memory of three hundred smiling families entered his mind. There was an older housing project set for demolition within a year to make way for a collection of high-scale high-rise condominiums. After catching the story on the late news one evening, Julian decided to do something about it. He'd met with the committee supporting fair housing for the city and in no time flat, his name was on the ballot for councilman. Julian won in a landslide and his constituency loved his hard-line take on doing the right thing. That was the beginning for him and he'd never looked back.

By the time he'd showered and changed into his favorite business suit, the gray flannel three-button number with thin pinstripes, Julian knew that he had at least three hundred reasons for getting involved. At 9:30 sharp, he walked out of the makeshift office at the old bakery on Fourth Street that served as his campaign headquarters. Every media outlet in New York was represented. Cameras rolled and reporters inched closer than they were given permission to. Someone from Julian's staff had been sent out beforehand to explain the order of business, which included him reading a prepared statement and a short question-and-answer session to follow.

Julian was calm as he stood firm and poised at the podium stacked with a bouquet of microphones. He said hello to all those in attendance, eager to hear what else he had to say, and then he methodically unfolded the sheet of paper that he and Kelly hoped would give him his say, despite how Natalie Huffman spun it in the morning newspaper. Julian glanced over the intro as he began to read.

"I would first like to thank you all for coming, although I do wish that it could have been under better circumstances." After some of his staffers chuckled uncomfortably, Julian sighed and folded up the statement before placing it into his breast pocket. "Okay. We all know why we're here today, so some cleverly written apology to those who believe in me isn't fair to them. I'll come straight from the heart, which is something I've done every single day since becoming a member of this great city's government, and I'm proud of that. I'm sure you'll hear soon enough that I was involved in an altercation with a famous ballplayer, who up until then was counted as one of my best friends. Needless to say, I'm not proud of those actions in the least. Friendship is priceless, I know that. I'm regretful to have lost a long-term friend in the process and displayed the kind of poor judgment I've frowned on my entire life. With that having been said, I apologize wholeheartedly and pray that you'll find it in your hearts to forgive my random act of stupidity. I can guarantee those of you who don't know me that I'm all for building relationships, not tearing them down."

Immediately, reporters started flinging questions and hurling accusations about the illegitimate child who was hinted at in the hot-off-the-presses *New York Weekly* column written by Natalie Huffman. "Is it true?" a tall blonde asked from the front row.

"Mr. Blake, would you like to comment on that relationship?" another quipped arrogantly.

"Where's the child?" another of them shouted from the back. "Where's the mother?"

Julian was relieved that neither of them had learned of the names

Natalie omitted from her story labeling him as a mad-dashing estranged father who secretly kept her out of his life as a way to keep her out of the headlines. At least Natalie was caring enough to leave Brittany's name off page 6, and Victoria's and Alex's as well. She couldn't very well expose them without smearing the child's name simultaneously. For that, Julian was eternally grateful.

When the barrage of questions continued to come at him, full speed, Julian straightened his silk tie and stared directly into the cameras to his left, where the top news affiliates were placed according to his directive. "I'm not here to discuss my personal life beyond what I've already shared. Not only is it not necessary, it also wouldn't be fair to a loving family and an innocent young lady whom I care a great deal about. Look, I do not have a drinking or drug problem, it's impossible for me to run around on a wife I do not have, so I won't make it a habit of discussing my personal life and allowing it to become the issue, when making this city a better place to live, work, and visit is. Allowing my personal life and those close to me to be used to sell advertisements on TV and in the newspapers wouldn't be fair to me or to them. Please don't let tabloid fodder overshadow the good I've done for New York and stifle my intentions of doing even more. If all this city really wants is to read about someone else's personal life and not what his accomplishments are, then I'm not the man for the job. If New York City residents are only interested in drama, there's plenty on the daytime soaps." The crowd chuckled. "But I don't believe that's what they really want. I believe they want a candidate willing to go to bat for them, to stand up for what they believe in, and I believe wholeheartedly in a person's right to privacy—not only my own but everyone else's as well."

"Councilman Blake, does this mean you'll continue seeking the mayor's seat? Do you believe you still have a chance to pull off a party nod?" the blond female reporter who'd opened the initial questioning asked, although this time behind a bright smile.

Suddenly Kelly appeared beside him. She'd been waiting behind the closed office doors watching the press conference on the small television set next to Julian's desk. Before answering the last question, he turned to Kelly and looked into her eyes swelling with love and admiration. Julian grasped her hand in his and smiled. "I'll be here to keep 'the thing, the thing' as they say. And we all know that *the thing* is taking care of business, *New York's* business. No further questions, thank you."

More dedicated than ever, Julian's trusty campaign staff members lined up to form a human barricade between their favorite candidate and the media hawks groping for sound bites. The parting shot from the press conference showed Julian and Kelly retreating casually hand in hand.

Thirty-four

Raja watched the news conference alone. Julian looked tired and withdrawn, and despite everything that had happened, she felt for him. It had taken a lot of soul searching and talking things out with Justine, but she'd come to realize that sometimes it was impossible to control what was in your heart, regardless of the situation you found yourself in.

Just take her and Calvin. There was no way she could have predicted the love they still shared, or even verbalized or acknowledged the fact that despite the time and distance that had kept them apart, her heart still belonged to him. Maybe, she concluded, Julian and Kelly found themselves in a similar position. Knowing both of them the way she did, she just wouldn't allow herself to believe that they deliberately set out to hurt her, and in a way she owed her newfound happiness to both of them. After all, if she had been as committed to Julian as she'd thought, and if the doubts about his relationship with Kelly hadn't nagged her so doggedly, there would never have been room in her life for Calvin.

"Okay, Julian," Raja said out loud, standing before the television with a wistful half smile on her lips. "Yeah, you played the sista a little bit there, but the sista played you too. And true, you shouldn't have led me on when you knew you had feelings for my girlfriend, but I have some pretty strong feelings for Calvin, too, and he's your friend as well." Raja grabbed her purse from the back of the chair and took a backward glance at the television screen before heading out the door. "No harm, no foul, Mr. Councilman. You're still cool in my book. Not cool enough for Raja Monet Jackson, of course, but you're great for Kelly. Let her worry about your proclivity toward white women. Calvin's favorite color is black!"

Thirty minutes later Raja was standing in Kelly's office.

"I saw you guys at the press conference—"

Kelly stood. "Raja, I know how you must be feeling, and I'm sorry. Neither of us meant to hurt you. I feel awful about everything that has happened, but I swear to you, I tried so hard not to love Julian. Especially after I introduced the two of you." She pushed a strand of hair out of her face. "I—I—I just don't know how things happened, but they did. I still don't understand it."

Raja held up her hand. "No, Kelly. Some things just can't be explained, and what we feel in our hearts is one of them. I'm sorry too. Sorry if I stood in the way of your true desire, because Lord knows I'll never let anything else stand in the way of what my heart craves most."

Kelly whispered, "Calvin?"

Raja nodded. "Yes, Calvin. The fight between him and Julian was terrible, Kel. I felt so torn, because even though I've long suspected the undercurrents between you and Julian, it hurt me to see two good friends going at it like that over a girl."

"I can imagine," Kelly agreed. "Just like it hurt both of us when we went at it over Julian. Again, Raja, I'm sorry."

Raja stepped close to Kelly and hugged her briefly. "Me too, but don't beat yourself up, Kelly. It would never have worked out between me and Julian. He's just not the man for me. Calvin is. And likewise, I'm really not the kind of woman Julian needs either. You are. Looking back, I can see that no matter what Julian told me, his heart was never with me. Maybe it's always been with you. Who knows? But the good thing is, you're both free to find out where your road can lead."

Kelly stood with her mouth open. "Do you really mean that,

Raja? I've never seen you give up so easily. You don't have a secret dagger hiding up your sleeve or something, do you, girl?"

Raja laughed. "Girl, no. No daggers. You guys have my blessings, so do it to the max. I've spent enough time harboring resentment and playing games. All of that is over. Calvin has asked me to move to L.A. with him, and I've agreed. I've been on the telephone most of the morning with a California bank that has a job opening that would be perfect for me."

"Girl, you're really going to leave New York?"

Raja nodded. "With a quickness. When love calls, you gotta answer. And that goes for me and for you too, Kelly. Take care of Julian. He has a rough road ahead of him politically, but he's the best man for the job. Besides, Calvin wants to marry me. He said we've wasted enough time apart, and he wants us to spend the rest of our moments together."

"I'm so happy for you, Raj. You deserve this."

"Thanks, Kel. For the first time ever, I really feel deserving of a good love. Calvin is wonderful, but best of all, he knows my heart."

"Thank *you*, Raja."

Thirty-five

At the window of her office, Kelly watched as Raja accepted a long hug from the man Kelly assumed was Cal, waiting outside the black limousine. He drew back and seemed to dab her tears before they climbed into the vehicle and were driven away.

Had Raja been crying? Why else would Cal have wiped her face? Crying seemed so out of character for Raja, but so was apologizing.

Kelly reflected upon their conversation, the haltingly delivered yet sincere words Raja had said. She'd listed her crimes, the accusations and the backstabbing—all acknowledged and then forgiven.

The agreement of understanding had come later. They wouldn't be friends any longer. She and Raja didn't hate each other, but with so much water under the bridge, they would never share the same level of girlfriendhood they'd once taken for granted.

Kelly returned to her desk, unable to work on the folders representing a new slate of clients, still thinking about the story Raja had given to Natalie.

Kelly had circumvented some of Natalie's glory by having Julian talk about the human side of himself, his success and his mistakes, reducing Natalie's thunder to a growl.

Earlier today Bree had mentioned that the gossip around town was that Natalie's job was on the line for her not bringing in "hot" stories. Kelly was sure that the call from Ronald Harper, Natalie's ex, may have helped that process.

Reaching inside the desk drawer, Kelly pulled out a manila folder and rifled through the pictures. They were of Julian's and Cal's fight. The photos had cost more than her mortgage for six months, but price wasn't an issue.

Julian getting into office was her only concern.

Staring at the frozen black-and-white images, she couldn't help but wonder, if Julian hadn't been fighting for love, why fight? He and Cal looked angry and Raja stunned.

For the first time in her life, Kelly felt jealous. Would Julian fight for her?

The question came, but the answer arrived with a blistering jolt. Of course he would. He'd had her back from the very beginning.

Kelly closed the envelope and returned the photos to the security of her desk drawer.

She didn't mind cleaning up messes if there was something good in the outcome. For Julian it was winning the mayoral race.

The photographer was three thousand miles away on a ten-day Kelly Taylor–sponsored vacation. No way would Natalie ever find him.

Kelly toyed with the corner of a client's folder, flipped it open, and was still unable to concentrate on the CEO of a major computer company who'd just been released from prison after serving time for insider trading. He wanted his life back and had hired Kelly to help him make it happen, yet it was no longer Natalie but Victoria who dominated Kelly's thoughts.

Now that she and Julian had exposed their truths, he was open about his standoffish relationship with Victoria, only she wasn't getting the message.

Victoria had tried everything from calling him, to leaving weepy phone messages, to threatening to expose their former relationship to the world.

Julian had continued to maintain the same level of responsibility regarding Brittany, but meeting Victoria privately was out of the question.

Although she didn't have a plan, Kelly knew she had to talk to Victoria one last time. She opened her Blackberry and dialed Victoria's private number.

"Victoria, this is Kelly, Julian's campaign manager. I'd like to meet with you today."

"I don't believe we have anything to say," Victoria commented crisply. "With the campaign nearing its end, my schedule is booked solid."

"Victoria, we need to clear the air. I'm sure there are things you want to say to me face-to-face."

She paused. "You're right," she said, the about-face a bit of a surprise. "I do have a lot to get off my mind. Be here in ten minutes." She gave Kelly the address.

Kelly arrived in fifteen. Victoria might think she had the upper hand, but not even she could control Manhattan traffic.

Kelly didn't know how she'd done it, but somehow Victoria had gotten hold of an office in a newly renovated brownstone on third. The smell of fresh paint greeted Kelly as she climbed the stairs to the richly appointed outer office. A college-age young woman greeted Kelly. "Hello, Ms. Taylor. This way, please."

Kelly followed her the ten steps to the double doors that had to be customized to fit the small frame.

The doors were opened and Kelly passed through only to hear them shut with the tiniest hush. She waited staring at the back of the white executive leather chair.

"Can we please cut the dramatics and get down to why I'm here?" Kelly stated, tired of the theatrics.

Turning her chair on the tip of her Chanel shoes, Victoria swiveled around. "You won't be here long. Where's Julian? It seems as if he has to have his women do all his fighting for him."

"You just made your first mistake. I'm not here to fight for Julian. I'm here to talk to you. Why are you chasing a man when you've already got one?"

"My husband and I are getting separated."

The surprise Kelly felt was short-lived. Looking at Victoria's face, she could tell the woman's mean streak extended well into not giving a damn about her husband's feelings.

"I'm sorry to hear that, Victoria, but some part of you must know that Julian doesn't want you. I'm not asking you to tell me anything, but if a man hasn't returned your calls, come by to see you, or responded to any attempt to contact him, he's sending a clear message that he doesn't want to be bothered."

"I am the mother of his child, damn it. He has to answer me. What if something was wrong with Brittany? I could be calling about anything and he's still ignoring me. He *has* to answer me."

Kelly watched the spoiled princess throw her tantrum and shook her head. Victoria wasn't behaving any better than a child who needed to be reprimanded. Except childlike adults often were allowed to act out until one person got good and damned tired and told them off. Kelly guessed she was that person.

"You're full of shit. How old is your daughter? Fifteen? I'll bet not once in her whole life have you called Julian for anything regarding Brittany. You want what you can't have."

"Because you got in my way."

"Not for fifteen years, Victoria. You had your chance, and Julian has made another choice. Grow the hell up and recognize what you have before it's gone for good."

"Julian was mine until you got between us."

"You're delusional, but that's fine. Think about this. You have a good husband who was still willing to raise your daughter as his own. What will happen when you end up back in Atlanta and have no Julian *and* no Alex? How are you going to support yourself? How are you going to maintain your lifestyle and rent office space you don't need?"

"My lifestyle is my business," she said, her face drained of color.

She could say what she wanted, but Kelly knew she'd struck a nerve.

"I earned the right to be on his arm. He deserves to be with his family. If I were you, I'd get tired of seconds and go and get something of my own."

"He is mine," Kelly said quietly. "For the rest of our lives we'll be together."

"Then he'll never see his daughter."

"That's what this was about all along. You don't have anything. And now you want to take away the joy of a father and daughter knowing each other. You're a royal bitch, Victoria. Think about this, while you run up credit cards and disregard the man who's proven his love for your strange ass. In three years your daughter will be able to make decisions without your permission. What do you think will happen when she finds out you blackmailed her father and wouldn't let him see her? Who do you think she'll hate, the man who's been paying support or the mother who manipulated their relationship for the past eighteen years?"

"I—I—she loves me. She'll never hate me. I'm her mother."

"You're a liar and a manipulator and filled with spite. Your daughter is probably as smart as her father. It won't take long for her to figure the truth out. So before you end every good thing in your life, why don't you stop yourself and think about your future alone?"

"You bitch."

Kelly nodded. "I've been called that before. But the truth is what I speak. You can be a woman for the first time in your life, come clean with Julian, Brittany, and Alex and then carry your ass back to Atlanta. Make a real life for yourself. Otherwise, you're going to get burned. Think about it and give me a call." Kelly put her card on the desk and walked out.

The penthouse suite Kelly had rented faced east and she was up with the sunrise. It was one of the few hotels in New York with a balcony, and they charged premium rates for east and west views because of the lovely sunrises and sunsets.

Kelly stood outside in the cool wind, her face raised toward the rising sun, and felt the spirits around her swirling with goodness. She didn't know what the day would bring, but it would be good, she just knew it.

Last night had been spectacular. She and Julian had made love until her body could give no more. They eclipsed the height of mountains and when their souls met, tears of pure love streamed from her eyes.

He was hers. She was his. They were one.

Julian lay inside sleeping amid an array of rose petals and she loved him fully, with her whole heart.

He'd wanted to witness the sunrise with her, but she let him rest for just a while longer.

She needed this quiet moment to commune with her God and thank him for her blessings.

The sun started up and she lifted her face, closing her eyes, waiting for the heat to kiss her skin, when strong arms encircled her waist.

Kelly gasped as shudders of love filled her.

Julian kissed her neck long and soft, and her body warmed even more.

"Darling, you're missing the sunrise."

He wrapped her in his arms and they watched it climb over New York.

"My God. There isn't anything more beautiful," she whispered.

"You are," he said softly. "Only you."

They stayed wrapped around each other until the sun settled above the earth, blazing in her glory.

Kelly's Blackberry bleeped and she hurried over, not sure why anyone would be contacting her this early.

She opened her e-mail from Bree and scrolled down.

"Julian!" she screamed. "You've got to see this."

Unable to contain her excitement, Kelly hurried over to him.

"What is it?"

"Alex. Late last night he withdrew from the mayoral race! You're predicted to sweep the election."

Several seconds passed before they hugged each other fiercely.

"You were going to win even with him in it."

"I wasn't sure," Julian murmured in her hair. "You always believed, though. You never gave up."

"I never will."

"I don't deserve you," he said, lavishing tender kisses on her lips and cheeks.

"Yes, you do."

Kelly's Blackberry bleeped again.

"Turn that damned thing off. We're busy."

Kelly snickered and read the quick message, then stopped Julian with a hand to his chest. "It's a message from Victoria. Brittany wants to meet you."

Julian hurried over to read the telephone message himself. He looked startled and then excited. "I have to go. I want to meet her too. Um. I have to do something—"

Kelly stopped his excited walk in circles. "Why don't you shower and get dressed? Then we'll go meet your daughter."

"Right." He walked off, then hurried back and captured Kelly's mouth in a loving kiss. "I love you. You need to know that."

Kelly nodded and urged him into the exquisite bathroom.

"I do," she said quietly. "Forever, I do."

"How do I look?" Julian asked for the fifth time as they sat in the café near their hotel.

"Like a million dollars wrapped in gold."

He smiled. "This tie isn't right," he said, fumbling with it.

Kelly took his hands, forcing him to look at her. "You look wonderful." She saw Victoria, Alex, and a beautiful teenager coming toward them. Kelly rose, bringing him with her. She squeezed his hands for support and gazed into the eyes of the man she loved.

"Your daughter has arrived."

Julian's eyes widened, then closed for a mere second. Then he turned.

Brittany held both her parents' hands as she stopped several feet from Julian. Kelly watched Julian and thought he was going to cry.

She moved to give him privacy, but he snagged her hand and held it. Brittany walked toward him alone, but looked back at her parents.

Victoria gave a tight smile and a nod and the young woman moved closer.

Kelly disentangled her hand from Julian's and let him face his daughter.

"My mom says you're my real dad."

"Yes, I am."

"I'm Brittany," she said, a little shy.

"Julian Blake. You're beautiful, Brittany," he said, unsure whether he should speak from his heart or hold the emotions in.

"Everyone says I look like my mom."

Julian looked at Victoria and Alex, who looked scared. He understood that emotion. He gave them a gracious smile. "You are beautiful. Just like your mother."

The Nixons gave him grateful smiles.

"Mom, Daddy," she said with a soft southern drawl, "do you mind if Julian and I sit down and talk, alone?"

Victoria lifted her head and saw that this was the life she was supposed to be living. Her daughter was going to grow up without her. Her eyes said it all. Alex took his wife's hand and kissed her fingers.

A tear slipped from her eye. The gesture had penetrated the cocoon of selfishness that had surrounded her for too long. "No, dear. Call my cell. We'll come back for you."

Julian's eyes were glassy as he smiled his thanks. "Thank you."

The parents nodded and Kelly tiptoed away as father and daughter headed into the café together.

Kelly watched the scene from a back booth in the cafe, her emotions racing in every direction. Joy, awe, fear, confusion. Was she ready to be a stepmom? Only time would tell, but she would give it one helluva try.

The Beginning